D1630609

BURDEN OF PROOF

I. W. Stewart © 2013

BURY LIBRARY SERVICE

000947488 4

CHAPTER ONE

Clotting blood had puddled and congealed on the oil-stained floor. The echoes of pain had finished their terror song, in the iron work above, and the torture of Andy Lewis was long over. Feral cats, previously too scared to venture into the workshop, were now sniffing the air and padding into the makeshift torture chamber. In a previous life this workshop had produced sheet metal fabrications, all hand crafted, metal formed and folded with heavy cast iron machinery. Now, it was a dormant reminder of a manufacturing heritage that little existed in the area anymore. Old factories were now the playgrounds of feline squatters and large rats. Homeless, wanderers were prohibited entry by the occasional uniformed security guard.

Each day the concrete crumbled a little more and the unpainted ironwork slowly transformed into the ferric-oxide of decay; unable to support its own weight it flaked into orange dust, disturbed only by pigeons. Timber window frames, no longer treated, rotted and held refuge for hundreds of scurrying woodlice, hiding from the light.

A large, green, metal-folding machine supported the body; its hand was trapped in the massive clamping plate and it held the puppet like arm over the lifeless moppet head, as if it was trying to pull itself up. Trapped in a grotesque pose was the body of Andy Lewis. His head, flopped forward, was gagged with grey gaffer tape and around his neck was a blue, nylon-rope necklace with a pendant of cardboard. Written on the sinister adornment was one word – JUDAS. Dried spittle had coated his chin and had mixed with blood, giving him a macabre, evil-clown look. His chest was marked with precision puncture wounds between the ribs, each one a potential kill. Where his feet should have been were now gelatinous, fleshy, mounds of meat. Sharp, white, bones jutted from the mess and coagulated blood shone, like a sick jelly sculpture.

As the cats crept back into their territory the new silence was interrupted by the arrival of an over-sized American truck. Complete with blacked out glass, and huge chrome wheels, the 4x4 barely squeezed through the factory gates. The muddy road had redecorated the glossy black paint as it rolled over the tyre tracks and footprints of recent visitors.

A rumbling bass rhythm leaked from the well fitted doors and windows, as the hooded driver pulled the over-sized beast to a stop at what used to be the reception. A heavy door opened revealing Ryan Knowles. Ryan wore a loose fitting Hilfiger hoodie that hid his gym-toned physique. A pock marked and sneering face peered out from the hood and his chino style trousers hung low on his backside. As he threw the door shut he took his phone from his pocket and called his brother.

"Where did you want me to meet you?" Ryan asked his brother, somewhat confused about the location and the reasons why he'd had asked him here.

Kyle answered quickly: "Inside the old metal work place. I'm already in here."

Ryan stood and thought for a minute before walking towards the broken door of the old reception area. In the entrance area, Ryan wretched at the smell of stale urine: that had come from years of use by the local homeless. He covered his nose and mouth with his hand and moved with pace into the factory area. Walking through the main assembly workshop, pigeons fluttered away in panic but the brazen cats gathered around his feet looking for an easy meal. Ryan kicked at the scavenging felines, muttering as he did: "get the fuck away you skanky little shits."

As he ventured further into the dereliction he shouted: "Kyle!" There was no response. Disturbed and confused he slowed his walk and took sometime to think. After a few moments he frowned but continued his walk deeper into the factory.

He crept into the metalwork shop and saw Kyle stood over the body of Andy Lewis at the folding machine.

"Andy! Andy! Kyle! What, what the fuck?" He stumbled over to the battered and executed Andy and crouched low to look at him. He choked back vomit and tears as he looked at Andy's feet and sucked air in sharply through his teeth. Looking round he saw no signs of anyone else there. At

Andy's side lay a hammer, it looked like any hammer, like his brother's hammer. He had a thought, he crouched down and looked closely at the hammer, on the base of the handle he saw the initials KK scratched into the rubber handle. "Fuck!" Still staring at the hammer lying in the blood-lake; the metallic, crimson fluids leeched onto his shoes, turning once clean, white trainers into an incarnadine sign of his brother's guilt. "Why Kyle? Have I missed something? Andy has always been loyal, one of us. You never told me he'd been fucking you off. Look at the mess man, how are we going clean this up?"

Kyle and Ryan had inflicted much pain over the past few years but Ryan had never seen anything that approached the brutality of what had happened here. The malevolence and psychosis needed for such a violent attack were well beyond anything Ryan could take and he walked away to throw up. As he gathered himself he glanced back over at the macabre scene. Kyle was almost serenely catatonic, detached, only the blood on his hands and shirt giving any clue as to his guilt.

"Kyle, come on what do we do?" Ryan asked his brother.

Kyle stared blankly at the bludgeoned body and then at Ryan: "I…I didn't do this Ryan." He stuttered through choking tears.

Ryan was confused and reached for his phone, desperate to sort out the mess, to protect his brother. As he started to look through his contacts he suddenly became aware of a dark figure running at his brother.

"Drop the weapon! Drop to the floor. Armed police!"

Kyle had no time to comply as the heavily armoured officer ploughed him into the floor.

DCI Sutherland joined the over enthusiastic officer and knelt next to the prostrated Kyle:

"Kyle Knowles, you are under arrest for the murder of Andrew Lewis." He smiled as he said it and pushed his knee into Kyle's side as he stood.

Moments later and Ryan was face down on the floor like his older brother. Cuffed and unable to move he couldn't understand what had happened.

Sutherland beamed with self-congratulatory pride, his step lighter than it had been for months he walked over to his DS, Howley, and patted him on the shoulder.

"Look at that Howley, we got the evil bastard. All his cocky posturing and talk of loyalty and the little shit has been caught killing one of his own. Oh, and as a bonus we have his little brother too."

Howley nodded in agreement; "looks like we have him sir. Who tipped us off?"

"It was anonymous, I usually don't bother with anonymous tips but I'm glad I did this time. God knows who, or why, they phoned but just look around, go over there and look at the mess he made of Andy Lewis. We've got him. A few forensic tests and BANG! That bastard is in prison. Smile Howley, you might even be on the news tonight."

With that he turned and strutted to the other team members. Sutherland's team gathered round their heroic leader and whoops, cheers and high fives were exchanged in ebullient enthusiasm. Kyle was dragged, like an unwanted bag of rubbish, to a waiting van as the celebrating team arranged drinks with Sutherland.

Howley watched him walk away and took some time to take it all in. Howley had been working in gang related crime for years and knew the Knowles well. It was hard to comprehend that he had finally been caught. An evil monster who preyed on the weak and flaunted his frequent escapes from conviction like medals of war. Andy Lewis had been Kyle's favourite, a lieutenant of sorts and now Howley would have to find out why Kyle had killed him. There had been no recent intelligence to suggest Andy was out of favour; Howley wondered what had changed. He walked over to Andy's body and looked past the carnage of human butchery and focused on the macabre necklace. JUDAS.

The obvious inference of the sign was that Andy Lewis had betrayed Knowles in some way. Of course in Kyle's world it was very easy to say, or do something, that he considered a betrayal. It was that motive that Howley wanted to establish, he needed a complete picture of what had happened, it was how he had been taught to work and would always work that way. The forensic team would soon arrive but Howley had seen enough to know that if the blood that soaked Knowles' clothes matched Andy Lewis's then it was pretty much a done deal; a life sentence for Kyle Knowles.

Howley turned away from the gruesome scene and marched across to DCI Sutherland and his excited team of armed officers. "Sir, shall I run some intel checks on his patch to see what sort of motive he had?"

Sutherland looked confused: "Steve, we've got him. Red-handed, it won't take forensics long to make the links. For Christ's sake if we'd been here two minutes earlier we'd have witnessed the crime. Is there something about this you don't understand? You've been working to put him away for years, you should be happy."

"I get all that sir, but it's just good to have a motive in these cases. His brief is an expert at getting him off; I don't want to lose him again." Howley replied.

Sutherland thought for a moment before answering: "Fine, you take the lead on it but I don't want it dragging out. I want this sewn up and with the CPS as soon as possible. I'll expect you to report anything you find, to me, the moment you find it. Let's get this to trial."

Howley knew that Sutherland was making a career play and simply nodded and said: "Understood."

CHAPTER TWO

Ollie James had missed the triumphant raid that had netted the notorious Kyle Knowles. Howley had tried to get the word out to him, but he had missed the call. As part of the team that had been working to bring down the Knowles family he should have been there, but Sutherland had moved so quickly on the tip that he was left chasing leads in Tin Town.

After interviewing several of Kyle's victims and illegal loan customers he was going over the notes. It was the usual list of crimes but also the usual list of non-committal statements and nobody was prepared to make a formal statement; the idea that anybody would stand in a court room and accuse Kyle Knowles and his brother of any heinous crime was, as ever, unlikely.

As he walked towards his car his phone beeped from his pocket and he quickly retrieved it and answered it: "Hello."

"Ollie, where've you been? Didn't you get my message?" Howley asked in an agitated voice.

Ollie moved the phone from his ear and looked at the screen: four missed calls and a voice mail. "I was interviewing people. What's the panic?"

"We just brought Kyle Knowles in for murder." Howley told him about the raid. "He killed Andy Lewis, the place was like a slaughter house…"

"Jesus, I don't know what to say." Ollie said as he let the news sink into his mind. "Andy Lewis was one of the faithful, are we sure he was the victim? Where did the tip off come from? Is there forensic to tie him in?" He asked excitedly.

"Sutherland wouldn't say who the tip off came from. And yes, it was Andy, I saw the body myself. I don't think the forensics will be an issue, he was covered in blood and it looks like the murder weapon is his hammer." Howley replied.

"Ok, I'll head over to the station and you can fill me in fully." Ollie said as he fumbled for his car keys.

"I'll be in the office. Bring some coffees we have work to do."

"Don't know how I always get stung for the coffees, but ok, see you in half an hour or so." Ollie said begrudgingly.

Still stunned with the shock of the news, Ollie slid into his car seat. As he drove out of 'Tin Town' he was soon going past one of the newer, privately owned, housing developments. This one was of interest because it was where Kyle Knowles had set up his home. Close enough to his patch to keep an eye on things but with all the ostentatious add-ons he could buy to let everyone know he was doing better than them. Ugly pillars, a shining driveway, electric gates and, of course, a black BMW parked beneath the over-sized satellite dish.

Diverting his route to the Altincham Road area Ollie soon found a coffee place that both he and Howley approved of, and pulled in. He ordered two black coffees and picked up a copy of the Manchester Evening News. The headline about a stabbing outside a club in the city caught his eye, because it was a Knowles related crime. Knowles had been pushing his business further north and this had led to a series of territory related scuffles in the city centre, as doorman assaulted doorman acting as soldiers for the manipulative machinations of Kyle and his rivals.

The clichéd Manchester grey sky made Ollie wish for sunnier climes and he scrolled through the song list on his iPod before settling on some northern-soul to lift his mood. His music choice soon eased his tension and he headed towards the gangs and organised crime unit at Wythenshawe Police Station.

Wythenshawe police station had been part of a new build programme, complete with a modern, clean, fascia. A swooping roof line and lots of opaque glass made it look a whole lot more welcoming than the older seventies style concrete stations that used to be the norm. Ollie slowed to a stop and passed his swipe card over the sensor. The barrier lifted and he edged into the too-small car park, hoping there would be some space left. Whilst the new building was brilliant in many ways the environmental laws involved in new builds meant that car parking was limited in an attempt to force more people to use public transport: it wasn't working. Luckily, all the marked cars were out and Ollie found a space near the maintenance garage.

Slinging his laptop bag over his shoulder and grabbing the coffees Ollie headed into the building. Using his pass he entered the building beyond the reception area and took the corridor past the offices used by uniform and entered CID. The CID office was a garbled wall of noise as various teams worked their cases. The chaos of the room was interspersed with freestanding whiteboards. Dry-mark pen scrawls mapped out the detective's investigations as cork and pins held the timelines of cases securely: CSI it wasn't.

Ollie nodded at colleagues, old and new, as he passed through. He approached the door to the gangs unit and was met by Howley.

"You took your time." Howley said.

"I know but I couldn't bring you an inferior coffee could I? You would have whinged all day." Ollie said with a laugh.

"Fair enough; where were you when I called?"

"I was down in Tin Town interviewing some of Kyle's loan customers, not that they'll admit or say anything." Ollie replied.

"Yeah, same old story," said Howley knowingly.

The two men moved to a large desk and sat with their drinks. They were the only people in the office, Sutherland having taken the rest of the team for a celebratory lunch and it was the first time in months Ollie had known the office to be so quiet. Neither man said anything about it because they both felt the same disdain for vulgar celebrations. There was a lot of work to do before they could call the case closed. The sort of premature celebrations that Sutherland was fond of showed a lack of respect and due diligence for the job.

Ollie asked Howley, so what now? Do you think Sutherland knows that Knowles's little empire of pain and suffering won't just stop operating because he is in prison?"

Howley nodded: "Somewhere deep within him he will know; but right now the newspaper headlines and adoration from our fearless leaders are clouding his judgement. This is his route into being nominated for one of the new democratically appointed police chief positions that are being brought in."

"Yeah I always considered him as more of a politician than a copper," noted Ollie.

As the evening drew down over the station, Howley told Ollie of the day's events.

CHAPTER THREE

Ollie James woke before his alarm and stared bleary eyed at his clock: 6.30. He rubbed his eyes and forced himself out of bed. The sun was barely risen and little light penetrated his blinds. He shook his duvet and straightened the pillows, before moving to the bathroom. The stark light stung his eyes for a second as he flicked the switch and he stood still for a moment as his eyes adjusted. After peeing he faced himself in the mirror and squeezed some toothpaste onto his toothbrush. He brushed his teeth, flossed and started to feel more alert. Rubbing his chin he decided to shave before showering and pulled his razor from the cabinet behind the mirror.

Clean shaven and minty fresh he pulled back the shower curtain and set the temperature for thirty nine degrees. The shower soon reached temperature and he stepped in. He hummed nondescript tunes as he showered and within minutes he stepped out and into a towel. From his wardrobe he took a freshly-cleaned black suit, a white shirt and a black tie. He laughed to himself as he predicted Howley's usual comment when he wore this, "you going to a funeral?" It wasn't funny the first time he said it, and it isn't funny after twenty or more times. He dressed himself and stepped down the stairs and into the kitchen. After putting some fresh coffee into the filter machine he dropped a piece of bread into the toaster and waited for his breakfast.

Ollie sipped at his coffee and looked through the notes he had taken during his meeting with Howley. Knowles would be interviewed and at some point taken to the magistrate's court for a remand hearing and to have the murder case kicked up to Crown court. He and Howley would interview Knowles, while Sutherland worked with the CPS counselor, on the request for remand statements and evidence.

He made some notes but he knew that ultimately the interview was likely to be short. Caught with the murder weapon in hand, which had been his personal hammer, and covered in the victim's blood there wasn't a great deal to add. It was also very likely that Knowles would remain tight-lipped throughout. They knew the how, they knew the when; all they could get from him now was the why.

Ollie drained his coffee cup and dropped it into the dish-washer before tidying his work together and heading out towards his car. Ollie climbed into his VW Scirocco, turned the ignition and headed to Wythenshawe station. The roads were just starting to fill up with commuters and he listened to Chris Evans on Radio 2 as he navigated his way from Sale, through Sale Moor, Northern Moor and onto the Parkway. After thirty minutes he was at the station. Pulling onto the car park he saw Howley's car and wasn't surprised that his former mentor had arrived earlier than him.

The dark clouds of the previous day were absent and the September sun was warm and pleasant against his back. Ollie wondered if the sunny weather was a good omen: a sign that the dark days of the Knowles were soon to be over.

The office was back to its usual state of activity. Plain-clothes officers, uniformed officers, admin clerks and detectives were all frantically collating intelligence and evidence for Sutherland. He was expecting the prosecutor and wanted as much information as possible to ensure Knowles was remanded. Knowles' remand and plenty of evidence to work with would be of great use, politically, for the ambitious Sutherland.

Ollie met Howley coming out of their office, "What's with all the activity?" He said.

"Sutherland wants a solid foundation for the remand hearing, so he's got the team looking for evidence of flight risk and so on." Howley replied thoughtfully.

"Makes sense. So I imagine Sutherland is going for the morning remand hearing which gives us a few hours to question our guest. So how are we playing this?"

"Let's keep it simple, his brief is already with him and he knows he's screwed so he'll either keep quiet or deny everything," Howley theorised. "Let's just go in, ask the obvious questions and then get out and do some legwork to prop up the forensics."

"I think you're right, he's not stupid, he knows he's on the harsh end of a murder conviction. He might want to fight premeditation but I can't see him getting anywhere with that."

Howley glanced out into the main office and saw that Sutherland was busy regaling, to anyone who would listen, his heroic arrest of Knowles. He shook his head and rolled his eyes. "Right, super-Sutherland is busy over there, shall we go down to the custody suite and have a chat with Mr Knowles?"

Ollie gave a gentle laugh, "is that how we have to address him now?"

"I think it's only appropriate don't you?" Howley joked.

"I'll remember that, so shall we head down to the custody suites?" He waited for Howley to move, "come on old man let's get a move on before Sutherland tags along and screws up the interview."

With that Howley opened the office door and stepped lightly out of the main office and into the corridor, Ollie had followed closely and the two men made their way to the custody suites.

CHAPTER FOUR

Grace Sterling strode confidently along Quay Street, coffee in one hand and a leather laptop bag in the other. Her charcoal suit fitted well and her red blouse boldly matched her red heels. Dark hair was tied back, sensibly, and her make-up was subtle. At thirty-three she had been with the Crown Prosecution Service for five years and was gaining a reputation as an aggressive prosecutor.

She finished her coffee as she walked past the Opera House theatre and dropped the cup into a nearby bin. The street was busy with city centre commuters, from business suited professionals to coffee-shop baristas and street cleaners, and Grace enjoyed watching the diverse work-force of the city as they started their day.

Grace left the street and entered the CPS office. The CPS office in Manchester was based in the art deco- Sunlight House, in the city centre. The early twentieth century design blended neatly with modern computers and the twenty-first century requirements of a multi-use building. As she made her way past the over-loaded desks and towards her own mess of work she was met by her friend and colleague Matthew Doherty.

Matthew had joined the CPS at about the same time as Grace and they had supported each other as they built their careers. Matthew wore his navy pin-stripe suit well and his athletic build was at ease in his well pressed shirt. With well-groomed, blonde hair and broad shoulders he was a fearsome shark in the courtroom and seemed to relish the adversarial face-to-face battles more than most.

"Hi Matt," Grace said as she dropped her bag on her desk.

"Hey Grace," he replied jovially. "The boss is looking for you, he's been out every five minutes; I think you better go straight to his office."

"Thanks for the heads-up, I'll go and see him now."

Grace left Matthew in the open office and paced through to the back of the room before knocking on the office door of Michael Blunt QC, Principle Legal Advisor. The Principle Legal Advisor effectively led the Manchester CPS team and directed the operational Specialist Prosecutors, of which Grace was one of ten in Manchester. After a couple of seconds Grace was called into the office.

Michael's office was a tribute to his successes in law. His walls were adorned with diplomas and honours, all glazed and dusted daily. In one corner stood a tailor's dummy that wore his silks and wig, and on all walls were newspaper clippings of his past successes in court. Grace tentatively stepped towards Michael and he gestured to Grace to take a seat and she quickly sat on the chair in front of his desk.

Michael was a very experienced QC and had been a member of the bar association for over twenty years. He'd been promoted to Principle Legal Advisor five years ago and, despite the constant offers, he resisted the temptation to relocate to London to further his career. His tailor-made suit hid a softening waistline and he was rarely seen with his tie anything but tight to his throat.

"Good morning Grace, how are you?" He asked.

"I'm fine thanks; Matthew mentioned that you wanted to see me."

"Yes, I have a new case I want you to look after. It's very high profile and would be your main priority until the trial is over." He reached for his cup and took a sip of coffee before continuing: "Do you think you can handle this sort of challenge?"

Grace felt a wave of excitement being chased through her body and answered:"Yes, I'm more than ready. What's the case?"

"I'm glad you're so confident because you will need to be. I had a call from the DCI Sutherland from the gangs and serious crimes division based in Wythenshawe. They arrested Kyle Knowles last night." He waited for Grace's response.

Grace was stunned and excited. For a moment she questioned her own ability to handle such an important case but just as quickly she banished the doubt and felt certain she was ready to take it on. "Knowles, as in South Manchester crime family boss Knowles?" She asked incredulously.

Michael noted her tone and said, "yes, that Kyle Knowles. Apparently caught red-handed by the Chief Inspector himself."

"You weren't kidding when you said high profile, the press will be all over this and the force will be desperate for us to get a guilty verdict."

"Indeed." He paused and churched his fingers habitually almost looking like a spy novel villain. "So Grace, I need to know- am I assigning you as lead prosecutor for this case?" Michael asked.

Without hesitation Grace nodded and said: "yes. Absolutely Michael."

"That's what I was hoping to hear. As ever I'll be there every step of the way and all press relations will go through me and only me, understood?"

Grace nodded again, "yes."

"Excellent; ok you need to get over to Wythenshawe station now and get ready for the remand hearing. The Chief Inspector assures me there's enough preliminary evidence to keep Knowles in remand."

"Ok I'll grab a taxi and go now. What about the cases on my desk now?" She enquired.

"Don't worry about them, this is your priority case now. I'll get Matthew to go through them and reassign some of them. When you're done with the Magistrates and Sutherland, come back here and we'll sort you a team out." He was making notes as he spoke.

"Right, I'll contact you as soon as I'm out of the magistrate's court." She started to leave the office but stopped at the door. "Thank you for this opportunity Michael, I really appreciate it."

"I'm not doing you any favours Grace, you have earned this. Now go, Sutherland is expecting you."

Grace closed the door behind her and punched the sky in celebration, whispering "yes!" as she did so.

CHAPTER FIVE

Ollie and Howley entered the stark, white, open area of the custody suite reception and nodded at the custody sergeant at the desk.

"Good morning gentlemen, I imagine you would like to spend some time with our most famous resident."

Howley smiled at the Custody Sergeant, "Morning Dave, I take it Mr Knowles has been keeping you busy?"

"Hello Steve, yes between the phone, his brief, the forensic team, the doctor, his brother and now you, it's been frantic."

"I'm sure it has, we don't get too many celebs down here in Wythenshawe, they're usually put up in Stretford." Ollie commented, "Have you got the custody book?"

The Custody Sergeant placed the large, well used book on the grey, formica counter top and flipped it open to the correct page. Howley filled in his details first.

"Which interview room can we use?" He asked.

"He's in room two with his brief, I think it's easier if you just use that." The Sergeant said.

"How long has he been in there?"

The Custody Sergeant nodded to the book, "I'd say about an hour but if you look back a few entries in the book you will get a more accurate idea."

"Thanks, was he any trouble?" Howley enquired.

"Not in the slightest, he was cooperative from the start. He didn't even want the doctor but I insisted."

Ollie was listening with interest and filled the next slot in the custody book. He then led the way from the Sergeant's desk as the detectives headed to the interview room. The custody suite was clinically decorated and the harsh lighting chased away any shadows. The sting of disinfectant, cleaning fluids made his eyes water a little and he wondered what odours hid beneath the acrid cleanliness. The wipe down seating areas and lack of sharp edges made Ollie think about sanatoriums and he decided it was appropriate for many of its guests.

The detectives gave a brief knock on the door of the interview room before entering the unlock code into the door lock and walking into the room. The interview room was sparsely equipped with furniture. The normally bare desk was covered with papers and a briefcase. On seeing the men enter, Knowles' lawyer began pushing the paper back into the case and soon the faux wood grain was all that could be seen. Built into the wall was a digital recording device and no member of the force was allowed to interview a suspect without recording the proceedings.

Kyle Knowles was usually a six foot, muscled wall of bravado, hate and self-assured swagger. The Kyle Knowles sitting in the interview room was merely six foot. His arrogant sneer was gone and his slumped form was almost foetal. His blood soaked clothes had been taken into evidence and he now wore a simple grey tracksuit. His eyes were framed by the black rings of a sleepless night and he barely even noticed the two detectives as they positioned themselves opposite him at the desk.

Howley positioned himself next to the recorder and a nod towards Knowles' brief let him know they would be starting the interview. The suited lawyer whispered in Knowles' ear and nodded back to Howley in agreement.

"Before I start can we have your name please?" He asked the solicitor sat with Knowles.

"Jeremy Allen," was the curt reply.

Howley pressed record: "It is 10.00am on the 9th of September, interview location is Wythenshawe Police Station and present are DS Howley, DS James, Mr Kyle Knowles and his solicitor Mr Allen."

Before the digital era the silence in the room would have been disturbed by the electric motors of the tape recorders, but now there was no noise. Ollie liked this silence, most of the criminals he had interviewed thought that silences were designed for them to fill. It was the silence that usually tripped them up. He watched Knowles and waited for him to break the hush: Knowles sat calmly in defiance of Ollie's theory.

Ollie began the interview: "So Kyle, you were arrested covered in Andy Lewis's blood and your hammer appears to be the murder weapon. So would you like to explain to me what happened?"

Knowles didn't flinch and his solicitor spoke for him.

"My client has no comment to make."

Howley ignored him and directly addressed Knowles: "So Kyle, what did Andy do to deserve the Judas tag? I thought you and him were tight, I was clearly wrong."

Knowles made no attempt to speak and his solicitor repeated his previous reply.

Ollie looked at Howley and raised his eyebrows. The two men had been expecting this and they knew no amount of questioning or cajoling would get a response. They could waste hours trying and they both knew there was no point in continuing.

Howley decided to call it. "Kyle I'm sure that your brief has advised you not to say anything but as this looks very much like premeditated murder any remorse shown now can only help when the sentence is passed. Admit to it now and maybe you will be in a jail close enough for friends and family to visit." He waited for some sort of response. "Ok, the time is now 10.10am and the interview is being concluded for the time being."

Howley and Ollie put their notepads away and stood. "I'm afraid you will have to conclude your business with Mr Knowles now Mr Allen; the Custody Sergeant will be in to escort him back to his cell after we leave." Ollie said.

Knowles was staring at Howley quizzically and finally broke his silence. "You the Howley who used to patrol up near The Black Boy pub back in day?" He mumbled.

Howley frowned and tilted his head towards Kyle; "yeah that's me, why?"

"My old man knew you, said you were an honest cop." Knowles said as he chewed the inside of his cheek; "Said when you bounced the beat things were done right. That still the way it is with you?"

Howley didn't know where this was going or why but answered: "That's always been my way. And yeah I remember your dad; he was a bit of wide boy but nothing in your league."

"No, my old man was small time, but that was a long time ago." His voice drifted and as suddenly as he'd broken his silence he went mute again.

"Is that it Kyle? You're here on a murder charge and you wanted to reminisce; I don't think so, come on what's on your mind? You ready to talk?"

Knowles rocked in his seat and looked at Howley. "I didn't kill Andy."

"What happened to no comment? Let me start the recorder again and we'll resume the interview." He reached over to turn the machine back on but was interrupted by Knowles.

"Don't bother, I'm done talking." Knowles said.

Jeremy Allen spoke before Howley or Ollie could respond and said, "Detectives my client has said as much as he going to today. I suggest you send in the Custody Sergeant."

Ollie whispered to Howley. "We're done here. He slipped; his lawyer won't let it happen again. Let's go and knock and some doors and see what we can find out."

Howley turned to Knowles and his lawyer. "Well gentlemen it seems our little chat is over. The Custody Sergeant will be here in a moment."

Howley felt uneasy, leaving the interview room, after the strange conversation with Knowles. There was something unusual about his tone, he seemed almost frightened. He remembered Knowles' father, he'd taken him in on many occasions but he always accepted it. He knew it was a risk he took with his chosen lifestyle and he never acted up when Howley arrested him. Howley in return treated him fairly and despite the rumours, of his colleagues less than honest methods, Howley never planted evidence or fitted up anyone. He wondered why Knowles had brought this up. His father knew that if he broke the law Howley would take him in but he also knew that if he hadn't Howley would only look for who did.

Ollie asked: "what's wrong Steve?"

"This all seems a bit strange. His dad was a real toe-rag, but he never kicked off when I took him in. He knew I'd never fit him up and back then it was pretty standard practice. So why did Kyle just bring him up?"

"I don't know; he's desperate Steve. He knows there's a ton of forensic evidence stacked up against him. He saw you and thought he'd try and muddy the waters." Ollie said.

"I don't know; this is all a bit odd. I was there at the factory and I was glad we'd got him, but something is bothering me."

Ollie nodded, "I know what you mean, but that doesn't mean he didn't do it."

CHAPTER SIX

Following the blitzkrieg arrest of Knowles, the crime scene was left for the Scenes of Crimes Officers, usually referred to as SOCOs, to investigate and analyse. Greg Milner was an experienced SOCO and was the supervisor for the Knowles' case. His small laboratory at Wythenshawe was a far cry from the public's, TV inspired, perception of criminal forensic laboratories. He couldn't run a DNA profile or hack computers. The bulk of any evidence found would be placed into protective packaging, ensuring no cross contamination, and the sent to various forensic laboratories. He could analyse some finger prints; but often they were also sent to the fingerprint bureau for analysis.

The SOCO lab at the station was clinically clean and organised specifically to ensure evidence was never contaminated. Everybody who entered the room had to sign in and out and only approved SOCOs were allowed past the deliberately high and obstructive reception counter. Inside the lab, Milner was organising the evidence collected from the factory and assigning catalogue numbers to the photos taken at the scene. Blood samples had been taken from Knowles' clothes and were ready to send for DNA recovery and analysis, along with a reference sample from Andy Lewis for them to compare. It would take two to three weeks to get the DNA results back.

The hammer retrieved at the scene was awash with Knowles' fingerprints and footprints photographed at the scene matched his trainers. All the evidence collected appeared to implicate Knowles and there was little else by way of physical evidence at the scene to consider.

Milner looked at the photograph of Knowles' wearing the blood soaked top. It looked like he had carried or held Lewis after the bloody torture because there was no spatter pattern to be seen, only a mass of blood soaked deeply into the material. Knowles' face was smeared and rubbed, and again had no spatter. This wasn't unusual, if a body had been moved or the assaulter had leant on or over the body, but some spatter would have confirmed Knowles' use of the hammer more positively.

The cardboard sign that had been recovered from the scene showed no obvious prints but Milner decided to see if the fingerprint bureau could recover anything with a newer technique using 'ninhydrin.' This chemical would cause the oils from any fingerprints ingrained in the paper to fluoresce a bright purple colour. If they got any fluorescence the prints would be photographed and run through the system.

Milner called the secure courier and arranged for the samples to be collected. He then completed his report and emailed it to Sutherland and the coroner's liaison officer. It would be a couple of weeks before he would add anything to the report.

CHAPTER SEVEN

The taxi ride from Quay Street to Wythenshawe station was uneventful and Grace used the time to research Knowles using her smart-phone. His public persona mirrored the sort of sentimentalised views that London's East end residents had of the Krays. He had been linked to serious assaults, drug dealing, loan sharking and three murders but nothing had ever stuck. His only convictions were from his early days: his apprenticeship and training for his ultimate role as Knowles gang leader. He was last arrested and released before trial for illegal money lending; she saw that Matthew had been the prosecutor and made a note to ask him about the case, any advantage she could gain on the case would be useful.

On arrival at the station Grace reported to reception and was soon collected by an admin assistant and taken to the gangs and serious crimes team control room. On entering the room she was warmly greeted by DCI Sutherland.

"Welcome to the gangs and organised crime division Ms Sterling." Sutherland said as he shook her hand.

Grace pulled out of the hand shake and said, "Hello Chief Inspector, I'm happy to be here."

"The remand hearing will be tomorrow morning. If you would be kind enough to follow me through to the other office I can show you the evidence collected and the preliminary forensics."

"Great; lead the way." Grace was eager to get started.

Sutherland led her to the office used by Howley and Ollie. On a large, beech table sat an innocuous looking box file. Grace was guided to a chair and she immediately began going through the contents of the file. Sutherland stood silently for a moment before saying, "I think everything you will need is in there. If you need any clarification with anything just shout up. Shall I get one of the admin clerks to bring you a coffee?"

"Yes please Chief Inspector that would be lovely."

"I'll have someone sort that out. Now if you'll excuse me I appear to have misplaced a couple of detectives." He left Grace alone in the office and went in search of Howley and Ollie.

Sutherland let the door to the office close behind him and stepped into the division's main office area. The excitement of the previous day's arrest had not subsided and there was a positive atmosphere about the work taking place. He looked across at the main entrance to the division and saw Howley and Ollie entering the room.

"I take it you two have been to see Knowles?" He postured.

"Just a few questions." Ollie replied.

"I don't know why you bothered. Nothing he says can change what we have. The DNA will be back next week. Forensics will match his prints to the hammer and he is going to be found guilty."

"Well a confession would have been the icing on the cake sir."

"And has he confessed?"

"No Sir, he has refused to comment."

Sutherland laughed, "of course he has. The little scrote knows how screwed he is."

Ollie and Howley both nodded in agreement.

"So gentlemen how do you intend to proceed?"

"We're going to go and talk to a few contacts on Knowles' patch and see what had changed between Knowles and Lewis." Ollie said.

"Fine, but as I explained to Steve I don't want a drawn out investigation, we'll let the forensics do the talking and get to trial as soon as we can." Sutherland's tone had changed and the two men knew that he would not give them much leeway in their investigation. "Consider this my respect for your old-school, gut-feelings…But do not push me too far."

Ollie nodded, "yes Sir. We'll get out there, shake some trees and see if anyone knows anything."

Howley backed up Ollie: "We'll be as quick as we can be and as I said yesterday I'll make sure you're kept up to speed throughout."

"Right I'm glad we understand each other. The CPS prosecutor is here, come in and meet her. No doubt she'll need you two over the next few weeks."

Ollie and Howley followed Sutherland and moved into the office where Grace had been left to assess the evidence collected. She was reading through the files and making notes on a yellow legal pad as the men entered and she barely acknowledged their entrance. A few seconds passed and Grace looked up from her work. She smiled at the men, ready to make an introduction but her smile faded on seeing Ollie.

"You're part of this case?" She asked Ollie with little effort to hide her disdain towards him.

"No hello? Well I'll say it, hello Grace and yes I'm a lead detective in the division." Ollie said. He was surprised to see her and spent a few seconds admiring her. They'd had a relationship about a year before but they'd both agreed it wasn't going anywhere.

Sutherland looked bemused and interrupted: "I take it you two know each other? Is that going to be a problem Ms Sterling?"

"Yes Chief Inspector; we know each other, and no it isn't a problem." Grace said through gritted teeth.

"Like she said Sir, no problem." Ollie conceded. "As long as she gets all her own way," he muttered under his breath in Howley's direction.

"What was that?" Sutherland asked.

"Nothing Sir, just agreeing with the counselor, there's no problem here."

"Right, good. This is far too important for personal issues to muddy the waters."

Howley, who had been observing the reunion, stepped forward: "Hi Grace, long time. You ok?"

Grace's demeanour immediately changed when she saw Howley and she smiled broadly at him. "Hi Steve, it's been too long. Are you ok?"

"I'm good thanks. So you're the prosecutor for this case?"

"Yeah, I'm going to sort the remand hearing tomorrow and then I'll start trial prep."

Howley nodded, "don't think you'll have much of a problem keeping him on remand and we'll have forensics back soon. We're going to see a few contacts and see if we can establish a motive. When we do we'll write it up and let you know."

Grace agreed: "yeah there's plenty to keep him on remand. Take care out there and we'll meet tomorrow."

"Ok, have fun with the Magistrates."

Ollie watched Grace interacting with Howley and remembered how pleasant and fun she could be. He smiled inwardly and then started to remember the fights and the tension between them. He remembered what an obstinate, unmoving cow she could be and he remembered how much she hated his way of working, at home or on the job.

CHAPTER EIGHT

Ollie and Howley left the station and headed across the car park. The sun had pulled itself higher in the sky and it warmed the men's backs. Ollie was thinking about Grace, about how good she'd looked and was staring blankly as they walked. Howley nudged him in the ribs. "Hey, where have you drifted off to?" He asked.

"Sorry, just thinking."

"Yeah I saw that. Forget her; you blew your chance with Grace last year. Focus on the job in hand," said Howley.

"I wasn't thinking about Grace."

"I'm sure. Right, back to business, where shall we go first?" Howley asked.

The men stood silently for a moment; unsure of how best to proceed. It felt like they were working the case backwards and with so much forensic evidence it almost felt like finding a motive was redundant. Ollie opened the car door and looked at his watch, 11.00am, "Do you think the family liaison officers will have told Lewis's girlfriend yet? What's her name? Amy something?"

Howley nodded, "yeah, let's head that way now. She lives in a maisonette up near 'Tin Town,' I have the address here somewhere." He opened the passenger door and slid into the car. He then opened his brief case and searched for the Amy's address. A few seconds later and he had the address in his hand. "Here it is. But before that, let's go and see what 'Brixton' McKenna knows."

Ollie nodded in agreement and started the car. It was a short drive across to Benchill to see Brixton and they both knew that he'd be in the White Lion by now. The two men didn't speak as they made their way to the Benchill estate, instead choosing to listen to Ken Bruce on radio2. The trees along Wythenshawe park's edges desperately held onto their few remaining green leaves and lolloping dogs fetched, lazily slung, frisbees for their owners.

The White Lion stood in solitude. Its neighbouring buildings had long since been knocked down or abandoned but the White Lion stood resolutely defiant. Built in the late twenties, as part of a new garden city development it had brought much needed housing to South Manchester, it once symbolised the heart of the community. As time moved on and society changed, the pub was no longer the heart of the community and by the eighties it had become a market place for stolen or fake goods. Pirated videos and then DVDs filled sports bags by the nineties and as the millennium passed a new generation of entrepreneur peddled Xbox games, Gucci bags and the ubiquitous green weed: cannabis.

Ollie pulled the car to a halt outside the White Lion and turned to Howley. "Right, last time we spoke to Brixton you managed to upset him and I ended up chasing him all over the estate. Do you think you can tread a little lighter today?" Ollie asked.

Howley laughed, "fine, I'll let you do all the talking."

"Thank you, I think that might be best."

The heavy door was pock-marked with scratched graffiti and the paint was thick and soft. Ollie pushed it open and walked into the bar. The bar was a fortress of dark wood and the landlord was securely positioned behind the pumps. On a tall stool, sipping at an early lager was John 'Brixton' McKenna.

John McKenna was six foot seven inches tall and sported a very close cut skinhead. His piercing, blue-grey, eyes and scowling mouth added fear to his imposing figure. In the early eighties he used a hockey stick, during a school hockey game, to break the legs of a kid who had called him Lurch. It was just after the infamous riots and his violent act had earned him the nickname 'Brixton.' After that he became more and more violent as a young Knowles befriended him and used him as teenage henchman.

"Hello Brixton," Ollie said, as he approached the well muscled hulk.

In a thickly layered, Mancunian-accent Brixton answered: "Hello Mr policeman, what can I do for you today?" He bristled with mancunian arrogance as he spoke.

"A few moments of your time and assistance."

McKenna laughed, "I'm here having a quiet drink so my time you're welcome to. My assistance though, will need to be bought…The usual fee will apply." He rubbed his fingers together.

Ollie took a ten pound note from his jacket pocket and placed it beneath McKenna's glass. "I'm sure that will keep your glass full for a couple more rounds. So what can you tell us about Andy Lewis and Kyle? Why did Kyle kill him?"

McKenna's eyes widened and he quickly replied: "Kyle wouldn't have killed Andy, no way man. Those two were tight, Andy was nothing but loyal and Kyle knew it."

"He was caught with the murder weapon and covered in Andy's blood."

"I don't care how he was caught, there's no way Kyle killed Andy." McKenna was adamant.

"Well that's the way it looked. Knowles met Andy at the old metal work place, tortured him and killed him. He even gave him a Judas necklace. So come on, what's been going on between those two?"

"I'm telling you Sergeant, there was nothing. I was up at Kyle's place last week. Andy and Ryan were there and it was all sweet. As far as Kyle was concerned, Andy was family."

Ollie listened and nodded. "What did Kyle have Andy doing lately?"

McKenna paused and scanned the room, to make sure nobody could hear him, before answering: "He basically ran the loan sharking. Kyle spent most of his time running the bouncers in town and Ryan pulls in the weed and redistributes it. So, Andy was usually on the home patch sorting the collectors and the heavies."

Ollie pushed, "so maybe Andy creamed off some of the takings and Kyle found out?"

McKenna shook his head: "No chance, Andy wouldn't. He wouldn't have to, Kyle had sorted him. He was family and about to be given a family home. He had plenty of cash, he was all good."

Howley had been quiet long enough: "That's a sweet story Brixton, but the facts all point to Kyle murdering Andy. He battered and tortured him with his hammer."

McKenna turned to Howley. "Listen old man, there's no way Kyle killed Andy. You've got the wrong man."

Howley ignored the old man slur, it wasn't the first time someone had said it, and shook his head. McKenna was usually on the money when it came to the Knowles gang. He'd been an informant for a few years now and his information had helped net several key players. He could be wrong; or he could be covering for Knowles. His loyalty was always questionable and he dwelled in a strange land between the law and the lawless.

Howley sighed loudly and said, "Ok Brixton, say I believe you; Knowles didn't kill Andy. Who did? Where do we look for this criminal genius who can so expertly fit Kyle up?"

"I wish I knew." McKenna said somberly. "Andy was a good guy and no way was there any hassle between him and Kyle." He picked up his glass and downed the last of his lager before standing and taking a packet of cigarettes from his pocket. "Walk with me gents."

Howley and Ollie said nothing and followed the hulking henchman outside. The sunshine was still warming the early autumn air and the fragrant aroma of late flowering rudbeckias masked the stale beer smell that tried to escape from the pub.

McKenna lit a cigarette and turned to Ollie: "I've been tight with Kyle and Ryan since we were sixteen. We've made a lot of enemies. There are some proper hard bastards in Gorton and Droylsden who have tried to pop Kyle. The Salford Quays gang has tried too but right now it's all quiet. There's a bit of push and shove in town over the door business but that's about it."

Ollie frowned, "so what are you saying?"

"I'm saying it wasn't one of those thugs, they haven't got the balls or the brains."

Ollie was exasperated; "so who?"

"Maybe one or two players within the gang would be smart enough and crazy enough to try this. If I were you I'd be looking into Jack Haworth, Adam Grey and Aiden."

Ollie and Howley recognized the first two names but both drew a blank at Aiden. Jack and Adam were both known criminal associates of Knowles. Americans might call them lieutenants to Ollie and Howley they were simply gang shit-bags. Ollie asked, "who the hell is Aiden? You've been working with me for years and never mentioned an Aiden." There was a hint of anger in his voice as he pushed the man mountain for an answer.

"Calm down Sergeant; he's hardly around and never been in the picture for anything we've talked about. He's a cousin of the Knowles boys; well I think he is."

"Right, so you think he's involved now?"

"Not sure. Just an unknown quantity and he used to do some fucked up stuff back in the day. But Jack and Adam have been noisy lately. They want more business on the North and have pushed Kyle about it. Adam is a vicious little bastard and Kyle thinks Jack has taken out a few Salford lads on the sly."

"I take it Jack is still running fags and green out of The Flying Horse?" Howley said.

"Yeah, he wants to be big time but has some weird agoraphobic thing going on with that place."

"What about Adam? Is he still running the bookies near Baguley park?"

"Mostly, but he has been running a prescription scam out of the back of the hospital too so he's mobile a lot. He's in a black Audi, not sure what type, they all look the same."

Ollie nodded, "yeah we know the car. What about Aiden?"

"I'm afraid I can't help you with that. He isn't from the patch. I will say though, he's a stuck up twat, who thinks he's better than everyone round here."

"And you say he's a cousin?"

"I think so but I can't say for sure."

"Really helpful," interjected Howley. "Can you tell us anything useful?"

"Look, I'm sorry man. He's a clever dick called Aiden who is sometimes at Kyle's place. That's all I know. And listen, if it was me I'd be looking at Jack."

Howley was becoming agitated and Ollie quickly said, "Ok Brixton, thank you for your insight, if you think of anything else, call me, yeah?"

"Scout's honour, Sergeant."

The two detectives climbed back into the car and pulled the doors closed. McKenna's refusal to believe that Kyle had killed Andy was preying on their minds and Howley was the first to break the silence. "Ok, I'll say it. What if he didn't do it?"

"From what you told me about the arrest there's enough forensic evidence to convict him. He was at the scene, covered in blood, and it looks like his hammer was the murder weapon. So the law of averages tells us he did it. But, there is no apparent motive." Ollie said.

"No motive and everything we know about Knowles, and all the intel we have, points to him trusting Andy Lewis. This murder makes no sense. And I'll be honest Ollie; I think we have to consider that there's a chance Knowles didn't do it. There's something iffy about this whole thing."

"I agree. So what now?"

"We stop assuming Knowles is the only suspect and we investigate this like any other murder. We look at what we know and what we need to know and build a case. Working it backwards was always the wrong way to approach this." Howley explained.

"What about Sutherland?" Ollie asked.

"Don't worry about Sutherland. We'll work the case then we'll go to him. For now, let him enjoy his moment. Let's not forget Knowles is a world-class scum bag so a few weeks or months on remand won't do him any harm. We let Sutherland and Grace push for remand and I'll report back to him, when or if we find anything."

"OK. Let's move on this. I'll drop you with the coroner and I'll go and see Amy Lawrence."

"Is it really my turn to see the pathologist?" Howley asked.

"Yes it is, and you know it. I got stuck with that freak they sent last time; it's your turn now."

CHAPTER NINE

Howley watched Ollie drive off to 'Tin Town' and turned to face the mortuary entrance. It was a forgotten corner of the hospital that had lost out on any refurbishment and sat somberly waiting for its silent visitors. The grey cement-slabbed walls and aluminium framed, blacked out, windows looked starkly out of place nestled amidst the newer red brick, and white upvc that the refurbishment works had blessed the remainder of the building with.

As he made his way to the entrance his phone buzzed in his pocket. He looked at the screen: SUTHERLAND. "Shit" he muttered to himself. He ignored the call; choosing to deal with his ambitious boss later.

Howley pressed the intercom and waited for a reply. His stomach growled at him and he made a mental note to arrange to eat at some point after his visit to the morgue. As he thought about places to eat the intercom buzzed into life.

"Hello," said a voice from the intercom.

"DS Howley for Christine Mullins."

"Come on in Sergeant."

The door lock clicked open and Howley pushed his way into the mortuary. The pungent aroma of alkaline cleaning agents invaded his senses and he winced as his olfactory organs adjusted. He signed in with the receptionist and waited for Christine Mullins.

Christine Mullins was the coroner's officer and acted as a liaison between the Home Office appointed pathologist and the police. Christine was a former police officer and Howley had known her for years. Part of her role was looking into unexplained deaths and establishing whether or not a post-mortem should be performed. If a post-mortem was required she would advise the coroner and they would order the post-mortem. Today her role was clear cut, the body had come in with obvious signs of foul play and she immediately ensured a home office pathologist was brought in to perform a post-mortem.

Howley didn't have to wait long before Christine appeared at the reception area. Christine was in her early fifties and wore her dyed, auburn, hair in a simple bob-cut. At a little over five foot and with a slight frame she had always looked out of place in her police uniform.

"Hello Steve," she said warmly.

"Hi Chris, how are you?"

"I'm good thanks. And you?" She replied.

Howley sighed loudly, "the usual: over-worked and under-paid." They both laughed together and Christine signaled that he should follow her.

They walked a short way through a wide corridor and into Christine's office. The office was filled with neatly stacked archive boxes and a collection of steel filing cabinets. Dominating the room was a large desk awash with files and papers. Family photos beamed out from picture frames and her screensaver was a slideshow kaleidoscope of even more family portraits and candid poses. She pulled out a chair for Howley and he sat. She walked round the desk and took her own seat opposite him.

"I take it you're here about Andy Lewis?"

"Yeah, has the doc finished the post yet?" Howley asked.

"He's just about done, I was in there earlier, poor kid took a real battering."

"I know, I was with the team at the factory. Looked to me like most of the damage was done before death. Has the doc confirmed that?"

Christine picked up a page of notes from her desk and said, "yes. All the bruising and broken bones appear to have been sustained before he died."

Howley felt sick, "I can't even imagine the pain he must have felt. So what's the official cause of death? Exsanguination from wounds sustained? Or a blow to the head?"

"Neither, he was stabbed directly into the lungs. There were six puncture wounds placed between the ribs and penetrating the intercostals. They appear to have been quite deliberately located. His lungs collapsed and filled with blood. He would have struggled to breathe for a few minutes before passing out and dying."

"Stabbed?" Howley asked with surprise. He'd not seen any stab marks at the scene and he was expecting to be told that Andy had been bludgeoned to death.

"Yes, with all the blood it's no surprise that you didn't see the wounds at the scene." She referred to the notes again. "A long sharp weapon, about fifteen centimeters long. Likely to be a knife but it could possibly be a screw driver or similar. But you will have to find a weapon to make a match I'm afraid."

Howley tried to picture the factory again and had no recollection of any knives or anything could be used as a knife. He made a note in his pad to check with the scene of crimes team if they'd picked up anything. If they hadn't they would have to find it.

"Are you ok Steve?" Christine asked the contemplative Howley.

"Yeah, sorry, just thinking."

Christine nodded, "I'll push the pathologist to complete the write up for you but it's pretty much as we've discussed. We're still waiting for substance tests on the bloods but that seems unlikely to change the cause of death."

"Ok, can I have a copy of your notes?" He asked hopefully.

"You know I can't really do that Steve, but if you promise to keep quiet about it then yes."

Howley rang Ollie as he waited for Christine to copy her notes. Ollie didn't answer and Howley guessed that he was probably with Andy's girlfriend. Having recently learned to text he applied his new skill and messaged him: **meet me for a late lunch in Sale. I have news. 14.30?**

Christine returned to the office with a copy of the notes and handed them to Howley. "Remember I didn't give you these," she said.

"Gave me what?"

"Quite."

Howley shared a few minutes reminiscing with Christine before excusing himself and leaving the mortuary. His stomach growled and he remembered the text he'd sent Ollie about lunch. He walked from the mortuary around the hospital to the taxi-rank. He was about to sit in a taxi when his phone buzzed again; it was Sutherland again. He knew he'd have to tell him about the stabbing at some point, but not now. He tapped the red button and sent Sutherland's call to voicemail.

CHAPTER TEN

Ryan Knowles was Kyle's younger brother. Like his brother he was tall and well muscled and shared the same thick, dark hair. Following a long night in the cells at Wythenshawe police station he was being driven home in a very conspicuous police car. He hadn't been questioned for long before being released without charge. They did, however, seize his car in their search for evidence. As the patrol car passed the brutal, diesel-stained, concrete façade of the civic-centre and supermarket, he stared blankly at the people milling around on the car park. He recognised some of the faces, old friends, ex-girlfriends and some of the runners he and Kyle used for money collecting.

As they drove away from the harsh design of the civic-centre and past Hatchett's wood the angular architecture faded and softer, red-bricked homes nestled comfortably amongst well established trees and open greenery. Ryan looked over to Big Wood and Little Wood and remembered his childhood, first playing in the woods and then hiding from truant officers as he skipped school, encouraged by his big brother, Kyle.

As they crossed the railway at Heald Green Ryan leant forward and spoke to the constable driving. "Just drop me near the library."

The driver suppressed the urge to rant about not being a taxi driver for scum-bags like Knowles and simply nodded; he knew from experience that there was little point in engaging with him. He slowed the car and pulled up outside of the library. Ryan didn't try and open the door, he knew it was locked and could only be opened from the outside and he waited for the pc to come round and let him out.

Ryan stepped out of the car and without walked away. His usual cock-sure stride failed him as he headed towards his home and his hands shook as he took his phone from his pocket. He found the number for his cousin, Aiden. He pressed call and put his phone to his ear. He took a deep breath and exhaled deliberately to calm his nerves. After a few rings his call was answered.

"Ryan, I told you not to call me at work." A nervous, whispering voice answered.

"I know, but I didn't know who else to call," said Ryan.

"Yeah I know what happened. But what can I do?"

"You can help, you know people." Ryan said desperately.

"This is different," the hushed voice fell silent before continuing, "but, I have come across some information that we could use."

"What? What can we do?" Ryan asked with optimism.

"I can't do anything, not yet, but you might be able to do something. Do you still have the Prodigy on the hook?"

Ryan felt a surge of excited expectation; "yeah, he's still into us for a few grand, why?"

"I'll let you know in a few days. Just keep calm and run things as usual. He'll be remanded so you need to stay sharp. This isn't his first arrest, or remand, so treat it like all those other times."

"I know all that Aiden, but something feels different about this. Something is way off. Kyle wouldn't kill Andy. It's a set up, it must be." Ryan said.

Aiden sighed heavily; "I know Kyle and Andy were tight but things change."

"They haven't changed. We were all together the day before. Everything was good, really good."

Aiden paused and thought; "I know mate, but we have to be realistic. You were picked up at the factory too, what did you see?"

Ryan closed his eyes and pictured the bloody scene. He shuddered as he visualised Andy's tortured corpse. "It was a fucking horror film man. I've never seen so much blood."

"What about Kyle? Where was he? Did he say anything?"

"He was covered in blood. He was just standing there looking at Andy, Andy's body."

"And what did he say?"

Ryan frowned as he thought about the factory, "he said he didn't do it. I asked him why he'd killed Andy and he said he didn't do it." He stopped talking for a minute and then said: "when I saw it, when I saw the blood and Andy, and Kyle's hammer I thought he'd done it. I was ready to help him clean up. Then I saw him just standing there and saying nothing. I didn't even ask him I just thought he'd done it."

Ryan's walk had slowed to a complete stop and he realised he was outside Christ Church. Built in the early sixties the contemporary design and, brown-red, brick construction was less obtrusive than many of the catholic churches that had risen during the same era. The star-shaped, stained glass window glinted in the sun and the double doors were slightly ajar. He sat on the wall and spoke into the phone: "Aiden, you gone?"

"I'm still here."

"It's all to shit isn't it?" Ryan said.

"It's not looking good mate. I wish I could say different"

Ryan knew his cousin was right, "I know, I better go now. I'll call Prodigy and tell him I'll need him. Call me if you hear anything."

"I'll keep my ear to the ground. Stay safe Ryan."

"Yeah, safe." He ended the call and pocketed the phone. He heard voices behind him and turned to look at the church doors. Three women were leaving the church, in their sixties and uniformed in rain coats with stout hand-bags. They seemed to talk in unison and they left through the wrought iron gate and ambled along Finney Drive.

Shortly after they had wandered off the parish priest appeared from within the church. Grey haired, and straight backed he had a calm look of wisdom and kindness. He nodded a greeting at Ryan. He then fumbled with the door locks and approached Ryan. "Are you ok?" He asked in a clichéd Irish accent.

Ryan nodded and replied: "I'm fine Father, just having a minute. Do you want me to move off the wall?"

The priest chortled. "No son, you're welcome to sit awhile. If you want to talk about something I can open up again?" He said.

"Thanks but I'll be ok."

"Well the church is always open if you ever change your mind." The priest patted Ryan on the shoulder and walked away in the direction of the library.

CHAPTER ELEVEN

Grace finalised her remand preparation and drained her third coffee cup of the day. A large, white-plastic clock ticked loudly and Grace became acutely aware of the time: 5.00pm. She needed to report back to Michael and help Matthew sort her case load out before the end of the day. She carefully tidied her papers together and closed the lid of her laptop before slipping her jacket on.

The piercing trill of incoming calls and the white-noise chatter of the main office seeped through the door. Grace readied herself for the assault on her senses and pulled open the door. She saw Sutherland flirting with some of the female clerical workers and she made her way over to him.

"Excuse me, Chief Inspector, I'm all set for the remand hearing in the morning." She told the preening Sutherland.

"That's excellent; do you foresee any problems with it?" He asked.

"No, it should be fairly routine. It would be very rare for someone charged with murder to be released on bail anyway and we have a lot of strong evidence that he may fail to attend trial or interfere with witnesses, not to mention his connection to at least four other ongoing criminal investigations." Grace explained.

"You appear to have it all in hand, I assume you'll be calling me as witness and arresting officer?"

"Yes, I'd appreciate it if you could meet me at the Magistrate's court about half an hour before the hearing. Say ten o'clock?"

"I'll be there."

"Thank you Chief Inspector, I'm heading back to the office now."

"Ok, take care Ms Sterling; I'll see you at the Magistrate's in the morning."

Grace left the gangs and organised crime unit and hurried through the main corridor, towards reception. As she walked she phoned for a black cab to take her back into the city centre.

Grace didn't have to wait long before her cab arrived and she tried to relax as the taxi driver piloted her from Wythenshawe and towards the city centre. Her feet were pinched by the shoes she wore and she slipped them off to rub her toes.

Twenty minutes later the cab pulled up on Quay Street and Grace pulled her shoes back on before stepping out onto the street. The matinee had started in the Opera House theatre and Grace could hear a vague bass thump pushing through the walls. She looked up at the sign to see what was playing and decided she was quite happy not to be watching Evita.

The CPS office was quiet, as prosecutors and their teams attended court, and Grace strode directly to Michael Blunt's office. Michael smiled broadly at her: "Hi Grace. Everything ok at Wythenshawe?" He asked.

"Everything is good. I've prepped for the remand hearing and Sutherland's team are bringing the case evidence together."

"Good, so we need to get you an assistant sorted out, don't we?" He asked rhetorically.

"I was hoping I could have Ruth Spalding?" She asked hopefully.

"Good choice, consider it done."

"Thanks Michael. What about my current case load? I didn't see Matthew in the office; did he get a chance to look through it before court?" Grace asked anxiously.

"Calm down Grace. Your cases are in good hands. Matthew had them reassigned before he went court. He might want a quick meeting to go over some points but otherwise your focus is on trial prep for Knowles."

"That's great I'll see Matthew later."

"Very good, now go and get yourself some lunch and go over your remand hearing plans. When you're happy with them get Ruth to bring me a copy." Michael said.

Grace stood and walked out into the open plan area looking for Ruth Spalding. At the coffee machine Grace saw the thick, golden curls of Ruth and she walked over to her.

"Hi Ruth." Grace said

"Hi Grace, I heard you got a big murder case."

"You heard right and I've asked Michael if you can be my assistant."

"Really?" Ruth asked excitedly.

"Yes, and he's agreed."

"That's brilliant; I can't wait to get started."

"Well come with me to my office and I'll talk you through what has happened so far." Grace replied.

Grace turned and walked towards her office; Ruth followed closely. Grace's office was neatly arranged and her desk held no mess. Yellow legal pads were stacked military-straight and her chair had been left neatly tucked under the desk. There were no pictures or any sign of personalisation on the desk. She walked round to her chair and sat; Ruth followed suit and sat opposite her.

Ruth was a legal assistant and had been part of the Manchester office for three years. Her effervescent personality and the seemingly limitless energy she applied to her work meant she was in demand amongst the prosecutors. Her curly hair and fresh face could have been an obstacle to being taken seriously but anyone who spent any time with her soon realised how serious and intelligent she was and she soon became the most sought after assistant in the office.

Grace quickly brought Ruth up to speed and they checked over the remand plan that Grace had prepared at the station. Confident the remand hearing would go to plan Ruth made copies and took them to Michael Blunt. As she walked across the office she beamed with pride and self-satisfaction about her inclusion on the Knowles' case.

CHAPTER TWELVE

The roads through the estate were quiet and Ollie almost wished for a delay as he contemplated the task ahead. As he rounded the final corner into Amy's street he saw the patrol car parked outside and realised the family liaison officer was still present.

Amy lived in a maisonette above a fishing tackle shop. The exterior brickwork was battered, and poorly maintained windows shed paint layers, with every winter that passed. Optimistic neighbours had hung washing out to dry across the elevated back yards and the shop next door had been boarded up so long the plywood had started to fade. Grubby net curtains, yellowed with smoke, and greyed with filth, adorned the windows above the shop fronts and long gone radio stations were remembered with stickers that had been applied sometime in the early eighties.

Ollie reached into his bag and took out his note pad and pen before stepping out of the car. The way into the maisonettes was around the back and he walked down the side of the tackle shop and found the right gate for Amy's stairs. As he opened the gate he was greeted by a uniformed officer who asked him for identification.

"Ollie James, gangs and organised crime." He said as he showed the constable his identification card.

"That's fine sir. She's just up the stairs; the liaison officer is with her."

Ollie nodded and climbed the stairs quickly. Amy's door was a shade of blue that only local councils used and her letter box rattled with every wisp of wind. There was no door bell so he tapped gently on the narrow, frosted, window.

Before he had finished knocking the family liaison officer answered the door.

The family liaison officer was, like most, a female, uniformed, officer. Ollie recognised her and said: "Hi Julie. How is she?"

Julie answered quietly: "She's ok. But go easy if you're here to interview her."

"I will. Is she through here?" He asked pointing at an internal door he assumed led to the living room.

"Yes do you want me to come in with you?"

"Yeah, she might need a hand to hold." Ollie said.

Ollie pushed the door open and stepped into the living room. The living room bore no relation to the shabby exterior of the building. A large leather sofa fought for domination of the room with an over-sized plasma television and the coffee table was a tasteful arched square of beech wood. Either side of the sofa were two large armchairs, that Ollie assumed were recliners.

Huddled deep into the corner was Amy Lawrence. Knees drawn up, she looked sorrowfully at Ollie through blood-shot eyes. Her blonde hair was scraped back tightly into a pony tail and her body shuddered slightly as she cried to herself. She had pulled the sleeves of her loose fitting jumper over her hands as if the grief had chilled her. Ollie sat on the edge of one of the armchairs and angled himself to face Amy directly.

He spoke softly: "Hi Amy, I'm Ollie James; I'm investigating Andy's death. I would like to ask you a few questions please?"

The clearly devastated girl sniffed and nodded. "Ok." She said almost inaudibly.

"I know this is hard for you but I really have to ask."

She nodded again but said nothing. Ollie could sense she was waiting for him to ask a question.

"Amy did you know what sort of things Andy did for Kyle Knowles?" He asked.

Amy sat up straight and moved her feet from the sofa to the floor. She leant forward and blew her nose, took a deep breath and answered clearly: "He ran the loan sharking for him."

"Ok, and on the eighth was that why Kyle asked him to meet him? To talk about the loans?"

Amy paused and thought. "He didn't say, he just said he had to go out."

"So, Kyle called him when?"

"It wasn't a call, it was a text. I think he got it about six." Amy replied.

"Ok and had Andy had any problems with Kyle recently? Were his takings down or anything like that?" He probed.

"No, he always brought the cash in." Amy was still calm as she spoke.

"So what was causing problems for them?"

Amy frowned and glared at Ollie. "There was no problem. They were tight. Andy loved Kyle like a brother and Kyle treated Andy good. Why are you asking about problems? There was no problems." Amy was crying again and Julie sat with her and placed a comforting arm around her shoulder.

"I'm sorry to upset you but I have to find out why Kyle killed Andy." Ollie explained.

Amy sobbed hard into Julie's shoulder and her body shuddered with every breath. She shook her head and spoke through gasps of air. "Kyle wouldn't have killed Andy. They were best mates, brothers." Tears streamed from her eyes and her voice was broken. "I don't know who killed Andy. But I know it wasn't Kyle."

Ollie thought for a moment about telling her about the crime scene and the evidence but could see she was already too distraught for anymore anguish. He nodded and waited to see if she had anything else to say. After a minute or more of watching her cry he asked her, "Amy, if you don't think Kyle did it, who else could've done it?"

Amy shook her head frantically, "I don't know." She said desperately.

"What about Jack Haworth or Adam Grey? Or Kyle's cousin, Aiden?" He asked.

"I just don't know." She wailed.

Ollie knew she didn't have much more to offer. Her anger and grief were all consuming. "Did you ever meet Aiden?"

She sniveled and sobbed. "No, never heard of him."

Ollie nodded. "Ok Amy, I think that's all for now but if you think of anything else you want to tell me please call me." He handed her a card with his number on and stood to leave.

"Sergeant, Kyle didn't hurt my Andy."

Ollie looked at her. "How can you be so sure? Everything we know points to him. Are you keeping something from me?"

"I just know. Someone else killed Andy."

Ollie didn't understand how she could be so sure about Knowles' innocence. It was barely a day since her boyfriend had been brutally murdered. Knowles was found soaked in Andy's blood and his hammer had been used to torture and kill him and yet, through her grief she was sure Knowles didn't do it.

He thanked Amy for her time and reminded her to call him if she thought of anything else. He left the maisonette and stepped quickly down the stairs. As he walked to his car he checked his phone and found the message from Howley. He responded to the message and drove across to Sale.

CHAPTER THIRTEEN

Howley paid for his taxi ride and stepped out onto the street. It was busy in Sale town centre and Joe's café had few free tables. Howley pushed open the door and a traditional bell jangled above his head. Joe's was a typical greasy spoon and chalked scrawlings listed five different types of breakfasts, none of them vegetarian. The walls were a shrine to Manchester City and aged, yellowing, pictures of never forgotten heroes mingled with modern millionaire super stars. A broad, blue, tiled counter held a simple till and a large urn, that steamed and bubbled as water was kept constantly boiling.

Howley looked around and chose a free table. He picked up a laminated menu and began to read through the selection. A minute later and a waitress appeared to take his order. The waitress was a young girl with a tightly drawn pony tail and huge hooped earrings. Her blue apron covered a designer t-shirt and her wrist dripped with tacky, gold charms. She chewed loudly as she asked Howley what he wanted. Howley ordered a mug of tea and explained he was waiting for somebody to join him before ordering food. The girl nodded, chewed and left Howley alone.

The door bell jangled again and Howley turned to see Ollie step into the café. Ollie saw him and joined him at the table. "Why do we always end up here Steve?"

"Because it's honest, simple food and you know you love it." Howley said.

"Yeah, yeah. You just want to keep fur lining your arteries."

"Thank you, doctor. So, what did you learn from Amy?" Howley asked.

"As you'd expect she's a mess but is convinced Knowles didn't do it." Ollie explained.

Howley frowned and chewed his cheek. "Does that not seem strange to you? I mean, she's just lost her boyfriend and Knowles was found covered in his blood; what would you normally expect from someone in this situation?"

"I know where you're going with this and yes I was surprised that she hadn't instantly latched on to the obvious suspect and directed all her anger and hatred and blame on him."

"What are we missing here?" Howley pondered.

"I wish I knew."

As Howley scratched his stubbled chin and thought about Amy's strange reaction the waitress returned to the table. Howley ordered a sausage sandwich and Ollie opted for a baked potato, with cheese and onion. As the waitress left them they returned to their conversation.

"Well I had an interesting visit to the morgue. The hammer is not the murder weapon, he was stabbed." Howley said.

Ollie was surprised by the news, "Stabbed? Was a knife recovered from the scene?"

"I didn't see anything and the SOCO report hasn't come through yet. I think I'll go and see them after this."

"Good idea, I'm going to try and catch up with Grace. I'll fill her in on our progress." Ollie said.

Howley gave Ollie a sarcastic grin. "Of course that's why you're going to see her."

"She's the prosecutor, I'm a lead detective. What other reason could there be?"

"Just don't upset her."

Before Ollie could respond the waitress brought their order to the table. Howley added sauce to his sandwich and Ollie spooned a little mayonnaise onto his. They ate in silence as they contemplated the information gathered during the day.

Howley finished his sandwich and gulped the last his tea. "Did you press Amy about Jack or Adam?"

Ollie sipped his coke. "Yeah, drew a blank. Same when I asked her about Aiden. She's a total wreck, barely coherent."

"No surprise and yet she still managed to proclaim Knowles' innocence."

"I know, and with no hesitation; which makes me think there's something we're missing. Do you think someone got to her?"

"It's not impossible, but the family liaison officer has been there from an hour after we found Andy. She could've been texted or facebooked or any of that crap I suppose."

"If nobody got to her, then what?" Ollie asked.

"Then we're still missing something."

"Add it to the list of things we don't know."

Howley thought for a moment, "I think we need to pay a visit to Ryan."

Ollie nodded. "Yeah, if nothing else he can give us a lead on Aiden."

"He'll be at the court tomorrow to support his big brother. We can grab him there." Howley suggested.

"I'm not sure how cooperative he'll be after he sees big brother remanded."

"We can but try." Howley said sagely.

"Quite."

As the two men talked through the case the café had lost several customers and the clatter of cutlery on crockery had all but gone. The over-worked cook was spraying the stainless hob with cleaner and the waitress was outside leaning against the window, having a smoke break. The men sat in silence for a moment as they worked through each other's contributions to the investigation.

Howley spoke again. "I've been thinking about the unknown cousin, Aiden. If he's family Ryan won't give him up easily so on your way to see Grace, drop into the office and get one of the civilian intel officers to do a family search. We may know this guy under a different name."

"I had the same thought. We've been following Knowles for so long we must have something." Ollie said.

Howley nodded, "yes, but family links are easily lost these days. Divorce, remarriage, affairs, they all extend the family. This Aiden could be a cleaner at the station and we'd never know. Hell, he could be a cop"

"Well, you never know we might find something. I'll speak to a few contacts up on the estate too and see of anyone knows anything."

"Ok, good."

"So what are you going to tell Sutherland? Does he know the cause of death?" Ollie enquired.

"I asked Christine not to rush the report over. Let's get Knowles in remand, he's still the number one suspect."

Ollie frowned. "Don't you think we should tell Grace and Sutherland? Are we not withholding evidence?"

Howley shook his head. "Technically, yes. But we both know Knowles is a shit-bag and the estate will be better for a while with him locked away."

Ollie sighed. "Technically Steve? Definitely."

"Come on Ollie if I hadn't been to see Christine the chances are that Sutherland and Grace wouldn't have found out until after the hearing anyway."

"Yes but you did and you know it wasn't the hammer that killed Andy. Grace is basing the whole remand hearing on the evidentiary strength of Knowles' ownership of the hammer."

Howley nodded. "I know and the hammer was still used to inflict dozens of perimortem injuries. It doesn't change the fact that we'd still have Knowles in custody and we'd still be putting him in front of the beak for remand."

Ollie thought about what Howley had just said and nodded. "Ok I'll keep quiet about it when I see Grace but what do you think Sutherland will do when he receives the report from the coroner?"

"At this point all we know is that Andy was killed with a knife but that doesn't preclude Knowles being the killer. If SOCO have a knife from the scene we'll soon see if it's linked to Knowles. If SOCO didn't turn up a knife then we need to get back into the factory with SOCO and see if we can find it." Howley conjectured.

Ollie agreed with Howley and looked for the waitress to ask her for the bill. The door bell jangled again and Ollie looked to see the waitress return from her break. He raised his hand a little and mouthed "bill please" to her.

As he waited for the waitress to bring the bill he took out his phone and found Grace's number. He put five pounds on the table and told Howley he was stepping out to make a call. Howley grinned knowingly, "say hello to her from me." Ollie rolled his and eyes and gave his friend the vee-sign as he walked towards the door.

Outside the café Ollie called Grace. The phone rang out and went to voicemail. Ollie thought for a moment and then decided not to leave a message and ended the call. As he put the phone back into his pocket Howley emerged from the café and joined him.

The afternoon's traffic had begun to build, as schools and colleges finished for the day, and the usually short drive to the station was marred and delayed by buses and anxious mothers, too scared of the modern world to allow their precious darlings to catch the school bus or even walk. As they eventually arrived at the station the two men went their separate ways and agreed to meet early the following day.

CHAPTER FOURTEEN

Howley left Ollie and allowed his pace to fall to a stroll as he made his way to the SOCO lab. The lab was located on the top floor and Howley's knees creaked as he climbed the stairs. After completing his weary climb he moved quickly into the SOCO lab and waited, in a small glass-walled vestibule area that allowed him to see the SOCOs busy in their clinical environment, for someone to let him in.

There was a strong chemical smell emanating from within the work areas and Howley could hear a camera snapping shots of whatever evidence had been brought in that day. The work area was busy with at least three SOCO teams, busy preparing reports and filling evidence bags. White coats blurred past, hurrying to meet the demands of pressured investigating officers and the phone seemed to be constantly ringing. In the furthest corner of the lab Howley could see the supervisor of the SOCO team that had attended the factory crime scene. He waved to him and Milner returned the wave before finishing whatever he was working on and making his way over to Howley.

Milner opened the door and Howley stepped into the laboratories. Milner was carrying a file and he was fully prepared for any questions Howley had. Howley had worked with Milner before and knew he was an excellent SOCO. He was one of several SOCOs at Wythenshawe who had been constables before moving into the labs. It meant he understood the pressures faced by the investigating officers and rarely complained about tight deadlines. He was also one of the most thorough crime scene investigators and if there had been a knife at the scene Milner or his team should have found it.

"Hello Sergeant, I assume you're here about the Knowles' case." Milner said.

"Just one question." Howley told him.

"Ok, fire away."

"Nice simple one this. Did you find a knife at the factory?" Howley asked.

Milner's brow furrowed in thought and he shuffled through the file in his hand before responding. "No, I couldn't recall anything and there's nothing listed here for either the immediate crime scene or the factory as a whole. Why do you ask?"

"I've been to see the coroner's liaison today and the hammer wasn't the murder weapon, he'd been stabbed. We're looking for a narrow bladed knife." Howley explained.

Milner's eyes widened. "Right we need to get back there now. The area's still taped off but I don't know how many officers we were able to leave there and whether they're still there or not."

Howley nodded and realised he'd just set himself for a long night with a torch in his hand. "Ok we can get across there in less than an hour. Have you got a team ready to go or is it just me and you?"

"We're stretched to the limit Steve, I'm afraid it's just us two. Give me a few minutes to grab a kit and we'll take a van and go. Are you ok for gloves and a torch?"

"Yeah I'm fine I'll meet you down in the car park." Howley said as he moved towards the door.

"Ok, be there in five."

Howley left the SOCO labs and descended the stairs. Back on the ground floor he dashed through the corridors towards the gangs and organised crimes room, hoping to catch Ollie before he left. The corridors were bright white and fluorescent lit, making Howley squint with discomfort as he squeezed politely past dawdling officers who crowded the narrow spaces. After several shouts of 'pardon' and 'excuse me' Howley reached the unit's doors.

Through the doors Howley could hear that the earlier frenetic energy had now subsided into a more subdued murmur. He pushed the door open and turned his attention directly to the civilian intelligence officers; stood amongst them was Ollie. Howley walked over to his colleague. "Guess who's about to spend the evening searching an old factory?"

Ollie laughed. "Ouch. Who's your hot date with?"

"Well that's the good news; it's Greg Milner."

Ollie nodded. "Well that's good; he's a very attractive and intelligent man" Ollie smirked and checked his watch. "Grace will be on the train now; so I won't be able to crash your date night. But if he gets too handsy for you I can come back later?"

Howley shook his head. "You're so funny. Why don't you try jokes like that on Grace and maybe she'll have you back?" He said sarcastically. "I'll give you a call when we're done at the factory."

"Ok, I'll check my emails and head down to Grace's place. If you're not done by nine I'll bring you and your date some coffee and donuts." Ollie quipped.

"Yes, yes you're hilarious but at least Milner will be civil with me. I doubt Grace will be so accommodating."

"She'll be fine. She was as culpable as me."

Howley laughed. "You really don't get women do you? It's not the breakup she was upset about. It was your instant rebound into bed with that WPC that upset her."

"We were over; I didn't do anything wrong."

"You're an idiot."

Ollie winced at the insult. "Thanks for that Steve."

"Right I need to get down to the car park. You just be polite and pleasant to Grace and hope she doesn't slap you." Howley said.

"Ok, take care."

Howley nodded and left the office. As he walked out onto the car park his back twinged and not for the first time recently he wondered if he should think about retiring. The car park was busy with marked vehicles and Howley didn't see Milner immediately. Moments later one of the vans moved in his direction and Howley recognised the driver as Milner. The van stopped for him and he climbed in next to Milner.

CHAPTER FIFTEEN

Ollie looked up from his computer and saw that the office was manned only by those few staff on the late shift. The intel officers had found no links between Knowles and anyone called Aiden; but the search would continue the following day. He closed the computer down and threw his, vending machine, coffee cup into the bin. He rubbed his eyes and yawned as he stood from his chair. From his untidy desk he grabbed his phone and then checked his messages: none. He contemplated calling Grace before heading to her place but decided against it and sent her a text instead.

The bright, viper-green, paint work of Ollie's Scirocco made him smile as he approached his car. His choice of cars had always been specific and his love of sporty models had, for about six months, earned him the nickname of Gene Hunt within CID.

It was a forty minute drive to Grace's home in Macclesfield and the traffic was busy. Ollie listened to Simon Mayo's drive time show as he maneuvered his way from the confines of the M60 ring road and out onto the Buxton road. The stop start traffic through Hazel Grove irritated him and only when he was clear of Poynton could he push his foot into the carpet and make some progress. The open fields that the road cut through were lushly green and the rail line that ran alongside the road was quiet now.

As he approached the outskirts of Macclesfield the satnav popped up with a message asking him if he wanted to navigate to Grace's; it was a reminder of his frequent visits before they'd split up. He dismissed the message; as he knew the route well enough himself. He continued his drive into Macclesfield and headed towards the famous Hovis Mill, which was now a modern apartment building. Grace lived near the mill and within walking distance of the station.

Many of the predominantly Georgian houses, which made up much of Macclesfield, had been converted into flats and apartments. Those that hadn't were huge homes for those fortunate enough to live in them. Amongst the conversions was the building Grace lived in. Ollie pulled up outside the building and cut the engine. He looked up at her apartment window and wondered if seeing Grace was a good idea.

***

Grace was sitting in her favourite seat on a comfortable, leather sofa. She was sipping at a herbal tea and watching a regional news show. Her designer shoes had been kicked into a corner, her suit lay on the bed and she was relaxed in jeans and a t-shirt. She was waiting for Ollie to arrive and had her remand notes ready, along with a fresh yellow legal pad and a pen.

She was nervous as she waited for Ollie's arrival. It had been a year since she'd last been alone with Ollie. She heard a car pull up outside and she peered through her window. She recognised Ollie's car.

Ollie wandered across a well kept lawn to the entrance of the apartments. He pressed the intercom for Grace and waited for her to answer. Seconds later she answered.

"It's open."

Ollie nudged the door open and stepped into the large hall area. The chipped and faded stair case dominated the room. Next to the stairs stood a sad looking yucca-plant, with browned leaf ends. He took the stairs two at a time and was soon outside Grace's door.

Grace opened the door and Ollie asked, "May I come in?"

"I think it'd push the boundaries of professionalism if we did this on my door step. So yes, you may come in." She said tersely.

Ollie followed her into the apartment and felt a pang of regret. He looked around the once very familiar living room and noticed the wonderfully comfortable sofa he used to enjoy slouching on with Grace. "I see you decided to keep the old sofa." He said. "I love that sofa."

Grace's response was cold and simple. "Were you expecting otherwise? A clean sweep maybe?"

"No, I just remembered you used to talk about getting something different." Ollie said calmly and warmly in an attempt to break the frosty wall Grace was putting up.

"Well I didn't. You can sit down on it if you like it that much."

"Thanks, I don't suppose there's any chance of a coffee?" He asked hoping she'd see the humour in his request.

She didn't. "You're right, there isn't."

Ollie pushed his luck a little more. "But it's so cold in here."

"Not funny Ollie." She almost snarled. "Can we get on with this please?"

"Ok first things first. Do you need anything urgently from me for the remand hearing?"

"No, everything is in place." She answered.

"Good, so I assume you went through all the evidence from the crime scene, so you saw the obvious missing piece?"

"Do enlighten me Ollie."

"There's no motive." Ollie said.

Grace considered what he'd just said. "The man was found in the middle of a massacre holding what appears to be the murder weapon, and not just any man: Kyle Knowles. That'll be enough; I'll paint a vivid picture for the judge. Don't you worry."

"Well yes for remand purposes that's fine; but for trial you'll want as much on him as possible." He said.

Grace sipped her tea and fidgeted in her seat. She nodded in agreement but didn't say anything. Her lips were pursed tightly as she fought back emotions she thought long gone and she found it hard to look at Ollie. Ollie noticed her discomfort. "Are you ok Grace?"

Grace took a sharp breath. "Why are you here Ollie? Really? Is it to hurt me more or to apologise? I don't understand Ollie; we could have exchanged emails about the remand hearing."

Ollie was stunned by her sudden challenge and was unsure how to answer. "I'm here to make sure you're kept in the loop." He thought for a moment, "and to apologise if I can."

Grace shook her head; "I don't believe I just heard you say those words. Do you even know why I was hurt?"

"I do." He said almost inaudibly.

"Well that's progress I suppose. If only you'd been more thoughtful before you jumped into bed with that WPC."

Ollie wanted to respond and remind her that they had agreed to split up; instead he gave a sheepish half smile and nodded. "I know; I was a total dick. I'm sorry Grace."

"Ok, you're sorry. That doesn't change the fact that you made me feel like a worthless piece of shit. But fine; you're sorry and I'm grateful for the apology." Grace said quietly and calmly.

"Thank you. So we're ok to work together? To go at this case properly?" Ollie asked.

"We're ok. We'll be totally professional."

"Good. So you met Sutherland; I take it you got a good idea what he's about?"

"Oh yes, a shiny medal and a huge feather in his cap in his push for commissioner." Grace said sarcastically.

"Yeah that's about right and he's really not interested in anything else. So don't let him push you into trial unprepared."

"I have never let anyone push me into trial unprepared." Grace said with a hint of anger.

"Sorry, I know."

"Ok, so back to motive. Just what sort of motive does a bastard like Knowles need?" Asked Grace.

"I don't know but it's all very strange. Even the victim's girlfriend doesn't think Knowles did it."

Grace had picked up her pad and had begun making notes. "Strange, but it doesn't mean he didn't do it. She could have been threatened."

"Agreed, but we also got the same reaction from one of our more reliable informants."

"Informants are notoriously flakey, even the good ones." She continued to write as she spoke.

Ollie looked over the top of her pad and saw that she'd started scratching notes around the word motive. "Yes and we'll carry on chasing down leads. We're going to pick up the brother tomorrow and see what he can reveal."

Grace listened intently and scribbled notes. "Right, so we have the immediate physical evidence, which will probably be backed up by forensics, but we're lacking motive. Anything else?"

Ollie shook his head. "No that's about where we're at."

Grace thought for a minute. "Ok, I'll have no problem getting him remanded tomorrow and that'll give us fifty-six days, before we have to apply for remand again, to build the case. The forensics are going to be the building blocks for this case but a motive would be very useful."

"It would indeed."

"Is there anything else?" She asked.

"No I think we're all up to speed." He confirmed. "Oh I don't suppose Sutherland told you who called in the tip?"

"No, I thought it was anonymous."

"You can certainly call the number and remain anonymous but it records the numbers. I just wondered if he'd called it back." Ollie explained.

"Well he didn't say anything to me."

"Ok, I'll add that to the list of things to do."

Grace stood from her seat and took her empty cup to the kitchen. She looked at the stainless steel coffee maker. "Do you still want that coffee?" She shouted through to Ollie.

Ollie looked at his watch. "No thanks. I promised Steve I'd catch up with him for nine."

"Ok." Grace found herself disappointed with his response.

Ollie moved into the kitchen. "I'll leave you alone now; I know you like to focus the night before court."

Grace smiled softly. "I do. I'm surprised you remembered."

"I remember everything from our time together."

She felt a sob building in her throat and she took a deep breath through flared nostrils to suppress it. "You're very sweet Ollie."

"I try."

"Right, as you said I need to focus and you better get a move on if you're meeting Steve." She thought for a moment. "What are you meeting Steve about at this time?"

"Just to review today's findings and make a plan for tomorrow." Ollie hated lying to her but if she knew about the murder weapon it would create problems for her in the remand hearing, ethical and technical.

As they spoke they walked to the door. "Ok, take care and say hello to Steve for me."

"I will. So are we good?"

"We're fine Ollie. Consummate professionals."

He laughed. "Very rarely am I called professional."

"I know; I was referring to me more than you." She joked.

"I thought as much. Right you get back to your meditation or whatever it is you do and I'll get on the road."

"Good night Ollie. Don't drive too fast." She said in a tone Ollie found familiar and comforting.

"Good night Grace." Ollie pulled the door open and stepped out onto the landing area. As he did so Grace pushed it closed behind him.

CHAPTER SIXTEEN

Howley and Milner were anxious to get to the factory and begin their search. They both knew the importance of finding the murder weapon; without it the case against Knowles could potentially be considered circumstantial. There was also the concern that the crime scene was now contaminated and even if they found a knife its validity could be called into question. They both hoped the scene had been kept secure.

The road to the factory had decayed and was more mud than tarmac after years of abandonment. Howley could see a myriad collection of different tyre tracks. "Did you take any tyre track casts?" He asked Milner.

Milner smiled. "You really are old school; we just take photos these days. And yes we took photos, we tied one set into the big Lincoln Navigator that Ryan Knowles drives and we have the rest on file for comparison should we need to."

"You learn something new everyday." Howley said.

An almost full moon leant some silvered light to the dark track and Howley could make out the angular roofline of the factory. The few south facing roof windows, that were unbroken, glowed subtly with almost mercurial liquidity. The rest cast ugly shadows into the vacant factory below.

Milner drove the van further along the muddy track that led up to the factory entrance. Ahead of him he saw the blue and white crime scene tape still in tact and he was greeted by a uniformed security guard. The guard was one of a four man rota that the estate management company had agreed to post to the factory for a period of two weeks. The guard asked for their identification and then showed them where to park. Greg parked the van and the two men stepped out onto the muddied track.

Howley approached the security guard and established that the scene had been kept secure since the SOCO team had left. The guard had a log of all visitors and there were no anomalies. They had also set up a temporary CCTV system; Howley felt reassured that the scene had not been touched and he followed Milner into the factory.

The dark factory creaked and the wind gusted in howls through cracked windows and roof panels. The feral cats scattered as the men shone torches into dark corners. A bat flapped clumsily in front of Howley as it altered its, insect hunting, trajectory to avoid hitting him and Howley flailed his arms unnecessarily to fend it off. After an hour of checking the factory areas that surrounded the crime scene the men had not found a knife.

Howley walked through the workshops and found Milner. "I guess the only place to check now is the actual crime scene."

Milner nodded. "Yes but we were very thorough in there so I doubt we'd have missed anything."

Howley knew he was right. "I know but while we're here we may as well take a look."

"Yes. Tomorrow we'll hit the exterior but if we missed it the other day I don't hold out much hope. The other thing to think about is that if it's outside the any DNA will have degraded and fingerprinting might prove difficult." Milner said in a defeated tone.

Howley peered through the darkness towards the crime scene. The clean-up team hadn't yet been and the blood puddles remained. As the two men walked towards it the air became thick with the smell of butchered meat, rotting and rancid from the warmth of the day's September sun. Howley suppressed the urge to heave and stood still. He turned to Milner. "I don't really think we need to go in there."

Milner's face was pulled in disgust with the smell. "I feel confident we checked and double checked the scene. If there was a knife in there we would have found it."

Howley nodded. "I'm sure you would. Your team is very good and if I'm honest I suspect that if there'd been a knife anywhere in here or within the perimeter they'd have found it. We both know what this looks like."

"Let's not jump to conclusions Steve. A big guy like Knowles could've easily thrown a knife ten metres from a window. If the forensic medical examiner had been able to see the knife wounds at the scene we'd have looked specifically for a knife and having not found one inside we would have extended the search area. Which is what we'll do tomorrow."

Howley chewed his lip and thought. "Was there any sign that somebody else had been in here with Knowles? Or even before him?"

"Nothing definite. The place has been empty for so long there was lots of evidence of visitors. Mostly what appears to be kids who used the place as a refuge from the rain when they wanted to drink. Lots of fag ends and a few used condoms but as I said, nothing definite we can link to the time of the murder." Milner explained.

"So we can't say if there was anyone else here and we can't say there wasn't." Howley mused.

"I'm afraid so Steve. If you had another suspect we might be able to make a link but we can't do more than that."

From the entrance area Howley heard a shuffling noise and he put a finger to his lip to let Milner know he should be silent. He edged slowly to the wall and then tip-toed towards the noise. Milner took the hint and stood silently behind an old press. Howley heard the shuffling noise again and crept through the workshop and into the entrance area. A tall figure stood holding a phone as a torch. The figure turned. "Steve is that you?"

"For god's sake Ollie," Howley said in exasperation.

"That's no way to greet someone with coffee and donuts." Ollie said as he raised a sturdy paper bag from his side. "Although it stinks in here we should perhaps go outside with them."

"That's the most sensible thing you've said all day." Howley said. He then turned towards Milner and shouted. "Greg, come through Ollie's brought us some coffee."

Milner moved towards the two men and followed them outside. Ollie lifted the bag onto the bonnet of the van and handed Howley and Milner a coffee each. "So what did you find?"

Howley took a gulp of coffee before speaking. "Nothing. Greg's team were all over this place in the daylight and didn't turn up anything, so I don't know what we expected really."

"So where does that leave us?" Ollie asked.

"Well we have a missing murder weapon and a suspect who didn't run or attempt to hide." Howley said.

"So why did he hide the knife? And if he didn't, who did?" Ollie conjectured.

"Good questions and when we answer them we'll have this case solved. One thing's for sure this is not the open goal Sutherland thinks it is." Howley answered.

Milner had been listening to the two detectives while sipping his coffee. He'd seen Knowles' handiwork on a few occasions and he'd escaped conviction each time. To Milner it seemed highly likely that Knowles was guilty and even without the knife there was the hammer that was used to torture Andy Lewis. "If I may interject gentlemen."

Howley turned to Milner. "Of course Greg."

"There are many reasons Knowles would have thrown the knife and been caught at the scene with the hammer. We all know he's an evil bastard but even evil bastards have moments of remorse and regret. He could have returned to the scene burdened with guilt and remorse. Killing somebody the way Lewis was killed takes such a detachment from one's own humanity that when it jolts back, even if it's briefly, the shock can cause strange reactions."

Ollie was a little confused. "So what are you saying Greg?"

"Well there's no doubt in anyone's mind that Knowles is a sociopath, but the thing is, sociopaths are rarely psychotic. Yet Lewis's killing seems to be a psychotic act; so if Knowles descended into a psychotic rage at some point he would have come out of it." Milner explained.

Ollie thought he understood. "Ok so let's assume Knowles is running away and his psychotic episode is over. He realises he's killed Andy and he what? Goes back to apologise? To mourn?"

Milner nodded. "Basically, yes."

Howley considered what Milner had said. "So despite the missing knife Knowles is still the number one suspect?" He asked.

"I'd have to say yes. Obviously you have to complete your investigations but I'm sure you'll find he's the murderer." Milner said.

The air had cooled and Ollie turned his jacket collar up. The van window was covered in a light sheen of condensation and the coffee that remained in his cup was now too cold to drink. He tipped his cup to the ground and dropped the cup back into the bag. "Ok so I think the day has been long enough. Let's head off and start fresh tomorrow."

"Agreed. Greg you'll be here with a team looking for the knife?" He asked?

Milner nodded.

"Good. Ollie we'll meet at the station and then pick up Ryan after the remand hearing."

The men returned to their vehicles and left the factory.

CHAPTER SEVENTEEN

There was no pleasant rhythmic clatter on Grace Sterling's train. No verdant views of England. No friendly ticket inspectors with a warm hello. This was a modern commuter monster. Sitting with her legs crossed she toyed with her shoe as she waved her foot in the air. This was a nervous tick and was unconscious, a sign of Grace's mind at work. Another station; another jolt of discomfort, as her knee clashed with one of the many obstructions beneath the table. She worried that her tights would be in tatters and wished she'd worn a trouser suit.

Grace fought back nausea as hot, over-used, grease exuded its bitter odour into the over populated carriage. Compressed air closed the doors with an almost sci-fi shoosh and Grace was again jolted in a series of syncopated bounces, she risked a glance at the window and was faced with a gaudy flower bed in honour of some minor member of royalty who liked to visit on occasion. With a more settled rhythm underscoring the ride, she returned her focus to the laptop screen.

She scanned the plans for the remand hearing and started to envision the scene in her mind. The media had called him the Chorlton Charmer but this genteel nickname was a far cry from the toe smashing monster that Grace had read about in the police reports. Another beat out of rhythm and the wheeled composer finally ended its song with a diminuendo into Manchester Victoria Station.

As she left the train she reached for her phone and called her assistant, Ruth. After a few rings Ruth answered: "Hello." She said.

"Hi Ruth, just checking we're all set? I've just stepped off the train and I'll be over at the court shortly." Grace explained.

"Ok, I have everything sorted this end and DCI Sutherland is already at the court waiting."

"That's great, I'll catch up with you later." Grace ended the call and continued to walk through the station.

The high iron work with ornate details and, at eye level, intricate tiles proudly tell visitors to Manchester that this station was once a regal example of nineteenth century architecture and engineering. Grace still found it impressive, but always found that the franchised gloss of coffee bars and pushy credit card sales people took the eye away from the splendour. Grace always saw it though. She looked for details she'd missed and hoped it would always be this way and not replaced with an antiseptic modern version. She hurried past the formerly glorious ladies WC, complete with its own waiting area, and emerged on to Balloon Street complete with its huge modern bank and homicidal bus drivers. On the ground floor and basement of another noble Victorian building was a Starbucks.

Starbucks was the usual morning mix of business men, women, gothic students and shopping mums, stressed about nothing, chattering about celebrity gossip and gym memberships. Grace ordered her caramel latte and found a seat looking out onto the street. She could see the splendidly designed Urbis building and found herself enjoying its lines and metallic hue, despite its modernity.

As she scrutinised the daily papers she was thankful that, despite the best efforts of the popular media, the court case would not be like an American TV show. There were a multitude of little blue wi-fi signs all over the coffee shop but Grace wasn't here to work. It was time to sit and compose herself for the day ahead. It was a relatively short walk to Crown Square and Grace could have taken the train to Salford central, but she preferred the walk and she liked this particular Starbucks, because it was on the corner of the old corn exchange. She sipped at her coffee, confident that her prep-work would ensure Knowles was remanded.

CHAPTER EIGHTEEN

Ollie arrived at Wythenshawe station at eight. The office was quiet with only a skeleton crew working, and waiting, to be relieved by the day team. Ollie sat at his desk and checked through his emails, nothing about Aiden. He tidied his desk and lay open a pad in the clear space. At the top of the page he wrote- motive?

The noise in the outer office increased as officers and civilian support staff arrived for the day shift. Computers whirred into life and kettles were boiled as habitual work rituals were enacted. Some made coffees for a group whilst others were solitary and made a drink only for themselves. Younger members of the team eschewed tea or coffee and drank sweet cold drinks, a habit that Ollie didn't understand. The night shift workers handed over notes and passed brief pleasantries with their day shift counterparts, as they desperately tried to leave and find their beds. Ollie glanced across at the civilian staff as they settled to their desks and wondered which of them had taken the call that led to Knowles' arrest.

Ollie moved away from his desk and headed over to the civilian support workers. As he approached their conversation subsided and as he reached their desks there was only the noise of busily tapped keyboards. Ollie approached Louise Byrne, the supervisor. Louise was in her early thirties and had been with the team for two years. "Good morning Louise, just a quick query please. Who took the call about the Andy Lewis murder?" He asked.

"Actually that was me," Louise answered without hesitation.

"Do you mind if I ask you a few questions about it?"

"No, not at all," Louise said enthusiastically.

"Did the caller leave a name?"

"No but I did ask him several times, as per the protocol." She explained.

Ollie nodded, "and it was definitely a male caller?"

"Oh yes, without a doubt." She said.

"Did the system pick his number up?"

Louise nodded, "yes it was a mobile number. The prefix looks like a pay and go one."

"Did you call it back?" Ollie asked.

"Yes as soon as the call was over. There was no answer."

"Ok, so what was it about this call that got Sutherland to send a team into that factory?"

"We get a few calls about the different gangs and in particular about the Knowles' gang. They're usually victims or witnesses too scared to come in. They report some minor crime or other but disappear when we explain they'll be needed as witnesses. This call was different though." Louise said.

"In what way?"

"The caller was desperate, he had specific details and seemed genuinely distressed that Lewis was going to be killed.

He gave an address and said Knowles was going there to kill Andy Lewis. I immediately told DCI Sutherland and he took the team straight away."

Ollie frowned in confusion. "Why did he call us and not 999?"

Louise shook her head and a look of worry grew over her face, "I don't know. I never thought about that. Have I done something wrong?"

"No no, you did exactly what you were supposed to do. It's just something to think about." Ollie explained.

Louise immediately looked calmer. "So what do you think it means?"

"I'm not sure." Ollie said. "Is there an audio file of the call?" He asked.

Louise nodded. "Yes we record all calls."

"Great, will you email me a copy of it please? If the caller didn't give a name there's no data protection issue is there?" Ollie asked.

"I'll send it straight away." She said.

"Thanks Louise.." Ollie said. He then turned and walked back to his office.

Ollie pushed open the office door to be greeted by Howley. "Hi Ollie, now why were you flirting with Louise while I'm in here working?"

"I wasn't flirting; you have a one track mind. I was talking to her about the call that tipped Sutherland off."

"Fine I take it back. And what did you learn from the lovely Louise?" Howley enquired.

Ollie told Howley about his conversation with Louise. "So it leaves us yet another question. Why didn't our desperate caller ring the hotline and not 999?"

"It does indeed."

Ollie sat at his desk and opened up his email. Louise had sent the audio file. He turned to Howley, "I've got the audio file here. Shall we have a listen?"

Howley nodded.

Ollie opened up the audio player and adjusted the volume before clicking play. The first voice they heard was Louise's as she answered and introduced herself. This was followed by a frantic male voice in a heavily Manchester accented voice. "You need to get to the old metalwork factory down on Clay Lane. Knowlesy is going to kill Andy Lewis. I 'eard 'im tellin' his brother. It's 'appenin now. Someone needs to stop 'im he's gone mental."

Louise responded to the caller, "ok sir I need to confirm a couple of things. Do you mean Kyle Knowles?"

"Yeah love, you need stop pissin' about on 'ere and get someone down there." The man said anxiously.

"I understand you're upset sir, may I take your name sir?" Louise asked.

"Fuck that. Nobody is getting no name from me. Just get to the old metalwork factory."

"Ok sir you are entitled to remain anonymous but it would be useful if you would let me have your name so we can contact you after we've been to the factory."

"Stop asking for my name and just get someone down there before Andy's killed."

"Ok sir, please remain calm and a team have already been alerted to the location." Louise's voice had become less calm at this point as she realised the reality of the situation.

"Is someone goin' down there then?" The nervous man asked.

"Yes sir. Thank you for your call today." Louise ended the call.

Ollie looked at Howley. "Did you notice anything strange about that?"

"Do you mean that awful accent?"

"Yeah, it was obviously put on for the benefit of the call." Ollie said.

"It was, but why?"

"Maybe he didn't trust the anonymous hotline; or he knew we'd record it and didn't want one of us to identify him." Ollie conjectured.

Howley nodded in agreement. "So what does that tell us?"

"Well it implicates Ryan, so it's a line of enquiry for today when we pick him up. We also have to think about who would have been a position to hear a conversation like that. I think we need to see Brixton again." Ollie said.

"Agreed."

"Ok, so this morning we'll pick up Ryan and then this afternoon chase down Jack Haworth and Adam Grey."

"And I suppose you'll want to say hello to Gracie while we're there?" Howley jibed.

"I suppose we could wish her luck." Ollie answered wryly.

CHAPTER NINETEEN

Grace left the urban chatter of Starbucks and began her walk across the city to the magistrate's court. She chose to walk through St Ann's square and, like the previous few days, the air was warm and the British penchant for the weather brought the words 'Indian summer' to many lips. St Ann's Square was home to the Royal Exchange Theatre and St Ann's church. In the winter Grace loved to hear the Christmas Carols in the eighteenth century church. The year before Ollie had taken her to the carol concert and then to see a play in the Royal Exchange Theatre. She smiled to herself as she walked past them both.

From St Ann's Square Grace made her way onto Deansgate and crossed over to the Spinningfields area. The recently developed walkways and franchised restaurants were enveloped with velvety lawns and Grace recognised solicitors and barristers who were sitting and drinking before their court appearances.

The magistrates court was resplendent in Victorian elegance. Red brick and an arched doorway sat comfortably next to the modern angular glass and steel work of its neighbours. Grace climbed the steps of the magistrate's court and pushed open the door. Inside she was met by an airport type security check. A large metal-detector stood alone, guarded by two uniformed security officers wielding hand held detectors for those tricky visitors who set the alarm off. Grace placed her bags in a large plastic box and slid it past the frame, for one of the guards to search, and then stepped through it. No buzzer sounded and she collected her bags.

The dour room she'd stepped into seemed to hold negative energy within it. The enquiry windows housed world weary clerks counting money paid in for fines, or calmly dealing with the irate families of the accused. Grace walked past the pool of negativity and found the day's court hearing list on the notice board. Her hearing was at ten, in court five with District Judge Arthur Stapleton. She didn't recognise the name but didn't think it mattered.

She climbed the wide staircase to the first floor and found the small café. Sat in a corner reading The Times was Sutherland. Dressed in a very good navy suit he oozed smarm. He seemed ill at ease amongst the periwinkle-blue formica tables and functional, brown plastic chairs; Grace assumed he usually dined in more upmarket establishments. He looked up from his paper and gave Grace a well-practiced smile. She smiled back and joined him at his table.

"Good morning Chief Inspector." Grace said as she sat opposite him.

"It is a good morning. I take it you're all set for the hearing?"

"Yes, should be a formality but I'm fully prepared for anything his brief might throw at us." She explained.

Sutherland's face grew into a cat like smirk of self-satisfaction. "I'm glad to hear it."

"Has there been any new evidence pertinent to the hearing?" She asked.

"No, Howley and James are working the estate but the physical evidence stands."

"So the corpus delicti remains as was, that's good." She said.

"Corpus delicti? Remind me, my latin is a little rusty." Sutherland enquired.

"Ah, sorry it's a lawyer thing. It means the body of the offence." She explained.

"Of course and yes, the body of the offence remains unchanged at this stage."

"That's very good." Grace looked at her watch and realised she needed to meet Ruth. "Well, if you'll excuse me Chief Inspector I need to meet with my assistant and let the clerk know I'm here and ready."

"Of course, I'll see you at the bench."

Grace left Sutherland to finish his paper and headed out onto the corridors in search of Ruth. The upper floor of the court building was church silent as she passed through. Cleaners had left another layer of wax on already slick floors and the noxious odours of cleaning fluids burned her eyes. She looked down at the floor in an attempt to shun the chemical attack, but to no avail.

Looking down she could see a myriad dents and dints in the thick wax. Stiletto-slashes and steel-heeled vandalism pock marked the Victorian parquet floors, while flat, dusty, leather souls left spectral walkways of Italian footwear. In amongst the history were the banshee spirits of modern man. Sportswear logos, and names in perfect print, emblazoned on the top surface of the wax. Nike, Puma and Adidas all floated carefree above the formal wear of the courts work force. They lay with an ease that seemed to sneer at the ludicrous notion of smart dress, much like the modern Cro-Magnon that pushed the imprints in as they accepted fines and sentences with equal contempt.

As Grace descended the stairs to the security area she saw Ruth checking the notices and walked across to meet her. Ruth's exuberant hair had been tamed, and simply tied back, and she wore a dark trouser suit with a pink blouse. In her hands she had the legal files for the hearing and a small Biba gretal, embossed, leather bag hung from her shoulder.

Grace smiled at her assistant. "Hi Ruth, you all set?"

Ruth's enthusiasm was almost tangible. "Yes."

"Great, you need to let the Clerk to the Justices know we're here and ready for the hearing. While you're there ask if there's a free meeting room we can use while we wait." Grace said.

"Ok I'll go to the Clerk's office now."

"Thank you. I'm going to step outside and enjoy a little fresh air before the stench of this place gets into my skin. Come and find me when you're all sorted."

Ruth tottered towards the Clerk's office and Grace left the building and headed for a bench outside. Grace tried to remain calm and reminded herself that as a prosecutor for the CPS she'd prosecuted many violent and psychotic criminals, most at the Manchester Crown Court. But she had never felt this uneasy before. As she mentally prepared for the remand hearing her jaw was involuntarily clenching and she found herself flaring her nostrils to draw more air as she fought anxious psychosis.

Grace thought about Ollie and found herself wishing he was there. She optimistically scanned the road in both directions hoping he'd be there; but there was no sign of him. She hated him for getting into her head again and she stood in front of the court and angrily chastised herself for being so weak.

As she climbed the first step of the building she heard a distinctive engine and turned to see a bright green car, paying no regard for the vehicles prohibited signs, and knew instantly it was him. He pulled the car up in front of her and stepped out. "Hi."

"Hi Ollie, why are you here?"

"We want to speak to Ryan Knowles and I wanted to wish you luck."

"Thank you, I appreciate it." Grace said. She then peered into the car. "Hi Steve, you ok?"

"I'm good. Good luck today." Howley said.

"Shouldn't need it but thanks."

As they spoke an efficient looking parking officer was making his way towards them. Ollie looked at Grace. "Look, I'd better move. I'll call you later and update you on the investigation."

He bounced back into the car and gunned it past the ticket toting officer and away from the court. Standing, watching him drive away Grace felt alone. He wished her luck. He'd never done that before. As for the bail hearing she felt confident enough.

Driving away from Grace, Ollie felt out-of-sorts. He didn't doubt she was a good prosecutor but he wasn't convinced she had the kind of smarts needed to keep herself safe working this trial. Any fool could find out her address and the Knowles' gang had a history of threatening and attacking prosecutors.

Grace turned to the court entrance and headed back into the security check area. Her bag was rechecked by the same security guards and she was soon confirmed as safe to enter. The mahogany veneer stole what little natural light the tiny windows let in; only the occasional refracted beam giving a clue to the time of day. Ruth exited the office as she approached and was followed by the Clerk.

The Clerk was a tall officious looking man. His black suit was impeccably pressed and the trouser crease sharp. His green eyes peered disapprovingly over his glasses and he had an air of self-importance as he ran the court like a tsar. The Clerk pointed them towards a small room and then left them as he attended to his duties.

Like all prosecutors Grace had been given a small meeting room to use. Harshly lit with fluorescent strip lights and no natural light, Grace felt an oppression that teased and toyed with her growing anxiety. She looked across at her bubbly legal secretary and smiled, every time she looked at her assistant she reminded her of a hamster. Her youthful chubby cheeks, usually framed by cherubinesque curly hair, created a caricatured hamster in Grace's mind.

"Well we shouldn't have to wait too long now." Grace said. "Would you like me to go through what we can expect? You might find it useful in your studies."

Ruth gratefully accepted the offer and Grace spent the time waiting to be called into court giving Ruth a lesson in law.

CHAPTER TWENTY

Knowles was dressed for court and wore a suit his barrister would do well to afford. It was a good distraction, a disguise, in complete contrast to his usual Manchester City shirt and costly trainers. His normal inked displays of hatred were well covered and he had removed the vulgar displays of gold that usually adorned his neck and wrists. He even removed his earring, for fear it spoiled his good citizen costume. He had handed all his jewellery to his solicitor. The suit and lack of jewellery were insisted upon by his brief and Kyle was in no mood to argue.

Knowles sat in his cell with his brief, waiting for transport to the court. The stark walls held nothing of interest but Kyle stared at them blankly. He took a drink of tea from a plastic cup and asked his brief to call his brother on his mobile phone.

A few button pushes later and Kyle was calling his brother, Ryan. Ryan was the younger of the two Knowles brothers and was eager to support and impress his brother: "Ryan my brother, my best friend, how are you?" Kyle asked in a desultory tone.

"It's all good Kyle. Just wish you were here with me." Ryan told him.

"All in good time kidder. Were you thinking of coming to court today?" Kyle asked.

"Oh yes big brother, I'll always be there to support you. And I want to see the prosecutor; I've got some sweet surprises in mind."

"No Ryan. I don't want that. There's going to be enough trouble without you adding to it. I know you mean well but I don't want you planning anything or interfering with the prosecutor." Knowles pleaded with his brother.

"Are you serious? We need you out of there Kyle."

"Ryan listen to me. Do not threaten the prosecutor. Don't come to court today. Do you understand me?" Kyle's tone had regained some of its usual malice and Ryan could clearly hear it.

"Ok no threats on the prosecutor. But I want to come to court and see you."

Kyle thought for a moment. "I don't think it's a good idea. I want you to do something else for me."

"Anything. What do you need?"

Kyle stifled a sob as he spoke. "I need you to make sure Andy gets a good send off and make sure Amy is looked after. Tell her I didn't do it."

"Yeah, of course I will." Ryan said quietly.

"Thanks Ryan and don't worry about me. I'm waiting for court transport and then I'll be boxed away in the cells until the hearing starts. So seriously, don't bother coming today, just chill at your pad, phone the funeral directors and my brief will let you know where I've been remanded to."

"You don't think you'll be bailed?" Ryan asked desperately.

"I'm not even challenging the remand. There's no point." Kyle explained.

"What do you mean you're not challenging? Are you mental?" Ryan said with disbelief.

"I know what I'm doing. I'm not ready to fight yet. Trust me Ryan." Kyle said with confidence.

Ryan was confused but he knew better than to argue with his brother. He sighed deeply before responding. "Ok Kyle but I'll be at the remand centre as soon as I can and you can explain to me what you're thinking."

"Fine. Look I need to go now the transport will be here soon. Take care my brother." Kyle ended the call and handed the phone back to his nervous looking brief.

CHAPTER TWENTY-ONE

One of the court ushers called Grace to the court room. Sutherland met her and they entered the room together. The Judge's bench was a tall, dark-wood, monolith that dominated the room, and all other desks, including the clerk's, sat deferentially below it. To the right of the bench was the dock and Kyle Knowles was already there. His head was bowed and the arrogance Grace expected didn't seem to be present. In the centre of the room were the desks for the prosecution and defence and to the left of the bench was the witness stand. Grace and Ruth took their seats before the bench and Sutherland took a seat in the public area near the usher.

Adjacent to Grace was Jeremy Allen, Knowles' brief and Grace nodded to him. It was a simple, polite greeting that acknowledged a colleague, despite the adversarial relationship they were about to undertake. Grace had spoken to him the day before in her preparation for the hearing and his client had acquiesced to a paper committal hearing. This meant that original signed statements would be served to the court at the hearing. The evidence wouldn't be read or questioned. As soon as it had come apparent that the case would need committing to Crown court Knowles was informed, through his brief and the agreement was made.

Behind the bench a door opened and the honourable Judge Arthur Stapleton entered the court.

"All stand." The usher said loudly.

Everyone in the room stood and waited for the judge to take his place. He sat down and addressed the room. "Please sit."

The usher stood from his desk. "Number three on the list, your honour, Mr Kyle Knowles represented by Mr Jeremy Allen."

The judge simply nodded and looked at the Clerk to the Justices.

The clerk stood and faced Knowles in the dock. "Please tell the court your name and address."

Knowles lifted his head, stood and looked at the judge. "Kyle Knowles and I live at fifteen Franklin road, Wythenshawe."

The clerk read from his notes. "It is said that on the eighth of September you attacked and killed a Mr Andrew Lewis of Wythenshawe. Owing to the serious nature of the charges brought against you the prosecution are asking that the bench refuse summary trial and order that the case be committed to the crown court to be heard before a judge and jury. That committal is to take place today. You may sit down."

Knowles took his seat. Judge Stapleton gestured towards Grace. "Miss Sterling, your committal request please."

Grace stood and referred briefly to her notes. "Your honour, it has been agreed that this case is suitable for a short form committal under Section six. I submit to the court witness statements from Detective Chief Inspector Sutherland, Detective Sergeant Howley and an initial forensic report from Mr Gregory Milner a scenes of crimes officer. I would respectfully ask you to formally commit the accused to the next sitting of the crown court."

Jeremy Allen now stood and addressed the bench. "Your honour, following discussions with my learned colleague yesterday, and further with my client, I agree to the short form of committal."

Judge Stapleton nodded and spoke to Knowles. "Please stand up. You will be committed to the crown court to appear there on a date no sooner that the twentieth of December. It is my duty to remind you that if you object to any of the statements or depositions which formed the evidence for this committal being used in your crown court trial, you must notify the prosecutor and the crown court within fourteen days from today."

Grace now took her turn to speak. "Your honour, at this point the prosecution request that Kyle Knowles be remanded into custody. The defendant has a substantial police record that shows several previous violent offences. He has had many different addresses in recent years and is well known to the police as the figure-head of a criminal gang. It is the prosecution's belief that if he were to be allowed his liberty today there is a strong likelihood that he would abscond and fail to return to court. Additionally the prosecution feels that he is also likely to commit further offences whilst on bail." Grace paused as the judge made notes. "Present today is Detective Chief Inspector Sutherland who has agreed to make a statement in support of the prosecution's request."

Jeremy Allen interjected. "Apologies for the interruption your honour but there will be no need for further representations. My client does not wish to challenge the request for remand."

Judge Stapleton looked bemused. "This is rather unusual; whilst I must admit I would have been very reticent to consider bail for a charge of murder your client does have the right to challenge the prosecutions request. Have you explained this to him fully Mr Allen?"

"Yes your honour. I explained and I was of the opinion that we should challenge. My client however, wishes there to be no challenge at this point. He does though, reserve his legal right to challenge the request at the fifty six day review of remand." Allen said.

Grace listened intently and was surprised by Knowles' acceptance of the request for remand. She hadn't planned for this outcome. The agreement from Knowles for a paper committal meant she couldn't question Knowles and she wondered if the lack of challenge was some sort of ploy ahead of a 'guilty by means of insanity' plea at crown court.

Judge Stapleton addressed Kyle. "Kyle Knowles you will be remanded in custody until your trial for the murder of Andrew Lewis. The bailiff will take you from here to the holding cells, from there you will then be transported to Risley Remand Centre." Stapleton then turned his attention to Grace. "Miss Sterling please remember, onus probandi remains with the prosecution. Mr Knowles' lack of challenge is not an admission of guilt."

Grace nodded. The court was silent and Judge Stapleton glanced through his notes. "Well it seems we're all done here. The bench retires." He said.

The usher loudly said, "All stand."

Judge Stapleton left the courtroom and Kyle Knowles was escorted to the cells by the bailiff. Grace turned to Sutherland and shrugged her shoulders to show her confusion. She left Ruth to sort the paperwork on the desk and moved to speak to him. "Well Chief Inspector he's been remanded."

Sutherland nodded. "Yes he has, but his not challenging was a bit strange wasn't it?"

"It was very strange. I don't really know why he didn't challenge but we have time to build a case."

"We do indeed. What did the judge mean by onus probandi?" Sutherland asked.

"It means the burden of proof. He was reminding me I have to do my job properly if I want Knowles to be found guilty." Grace explained.

"Ah, yes. Well I'm sure we can we provide that proof for you."

Grace agreed with him and excused herself. She then helped Ruth with the papers before they left the courtroom and exited the building.

CHAPTER TWENTY-TWO

George Sutherland admired himself in the mirror. For fifty two he thought he looked good, he had kept his hair and the silvering that now covered most of it had given him the distinguished look of a politician. He liked that, with the changes the government were making he was ready to put himself forward as a candidate for democratically elected police-chief. He turned sideways on and, again, was happy with his reflection; trim and fit he had done a good job of looking after himself. Content that he was presentable he gave his suit one last brush and gave his hair a final blast of hair spray and strode out of his office and towards the press briefing.

The press briefing room had been erected with speed. The force logo stood proud on a blue back ground and the blue-cloth covered tables were cluttered with microphones, each one wearing a TV or radio station logo. The bottled water was chilled and the lighting, harsh and warm, had been set up by the TV companies. As Sutherland looked at the lights he wondered if he should have arranged to have had a makeup person in, to ensure he looked his best on screen.

The media interest in the arrest of Kyle Knowles was high and eager journalists were desperate to find out how the headline grabbing crime boss had finally been caught. The thronging journalists waited patiently, photographers were poised and camera men focused and refocused on the waiting chairs in anticipation. Local crime reporters, who had often written about the Knowles family, hoped that the nationals wouldn't steal their opportunity to pose some questions as the furore of interest swelled.

Sutherland looked out at the story-hungry journalists and was ready to feed them some scraps, but that's all it would be: scraps. In a meeting with the Chief constable, the press office and the Crown Prosecuting Service it had already been decided that there was too much at stake in this prosecution to allow too much detail to be given to the press and public. A brief statement and a couple of questions would be the sum total of this briefing. Of course if one of Sutherland's supporters in the press happened to squeeze in a question about his candidacy for the chief of police elections then he would have to give some sort of comment.

Moments later, Sutherland was joined by Chief Constable Edward Wright. Wright was a hardworking leader of the force and was respected throughout the force for his integrity and his hands-on approach to the job. Known, by reputation, as a tough cop in his day he was often seen in incident rooms ensuring manpower was used effectively and he was a staunch defender of overtime when big cases needed working hard. In contrast to Sutherland he was bald and had a slight paunch, luckily his immaculate uniform meant his public image was never harmed but on days like this, when Sutherland was clad in an expensive suit and had an air of dashing charm about him, he wistfully missed the vigour of his earlier days on the force.

"Ok chief-inspector shall we take our seats and get this over with?" Wright asked Sutherland.

"Yes sir, after you." Sutherland said as he gestured with a gentle wave of his hand.

"Thank you, now remember we reveal only the basics and promise another briefing at a later date." Wright reminded Sutherland.

"As discussed sir, like you I do not want public knowledge and rumour to ruin our case." Sutherland said in an almost patronising tone.

Wright nodded and moved steadily to his chair behind the microphones. Sutherland followed him and the two men sat down to a rally of flash-photography and garbled requests for information.

The Chief Constable waited for a few moments as the noise subsided and then cleared his throat. The crowd took this as their signal for silence and within seconds the room settled to a waiting silence. Wright shuffled his papers and began to carefully and clearly read the prepared statement.

"Welcome and thank you all for your patience. As you are all aware there has been an arrest made following the apparent murder of Andrew Lewis, a former resident of Benchill, Manchester." Wright paused for a moment before continuing: "On the 8th September a team of armed police officers, accompanied by the gang-crimes team, entered a warehouse unit in Wythenshawe and arrested a suspect for the murder of Mr Lewis. At that time the officers arrested Mr Kyle Knowles, a resident of Wythenshawe and his brother Mr Ryan Knowles. Subsequent to preliminary investigations and forensic tests Mr Ryan Knowles was released without charge but remains a person of interest at this time. Mr Kyle Knowles has been remanded into custody. All investigative efforts are, of course, continuing at this time."

As Wright finished his statement the room exploded into a furious melee of shouting as questions spewed from the mouths of appetite-whetted journalists.

Wright cleared his throat again and the room reacted as they had earlier. Once satisfied with the silence he spoke again:

"I understand you all have many questions but I'm sure you will understand that with this being a murder investigation there is a limit to the amount of information we can reveal at this juncture. We will however allow two or three questions and will endeavour to answer them to your satisfaction."

Sutherland had watched Wright carefully and had to admire the instant respect and gravitas the man attracted in a room. Now it was his turn. As they had previously agreed Wright would read the statement and he would field the questions.

Hands were thrust into the air and Sutherland would choose the journalists who would be allowed to put forward their questions. Amongst the crowd he saw Lisa Stanlow of the Manchester Times and gave her a knowing acknowledgement, a nod that was unseen by all but the most astute observer. Unlike Wright he didn't clear his throat for silence he simply raised a hand and soon the room descended into silence once more.

"Thank you again for your patience." He began. "As Chief Constable Wright has explained, this is an ongoing murder investigation and I would ask that you remember that when you pose your questions." He waited and watched as every hand hit the sky in unison. Without hesitation he pointed at a BBC news reporter and nodded.

The reporter immediately blurted: "Kyle Knowles has escaped prosecution on several occasions, what makes you so sure he will be convicted this time?" The question was expected and Sutherland had a rehearsed response.

"At this time Kyle Knowles is our chief suspect, the investigation continues and if Mr Knowles is guilty then I feel certain our justice system will find him thus." Sutherland said with a hint of glibness.

The reporter tried to follow up but Sutherland ignored him moving his gaze to a reporter for Sky News. The reporter mouthed silently: "me?" and Sutherland nodded.

The reporter looked at her notes and asked, "Who tipped you off? Had there been any indication that Knowles was in a feud with Andy Lewis?"

Sutherland was unhappy with this question but was expecting it nonetheless. "As you will all be aware the gangs and organised crime team have an information and helpline. A call came in that seemed genuine and worth following up. I felt it was our duty to take the tip seriously and as a result we were able to arrest Mr Knowles."

The Sky News reporter was quicker than the BBC and shot Sutherland another question: "But why respond so quickly to this call? Is it normal to send an armed team racing across the city based on an anonymous tip?"

Sutherland scowled and responded: "We take all calls to the information and helpline seriously, I'm sure you will understand that I can't reveal too much about the specifics of the call." Before the reporter could push any further Sutherland turned his gaze to Lisa Stanlow and pointed.

Stanlow knew the drill and without hesitation said, "Chief Inspector, did you lead the team into the factory?"

Sutherland did his best to stifle a smile and answered: "Well I was with the team, the armed officers have their own team leader and he led the initial breach. Once the area was secure I then began my investigation of the scene. It was a truly cross force effort and I am very proud of the outcome." He surveyed the room and saw that the gathered crowd were busily writing notes and he felt sure the reports would all portray him and the force in a positive light.

He took a deep breath and firmly said, "thank you ladies and gentlemen, I appreciate your patience and understanding. If there are any more questions please leave them with the press office and I will do my best to respond." With that he made a move to stand and leave the room. Stanlow saw the move and shouted:

"Chief Inspector, will this case prevent you from entering the race for Chief of Police?"

Sutherland replied, "no comment at this time, please, if there are any questions pertinent to today's briefing please leave them with the press office."

CHAPTER TWENTY-THREE

Ollie and Howley parked at a meter on Byrom Street. Walls of mirrored glass flashed the lazy autumn sun haphazardly into the car windows and both men reached for sunglasses before stepping out of the car. The slate grey paving, pavement cafes and al fresco cocktail bar gave the Spinningfield open space the feel of an Italian piazza. Above them, sharp, angular, modern multi-storey buildings clashed at acute angles fighting for space.

Business suited men and women bustled about the square carrying coffee cups and brown paper bags full of bagels or sandwiches. Loud voices shouted at mobile phones as Ollie and Howley strolled towards the magistrate's court. As they turned the corner onto Gartside Street the sun was lost behind the buildings and the autumn air felt cold.

The men were soon outside the court and there was no sign of Ryan or any of his thugs. "I'll go inside and have a look. You stay out here and keep an eye on the front doors." Ollie said to Howley.

Ollie dashed inside and headed to the first floor. There was no sign of Ryan anywhere. He ran back outside to Howley. "He's not in there. He mustn't have come." Ollie said.

Howley nodded. "Nothing out here either. Let's get across to the estate and see if he's home."

"Yeah and we'll have another word with Brixton too."

The men quickly returned to the car and headed away from the city centre and onto the ring road. The rush hour traffic had dwindled away and they were quickly in Wythenshawe again. Ryan lived near Wythenshawe Park, in a newly developed housing estate and as Ollie turned the car onto the park road he could see the development brusquely juxtaposed with older more weathered homes.

Following his call from Kyle, Ryan had smoked a joint and clambered back into his bed. He was lying in musty three week bedding and last night's t-shirt. He woke from his frazzled sleep instinctively, to the sound of Ollie's powerful engine. Guiding one eye open, with a sleep numb hand, he focused on the sound, for a moment he thought it was Kyle's car and he concentrated on the noise. He sighed with exasperation and exhaustion and shook his alien-feeling hand until the stabs of pins and needles dissipated and he could feel again. He stretched out his tingling hand to tilt the alarm clock and knocked a cold cup of coffee over and onto his pillow – "fuck!" He cursed and distracted tried to remember where he had put the clean bedding, or if he had any.

Ollie knocked loudly on Ryan's door and thought about the last time he'd dealt with him. After years on the force Ollie was used to being smacked in the face and the last person to take a swing at him at been Ryan Knowles. Ollie had goaded him into it; people were so predictable. At the time he'd interviewed a young woman with a broken nose. Ryan had hit her because she'd fallen behind with her loan payments and like most of the Knowles' victims she wasn't prepared to make a complaint. Ollie felt frustrated and chose to goad Ryan into hitting him; as a result Ryan was arrested for assaulting a police officer. Ollie smiled to himself as he recalled the memory.

Ryan assumed that the loud knocking was the police and he added no haste to his movement. He found some suitable jeans and a t-shirt, from a pile of unwashed clothes, and picked up his keys. He stepped slowly down the stairs and fumbled with his keys as he reached the door. After unlocking the door he pulled it open and sneered at the two detectives stood on his step.

"Fuck off!" Ryan snarled at Howley and Ollie.

Ollie raised his eyebrows in mock shock. "Well that's no way to greet an old friend."

"It's the perfect greeting for a pair of pigs showing up at my door on the day my brother is in a remand hearing."

"Pigs! Now that's just rude." Ollie said sarcastically.

Ryan shook his head and sighed. "What do you want?"

Howley knew there was history between the two men and didn't want the extra distraction as they interviewed Ryan. He nudged Ollie and Ollie responded by stepping back slightly. Howley was glad he'd understood the message. "Hello Ryan I'm DS Howley, we've never met but I really need to talk to you about your brother." He said calmly.

Ryan was distracted from his anger by Howley's calm and friendly approach. His face relaxed from its sneer and he looked directly at Howley. "Erm, ok."

"Thank you. Would it be ok if we did this inside?" Howley asked.

Ryan considered what Howley had said for a moment. "You can come in, but he can wait out here or in his puke green car." He said gesturing towards Ollie.

Howley turned to Ollie and nodded. "That's fine."

Ollie shook his head as he walked back to his car. Despite Ryan thinking he'd scored some sort of victory, Ollie knew this was the only way to get him talking, so he played the disconsolate, scalded puppy and slid into his car.

Content with Ollie's apparent put down Ryan smiled slightly. "Ok DS Howley come in."

Howley followed Ryan into the house and they moved into the lounge. An oversized plasma television hung on a faux chimney breast. It dominated the room and was clearly a status symbol. Black boxes with green and red flashing lights were untidily attached to the screen. Facing the huge screen was a black leather sofa and between the sofa and screen a glass coffee table strewn with ashtrays, filthy mugs and plates with dried food clinging to them. Howley could smell marijuana but ignored it; he had more important matters in mind.

"Ryan, I interviewed your brother yesterday and as a result there's a few things I need to talk to you about." Howley explained.

Ryan was lighting a cigarette and nodding. "Ok."

"Why do you think Kyle killed Andy?" Howley asked bluntly.

Ryan's face drained of colour and his angry sneer returned. "Kyle didn't kill Andy. He wouldn't. He couldn't."

"How can you be so certain?"

"I just know Kyle wouldn't hurt Andy. It just wouldn't happen." Ryan said.

"Ok so let's go back a day or a week. Was there any sort of fight or problem between Kyle and Andy?"

Ryan instantly shook his head. "Nothing, they were tight. We all were; Andy was like family."

"Ok but there's a witness who reports hearing Kyle tell you he was going to kill Andy."

"Fuck that. Kyle never said that. Who the fuck said that? Kyle wouldn't have hurt Andy. That's just a fucking lie."

Howley could see that Ryan believed that Kyle hadn't killed Andy. "Ok let's say for a minute Kyle didn't do it. Who did? And how did they get Kyle to take the fall?"

Ryan's head dropped as he thought about the question. "I don't know."

"What about Jack Haworth or Adam Grey?" Howley ventured.

Ryan's eyes narrowed as he thought about what Howley had just said. "I don't know, maybe. They've both been disloyal before and they're both scum. But I don't know if they've got the balls." He stopped talking and Howley could see a malevolent thought creep into his mind before he spoke again. "But I'll fucking well find out."

Howley quickly responded. "Don't do it Ryan. I can see what you're thinking and it won't help."

"It'll help me. If one of those shit-bags did this I'll fuckin' skin 'em alive. Was it one of those two fuckers who said they heard Kyle tell me he was going to kill Andy?"

"No I haven't spoken to them yet, just calm down. Listen to me for a minute Ryan." Howley said firmly. "When I was with your brother he asked me if I remembered your father. Your brother knew that back in the day I'd known your dad and more than a few times I'd arrested him. But he also knew I never went in for any bogus charges. He asked me if was still straight like that."

Ryan was confused. "So what?"

"So I think he was asking me to do what I'd always done, and to investigate this fairly and honestly. He knows the evidence looks bad but he knows I won't be taken in if it's bogus."

"Ok so you're an honest cop. I still don't get it." Ryan said.

"Just think for a minute Ryan. If Jack and Adam suddenly disappear and one of them is guilty then Kyle is still stuck on the end of a life term. Let me do my job and if Kyle didn't do it I'll find out." Howley explained.

Ryan knew Howley was right and nodded. "Ok but if they won't talk you can be sure I'll make them."

"I have no doubt you could do that. But don't. If you really believe Kyle didn't do this leave them to me."

"Ok. For now."

"Thank you." Howley said.

"It's ok Sergeant but I won't wait forever."

"I know you won't. There's one more name that came up. Aiden. I'm told he's your cousin." Howley tentatively asked.

Ryan seemed surprised to hear the name. "Yeah I've got a cousin called Aiden. What of it?"

Howley noted the surprise. "Could he have killed Andy?"

Ryan smiled. "No way. Aiden wouldn't kill anybody."

"Are you sure? I was told he did some fucked up shit back in the day."

"I don't know who you've been talking to but they've fed you some bullshit." Ryan said.

"Ok but I have to follow up any leads. What's Aiden's full name? and where can I find him?" Howley asked.

"He's a Knowles. Don't know where he lives or works though Sergeant. He just visits from time to time." Ryan said.

Howley sensed Ryan was lying. "You really don't know where he lives? Come on Ryan."

Ryan continued his lie. "Sorry, no idea."

Howley knew it was pointless to push him. "Well if you're sure?"

"I'm sure." Ryan said.

Howley nodded. "Ok Ryan. Thank you for your help."

Ryan stood and waited for Howley to do the same. As he stood, Howley could see Ollie sitting in his car waiting. He followed Ryan to the front door and walked quickly back to the car. He heard the door slam behind him as he opened the car door.

"So what's the story?" Ollie asked.

"Same one we keep hearing."

"What about Aiden?"

"He says he's a cousin but claims not to know where he lives or works. He did say his surname is Knowles though but I don't know if that was a lie or he thinks it really is." Howley said.

"And what about Kyle telling him he was going to kill Andy?"

"Denied it."

"Do you believe him?"

Howley nodded. "Yes I do."

"So what now?"

"Let's find Brixton again."

Ollie nodded and started the car.

CHAPTER TWENTY-FOUR

Grace and Ruth left the magistrate's court and made the short walk back to Quay Street, and the CPS offices. As they crossed the Spinningfield open space Grace could see the art deco stylings of the CPS office building. It was more graceful and interesting than the jutting, metallic monsters it shared the area with and Grace wished more of it was visible in the Manchester skyline.

As they strolled past a sandwich bar Ruth parted from Grace, to collect lunch orders for the office. Grace continued her walk to the office and took the smaller unmanned entrance, beneath the turret on the Atkinson Street side of the building. She swiped her magnetic card against the lock and entered the rear of the building. There was only one lift at the rear of the building and Grace pushed the call button.

Grace stepped off the lift onto the fifth floor and into the CPS lobby. She walked into the office and headed straight for Michael Blunt's office. Blunt had been waiting for her to return and eagerly anticipated her report from the remand hearing. "So, how did it go? I assume Mr Knowles is on his way to Risley?" He enquired.

"Yes." Grace said in an uneasy tone.

Blunt frowned, "is there something else you need to tell me about the hearing?"

Grace fidgeted with the hem of her jacket. "It was just a bit odd. He didn't mount any challenge to the remand application. I hadn't really considered that as a possibility and it's thrown me a little."

"It does seem strange but it's not unprecedented. Knowles is familiar with the legal system; he had to know bail in a murder case was very unlikely." Blunt suggested.

"Yes I did consider that." Grace agreed "but what if it's the start of an insanity play?"

"It may well be but we can only address that if it happens. For now, concentrate on the evidence and the police investigation." Blunt advised, "I believe your old flame is one of the lead detectives. Will that be a problem?"

"No problem. Ollie is a good detective; we've spoken and made sure there won't be any problems."

"I'm glad to hear it." Michael said almost inaudibly as he turned his attention to the emails on his computer. "Ok, well done today, get Ruth to file a report on the hearing before she goes home today."

"Will do." Grace said as she left Blunt's office.

Grace walked back into the communal office area. She needed a coffee and then she could catch up with the rest of her case load. Blunt had arranged for part of her existing load to be reassigned but she still had a substantial number of cases to deal with. She walked round the office space and into the compact kitchen area.

The small kitchen area was kept tidy and the fridge held the lunches of at least ten staff members; each one was labeled and it would be considered very poor etiquette to take someone else's lunch. On the wall was an always hot water boiler and next to it were three cafetieres. Grace scooped some ground coffee into one of them and filled it with water from the boiler.

As she reached for a mug a tall figure stepped into the kitchen. Grace turned to see Matthew Doherty.

"Hey." He said in a jovial voice.

"Hi Matthew."

"How did it go?" He enquired.

"It was ok. We went with a short committal and the application for remand was unchallenged."

Matthew looked bemused. "Unchallenged? By the judge you mean?"

Grace shook her head. "No, by Knowles."

Matthew seemed more perplexed. "What, he made no attempt for bail? I find that somewhat out of character. Whenever I've come across him in court he's pushed for bail. In fact, I think he's always managed to get it. Who was representing him?"

"Jeremy Allen." Grace answered.

Matthew's face looked like he'd tasted something sour. "Oh, that faggot. He usually gets him bail." He said with venomous vehemence.

Grace was stunned by Matthew's revulsion and use of such an offensive term. "Matthew! Faggot? Seriously?" She said almost scalding him for his indiscretion.

Matthew tutted. "Sorry. I just get so frustrated by that man. He has helped Knowles avoid prison too many times."

Grace nodded but felt no sympathy for him. "It's ok."

Matthew changed the subject and asked: "So what's next? Will you get him to trial in the first fifty six or will there be another application?"

"It depends on the forensics. The detectives are struggling to find a motive. Even Lewis's girlfriend doesn't think Knowles killed him, although there's still time for them to turn something up."

Matthew listened intently. "So you'll be looking to build the case on forensics and his being at the location with the hammer?"

"Yes, from the evidence I've seen so far there should be enough to build a case and get a conviction but having a motive would really help if the forensics raises any questions or doubts." Grace said.

Matthew smiled. "Well it sounds like you're on top of things but if you want any help don't hesitate to ask. I've lost too many cases to Knowles I'd like to see him face some justice."

"Thanks Matt." She said. "Anyway, I'd better get back to the grindstone, lots to do."

Grace left the kitchen and carefully carried the cafetiere and mug to her office. She placed the coffee onto her desk and flopped into her seat. Her in-tray was burgeoning with work that needed her immediate attention and she began to systematically prioritise the work. Before making inroads into the most urgent cases she sent a text to Ollie: **Knowles remanded. Meet me later and update me on your investigation.**

CHAPTER TWENTY-FIVE

Ollie and Howley knew that Brixton McKenna would be in the White Horse again and Ollie pointed the car in the direction of Benchill. The Indian summer had stretched another day and the green islands of lush grass, that were interspersed amongst the red-brick houses, added a sumptuous feel to an otherwise drab, urban estate.

As Ollie pulled up outside the White Horse and cut the engine his phone buzzed. He checked it and saw a text from Grace. "That was a message from Grace; Knowles was remanded."

"Well that's what we expected." Howley replied.

"All we have to do now is find the evidence to convict him at trial."

Howley considered what Ollie had just said. "If he did it, we'll find the evidence and if he didn't, we'll find out who did."

"You're really not convinced he did it are you?" Ollie asked.

"Something feels off. Knowles is a total scumbag, without doubt, but I'm not convinced he did this." Howley explained.

"I think I'd have to agree. If Milner turns up a knife with Knowles' prints or DNA, then I might be more inclined to place Knowles firmly in the frame. But right now I'm really not sure."

"Well he's not going anywhere for a while so we'll continue to do what we do and see where the evidence takes us."

The detectives stepped out of the car and headed into the White Horse. There were more patrons in the bar than on their previous visit but McKenna was sat on his usual stool at the end of the bar. On the bar in front of him was a half finished pint of lager and the remains of a bag of peanuts. He wore a short sleeved shirt and his forearms were a collage of faded tattoos. As the men approached he drained his glass and shook the empty glass at Ollie. Ollie smiled and was expecting to buy him another pint before he'd been asked.

"Hello detectives. What brings you here again?" McKenna asked.

"I just enjoy the atmosphere and company in here." Ollie quipped.

"I can understand that. Much more down to earth than the poncy cocktail bars you normally frequent I imagine."

"Very much so, and with colourful characters like yourself to liven things up it's a veritable charm-fest."

McKenna laughed quietly. "So DS James, what do you want?"

"The caller that tipped us off about the murder said he'd heard Kyle telling Ryan that he was going to kill Andy."

McKenna interrupted before Ollie could finish. "And you believe that crap?"

"Give me a reason not to."

"Oh come on. Even if Kyle was going to kill Andy he's not stupid; he'd never openly say anything to anybody." McKenna said.

Ollie nodded. "Let's imagine he was having an off day, who could have been around to hear something like that?"

"Ok I'll play along. Well first of all, even on an off day he'd never talk in public so the only way someone could've heard anything would be at Kyle's place or his car and there are only a few guys who get access to Kyle's place or his car." McKenna explained.

"Who?" Asked an agitated Ollie.

"Keep your cool Mr Policeman. After Andy and Ryan it'd probably be Jack Haworth and Adam Grey."

"What about the cousin, Aiden?" Ollie asked.

McKenna rubbed his forehead as he considered the question. "Not sure. He's not a regular on the patch and I don't know if Kyle would want him knowing too much. Kyle reckons he has a legit job and he once told me he doesn't want him knowing too much just in case."

"Just in case what?"

"Not sure. I think he was worried that he could lose his job or something."

Ollie pondered McKenna's response. "Ok, so basically you're saying Adam or Jack might've been in a position to hear something?"

McKenna nodded. "Yeah. But I still don't think Kyle did it. So I don't think anyone heard anything. Kyle's been set up, Adam or Jack must've set 'im up. Track those two twats down and I bet you anything one of them's done it. There's no way Kyle killed Andy."

"I keep hearing that. How can you be so sure?"

"I just know." McKenna said with a sigh.

Ollie looked at Howley and shrugged his shoulders slightly as a sign of confusion and frustration. "Ok Brixton thanks."

Ollie turned away from the bar and stepped round the lunchtime drinkers crowding the bar eager for a drink. Howley followed suit and the detectives left the pub and stepped out into the mild, autumn air. A group of kids, barely out of school were gathered round Ollie's car. They were part of a growing generation of kids who'd avoided school and were now an unemployable army of disparate, aimless, outcasts who had little hope of ever owning the sort of car they lusted after. As Ollie approached his car he answered questions about its power output and about how fast he'd driven it as the young men tried to imagine owning one themselves. As the detectives climbed into the car and shut the door behind them Howley laughed. "You know Ollie, I never get that with my old car."

"I'm sure you don't." Ollie said as he joined in with the laughter.

A few clouds had floated into the otherwise blue skies and a cold shadow brought a chill to the air. Howley felt a rumble from his stomach. "Shall we get something to eat before we do anything else?"

"Yeah, let's. Café Moorish?"

Howley nodded. "Sounds good to me."

Ollie steered the car off the Parkway and onto Sale Road. They drove through Northern Moor and into Sale Moor. Ollie parked the car in front of Café Moorish and the two men walked inside.

CHAPTER TWENTY-SIX

Greg Milner's team of SOCOs had arrived early at the derelict sheet metal factory. The clear light of morning did nothing to lessen the look of decay that the building bore. Broken glass shifted in rotten frames and twisted metal framing pinged in the unseasonal warmth.

Milner had set an initial search perimeter of twenty metres beyond the factory walls. The team wore white, tyvek, coveralls as they searched. Milner had taken a team of twenty and each one was diligently searching, their assigned area, square metre by square metre. Angry barbed brambles pulled at the coveralls and nettles stung exposed skin. Tweezers picked up anything that might be construed as evidence and every stone was upturned.

Milner checked all the door ways and obvious points of entry into the factory for evidence of a second person. As he'd told Howley there was plenty of evidence of visitors to the factory but establishing proof that one of the many footprints had been made that night was an impossibility. In a rear entrance way Milner took more photos and crouched to look for anything else of interest. He scooped some clearly recent cigarette ends and bagged them.

As lunch approached it had become obvious that they weren't going to find a knife. Milner felt frustrated; he'd known the chances of finding a weapon so long after the crime were slim but he'd hoped for some luck. He still felt sure Knowles was guilty and the knife could easily have been picked up by kids or one of the many homeless wanderers who frequented the area.

Milner wearily made walked to his van and took off his coveralls. He sealed the bag with the cigarette ends and labeled them ready for evidence logging back at the station. From the passenger seat he took a stainless-steel, vacuum flask and poured himself a cup of coffee. He sipped at the coffee and used his mobile phone to call Howley.

"Hello." Howley answered.

"Hi Steve, thought you'd like an update from this morning's search."

"That would be great."

"We set out a perimeter of twenty metres and covered every inch of it. We spent all morning literally combing the ground and we've found nothing. Sorry Steve but there's no knife here." Milner said with diffidence.

"Don't worry about it Greg. I wasn't really expecting you to turn up anything new today."

Milner sighed. "Yeah, I know it was a bit of a long shot."

"It was but thanks for calling me. Let me know if you get anything back on DNA and fingerprints."

"Will do. Catchup with you later Steve."

"Yeah, take care."

Milner pressed end and pocketed his phone. He felt uneasy about not finding the murder weapon and hoped the remainder of the evidence was enough to convict Knowles. He assembled the team and thanked them for their efforts before sending them back to their regular assignments and heading back to the station.

CHAPTER TWENTY-SEVEN

After their lunch Ollie dropped Howley at the station and headed into the estate to find Jack Haworth. Brixton McKenna had tipped him off that Haworth would be in the Flying Horse. Ollie knew the pub and had downloaded a picture of Haworth to his phone from the gang unit's intranet.

Ollie walked into the bar of the 'Flying Horse' and immediately drew the attention of Jack Haworth, Jack was a known associate of the Knowles brothers and had a history of violence, Ollie gave a small nod in his direction and walked to the bar. The 'Flying Horse' was the sort of traditional pub that was fast becoming extinct in Britain. No food, no family-friendly room, just a bar, a dartboard and a pool table. The smell of furniture polish mingled with stale beer to give a uniquely British pub smell.

He ordered a lager and waited for Jack to move. A few sips into his drink and he saw Jack move away from the bar and out to the smoking shelter. Ollie stood and made a deliberate show of checking his pockets: "Shit, forgot my cigs." He said loud enough for everyone at the bar to hear. He turned to one of the men who had been stood with Jack and said, "is there a cig machine in here mate?"

The man looked Ollie up and down before replying: "There is but it's over-priced. Go out back, go to the guy in the blue jacket and tell him Johnny said he could sell you some cigs cheap."

Ollie nodded, "got it. Cheers bud." With that he walked out to the lean-to that acted as a smoking shelter.

As Ollie emerged from the backdoor of the pub Jack immediately noticed and watched him as he walked towards the shelter. Ollie made eye contact with him as he approached him, "alright mate? Johnny said you could fix me up with some fags."

Jack nodded: "yeah man, cheaper than that machine in there. Four quid for twenty, I got Bensons, Regal or Marlboro. What can I do you for?"

Ollie smiled. "Cool, I'll take a couple packs of Marlboro." He said as he pulled a ten pound note from his pocket. "Glad I found you, smoking is getting so expensive I won't be able to afford to slowly kill myself." He laughed.

Jack laughed with him and asked, "so are you from round here? I don't recognise the face."

Ollie looked around and saw that they were alone. He reached into his pocket and put his hand on his ID badge and answered; "No, I'm from up near the supermarket." He pulled his ID out and showed it to Haworth. "You know the new building? The police station."

Haworth was taken aback and tried to run. Ollie grabbed his shoulder and dug his thumb deep into the joint. Haworth dropped to his knees in pain and Ollie grabbed his hand and twisted his arm behind him, holding him down on his knees. Haworth tried to move but as he did Ollie applied more pressure to the arm and Haworth submitted to the restraint.

"What the fuck?" Haworth shouted.

"Calm down Jack, I just want to ask you a few questions."

"What questions? I don't know anything about anything..."

"Oh come on Jack, you must have known you were getting a visit today."

"I don't know what the fuck you're talking about."

"You seriously didn't think nobody would want to talk to you about Andy Lewis's death? You're one of the inner circle Jack."

"I don't know anything," Haworth muttered.

"Don't play stupid Jack. Now I'm going to ask you some questions and you're going to stop being stupid."

"Fine."

"Where were you on the eighth between six and eight?"

"I was 'ere and then I was at home."

"I don't doubt there are plenty of people who'd say you were here but can anyone verify you were at home?"

"I was on my own. Why are you asking? Kyle killed Andy, why do you want to know where I was? What's that fucker said?"

Ollie ignored Haworth's questions. "So what time did you leave here?"

Haworth shook his head. "I don't know, about quarter to seven. What did Kyle say? Did he say I did it?"

"And it's what? A five minute walk to the metal work factory from here?"

"What the fuck are you sayin'? That I killed Andy? Fuck that for an idea."

"How did you get Kyle to the factory? Did you make Andy call him? It was a very clever plan Jack."

"I didn't kill 'im." He shouted.

"You've been a busy boy Jack, looking to expand into the north of town. Did Kyle piss you off when he told you to stop pushing so hard?"

"You're full of shit, me and Kyle were good, Andy was a mate. I didn't kill no one."

"I don't know Jack. The way I heard it Kyle wasn't happy with your taking out some of the Salford boys."

"We 'ad words sure, but we straightened it all out. Come on you caught Kyle; it wasn't me."

"So you think Kyle did it?"

Jack paused before answering. "I don't know anyone else who would, and it wasn't me."

"You didn't really answer the question. Do you think Kyle killed Andy?"

"If you'd asked me a few days ago I'd have said no but things change. Doesn't take much to piss Kyle off."

"And did Andy piss Kyle off?"

"I didn't say that. I just think it's possible."

Ollie wanted to explore the idea more. "Had you ever seen Kyle lose it with Andy?"

Feeling like the spotlight of accusation had moved from him, Jack quickly responded. "No but I've seen him lose it plenty of times."

"Really?"

"Oh yeah. One time Adam Grey was up at the house and he'd fucked up with a boxing bet. Kyle nearly killed him. He twatted him so hard round the back of the head, with one of those wooden hammers; you know the ones they use for meat and I thought he was going to die. The blood was everywhere. I remember Kyle burnt his rug after. Adam had to have a hundred stitches in his head and all his hair at he back shaved off. One minute he was calm the next he's laying into Adam like he's a piece of meat."

Ollie listened intently. "And is that normal? If someone screwed up they were beaten to a pulp?"

"Not usual but it happened. Usually when he loses it, it's all verbal and a slap."

"So why the violence with Adam?"

"Dunno; he just flipped. Adam has a big mouth though. He could've been winding him up before the fuck up."

Ollie nodded. "So what sort of things wound him up?"

"I don't know really, but Adam has a way of getting under his skin."

"So there was no love lost between Adam and Kyle?"

"I don't exactly know why, but Kyle puts up with a lot of shit from Adam. I don't know why he hasn't cut him loose."

"So you think Adam has something on Kyle?"

"He might have. No one else who winds Kyle up stays around for long."

"And you haven't heard anything? Come on Jack you must've heard something."

"Nothing." He looked at his watch. "Are we done now? I've got things to do."

"Ok Jack but I'll be checking the factory for your prints and if you were even near it I'll be down on you like a ton of bricks."

Ollie stepped back from Haworth, turned and headed away from the smoking shelter. He walked to his car and slid in. Before setting off he sent a text to Howley: **Haworth is a dead end but Adam Grey just became more interesting. Heading to the bookies to look for him.**

CHAPTER TWENTY-EIGHT

Howley drove onto the block-paved driveway of Kyle Knowles house and cut the engine. He looked up at the overtly ostentatious pillars, which stood sentry either side of the door, and shook his head with disapproval. He walked to the door and knocked loudly. Nobody came to the door and Howley knocked again. He moved to the right of the door and stared through the window; the house looked empty. The intel the gangs-unit had on Knowles stated he lived alone.

Content that the house was empty Howley used the key he'd taken from Knowles' possessions at the station and let himself in. Inside, the house was decorated in muted tones and the flooring was a mahogany-red hardwood. Howley made his way into the lounge area and was met by the obligatory over-sized plasma screen that dominated the room, but everything else had a show house feel to it, too clean, too impersonal. He sat on a soft, cream sofa and surveyed the room. On shelves throughout the room were pictures of Kyle with his brother and what appeared to be his mother. There were also pictures of Kyle's father; Howley looked closely at them and noticed how similar Kyle looked to his father.

Howley moved from the lounge and into the kitchen. Like the lounge the kitchen barely looked lived in; gloss white cabinet door fronts hid untouched plates and cutlery. The oven had never been used and only the kettle and microwave seemed to have had any use. Howley looked through draws and cupboards, not really knowing what he was looking for. He found nothing of interest in the kitchen and headed for the stairs.

On the first floor he found three empty rooms and Knowles' bedroom. He stepped into the bedroom and found a perfectly made bed and custom fitted furniture. Like the lounge there were family pictures, but no signs of any girlfriend. Howley opened a draw in a unit next to the bed. In the draw he found a collection of photos and a small metal cashbox; he pocketed the photos and grabbed the cashbox.

Leaving the bedroom he briefly looked through the dining room as he made his way to the garage. The garage was empty except for a workbench against the longest wall. The bench was untidily covered with tools and spray cans of WD40. There was no hammer amongst the tools and no apparent system to keep track of the tools. After a few minutes browsing the bench he left the garage and headed to the front door.

He locked the door and strolled to his car, carrying the photos and cashbox with him. He placed his haul on the passenger seat and sighed. He picked up the pictures and glanced through them, then tried the keys he'd taken in the cashbox; none fitted.

After a few moments reflecting on his day he picked up his phone and called Ollie. Ollie answered quickly. "Hello."

"Hi Ollie, I just got your text. I'm done here so I'll meet you at the bookies."

"Ok Steve. See you soon."

Howley ended the call and drove to meet Ollie.

CHAPTER TWENTY-NINE

Knowles had a majority share in a legitimate betting shop, near the concrete shopping centre; whether everything that went on in the betting shop was legitimate had been the subject of many investigations for years. The front of the shop was clad with faded pictures of horses racing and shiny cups being held aloft by sporting heroes. Overhanging the edge of the flat roof was an industrial sized satellite dish, beaming sporting contests from around the country, and at times the world, onto a large screen that mesmerized hopeful gamblers, cheering on their horse or team.

Ollie stood outside the betting shop, leaning against the scratched glass, waiting for Howley. The shop was busy with punters betting on horse racing from Doncaster and Haydock. Ollie looked through the scarred glass but hadn't seen Adam Grey. He'd spotted a couple of faces he knew were associates of Knowles and Grey, but not Grey.

Ollie heard the familiar sound of Howley's high mileage Mondeo and looked along the road to see his partner heading towards him. He waited for him to park up and greeted him as he stepped out of the car. "Hi Steve. Did you find anything at Knowles' place?"

"Nothing much. I grabbed a cash box that we can open later but other than that there was nothing there."

"Well Haworth has a flakey alibi and no great love or loyalty for Knowles."

"Do you think he had anything to do with the murder?"

"I don't see him being clever enough to set Knowles up. If he wanted to hurt Kyle he'd kill him. He's another unpleasant little scrote but I don't think he played a part in Andy's death."

"So in your text you said Grey had become more interesting?"

"Yeah, apparently Knowles gave him a real beating." Ollie said and then explained to Howley what he'd learnt from Haworth.

Howley listened carefully to what Ollie said. "Ok so Grey has a motive and desire to hurt Knowles. So why not just kill Knowles? Why kill Andy?"

Ollie shook his head. "I don't know, but it's the only decent lead we've had so far. Let's see what Adam has to say for himself."

"Ok. Is there any sign of him?"

"Not in the front of the shop, but his car's round the side. So he's probably in the back."

"Good, let's go."

Ollie led the way and the two men walked into the shop. A group of men watched a horse race on the big screen, while others filled in betting slips. Nobody turned to look at the detectives as they walked through the shop to the counter. At the counter Ollie was met by a large, sweaty man wearing a Manchester United shirt two sizes too small for him. "Hello Officers. Can I help you?"

"Hello George, don't know if you remember me but I'm DS James and this is DS Howley. Is Adam about?"

The big man frowned. "You're kidding right?"

Ollie was confused. "What do you mean?"

"We thought he was in custody."

"Why would you think that?"

"He went out for a fag the other day and didn't come back. Round 'ere that usually means you've been lifted."

"And nobody bothered to check?"

"No one 'ere is his mother."

"Fair enough. So when was the last time you saw Adam?"

"Tuesday I think." He scratched his head and chewed his lip. "Yeah it was Tuesday 'cause someone won big with King Kenobi at Leicester. It was just after that race he went for a fag. When he didn't come back I just thought he'd been lifted for something."

"Well he's not in custody so do you have any ideas where he could be?"

"Dunno. His car has been outside since then, so I don't know."

"Where does he live?"

"Over the other side of the Parkway, just into Benchill. I've got his address on me phone somewhere, I'll write it down for you."

As the big man started scrolling through his phone and scrabbling about for a piece of paper, Howley wandered away from the counter and out of the shop. He stepped from the front of the shop and found Adam Grey's car, an Audi A5. He tried the car door and to his surprise it opened. He slid inside and found a pack of Marlboro light cigarettes and a bronze Zippo lighter. He looked in the glove box, and in the back seats, and found nothing. He looked around the cabin and found a boot release button, pressed it and stepped out of the car to search the boot.

With Adam Grey's address in hand Ollie left the betting shop in search of Howley. He rounded the corner to where he'd seen Grey's car parked and saw Howley stood at the rear of the car with the boot open. "How did you get that open?"

"The car was open; I pressed the boot release switch."

"That's strange. Who'd leave a car like this unlocked?"

"It gets stranger. Come and have a look."

Ollie joined Howley at the boot of the car and looked in at what Howley had found. Howley pointed at a coil of blue, nylon rope and some flattened cardboard boxes.

"Holy shit, is that the same as at the factory?"

Howley nodded. "Looks like it. We better get Milner down here to look at the car as soon as possible."

"I'll give him a call, then I think we better go back inside and have a longer chat with big George."

"Yeah, why don't you go inside and I'll ring Milner and wait with car 'til he gets here?"

"No problem."

Ollie left Howley and stepped back into the betting shop. He marched to the counter and told George he needed to see him.

"What is it now? Need me to draw you a map?" George said.

"Want to tell me why you lied to me?"

"I didn't lie." The big man bristled with imminent violence.

"Ok, calm down big man. So you're telling me Grey hasn't been back at all? Did you know his car was unlocked?"

"I haven't checked it. Why what's the problem?"

"That's a thirty thousand pound car out there. It's been left unlocked, apparently since Tuesday. Do you see my problem now?"

"No."

"Really? You don't find that strange? An expensive car has been stood, unlocked, for all that time and it's not been taken or vandalised?"

"Things have improved a lot round here."

"You're a funny guy George." Ollie's face tightened in frustrated anger. "Where's Adam?"

"Seriously Sergeant, I haven't seen him since Tuesday."

Ollie nodded content George was telling the truth. "Alright George, so tell me, would Adam usually leave his car unlocked?"

"Nah, he'd never leave it unlocked."

"And you're sure he's not been back?"

"Positive."

"Ok George, thanks for now."

Ollie walked back out to Howley and took a cursory glance around the car. "Did you find anything else?" He asked.

"Just a packet of cigarettes and a lighter in the front."

Ollie thought about the day's investigation and thought that Kyle's guilt was looking more and more doubtful. "Ok, I'm going to go to Adam's place and see if I can turn anything up. Are you ok dealing with this and handing over to SOCO?"

Howley nodded. "Yeah no worries. When you're done at the house why don't you go and see Grace and get her up to speed and I'll update Sutherland?"

"Alright. I'll get going. If you need me just call."

"You're very sweet, but I think I'll manage." Howley quipped.

Howley watched Ollie drive off and didn't have to wait long for Greg Milner to arrive. Milner was in a tow-truck and was accompanied by an assistant. The two SOCO members soon had the car taped off as a crime scene and took a rapid succession of photographs. Milner approached Howley. "You ok Steve? You look tired."

"I'm alright just a bit fraught." He nodded towards the truck. "So I take it you're going to take the car back and process it at the station?"

"Yeah. It'll be easier to do a thorough job there. It's late now but I'll get it processed first thing in the morning. As soon as I know anything I'll call you."

"Thanks Greg, much appreciated."

* * *

Howley left Milner with Adam Grey's car and trudged to his own car. He flopped into the driver's seat and rubbed his weary eyes. The over-powering, acidic, aroma of sweet-pine air-freshener did nothing to disguise the musty smell of damp carpets rising through the car. After ten years of ownership Howley felt comfortable and happy with his car and made a note to see a garage about getting some welding done.

Steve Howley lived in Urmston and apart from the usual heavy traffic, past the Trafford Centre, he had a trouble free drive from the betting shop. He looked at his watch, it was after six; he decided to spend some time thinking the situation over. Sutherland could wait till morning.

Howley grabbed his papers and folders from the car and shuffled to his front door. He tucked the mess of papers under his arm, as he keyed the door, and pushed into the house. The small hallway was lit by a low wattage bulb and Howley failed to see the cat, standing heavily on its tail as he passed. The kitchen table provided a home for the paperwork and Howley dropped it squarely onto the wooden top.

Howley looked at the mess of papers he had dropped on the kitchen table. He needed to create some sense from the investigation for the ambitious DCi. What he had discovered would mean that Sutherland's hope for a clear cut, easy conviction wasn't going to happen.

He roughly collated the case notes and downloaded the forensic reports and post-mortem report, before stabbing at the keyboard to create his synopsis. It was brief. All the evidence collected so far cast doubt about Knowles' guilt. There was sufficient doubt to consider that someone else killed Andy Lewis. The missing knife and no apparent motive, alongside the recently discovered rope in Adam Grey's car meant there were still more questions to be answered. Knowles had been found with a hammer and Andy's blood on his hands and clothes. He always maintained he had picked up the hammer at the scene. This was suddenly far more believable. And with that came an obligation to investigate further and to keep the CPS informed.

Content with his work he decided not to put off the call to Sutherland. He picked up his phone and found Sutherland's office number. After a few rings there was an answer. "Sutherland," came the jaded greeting.

"Hello Sir, its Howley. Have you got a minute or two?"

The DCI sighed audibly before answering "I'm trying to get home on time for a change Howley so keep it brief."

Howley could tell this wasn't going to be easy. "Ok, there's a few things come up with the Knowles' case. There's some doubt about Knowles' killing Lewis." He waited for the back lash.

Sutherland held his breath, confused and annoyed, he tried to make sense of what Howley had just said. "What the hell are you talking about Howley?" He spat back at Howley.

"The pm report was sent out today and the cause of death is stabbing. We've been back out to the factory looking for a weapon but found nothing." He waited for a reply. A few moments later and Sutherland was still silent. Howley continued: "As well as that there's no apparent motive." He paused and waited.

"The knife could have been picked up by one of his scrote pals trying to protect him. It means nothing." Sutherland proffered.

"Yes that's true. But if Knowles claims he never did it, and there's no knife linking him to the stabbing, then I'd say it means a great deal boss." He thought for a minute before continuing. "It's not just the lack of a knife though boss. I don't think he did it. I spoke to Amy Lawrence just hours after Andy's death and she resolutely refused to believe Knowles did it. There's another story here and we don't have all the details yet. One thing's for sure; we're nowhere near ready to present evidence for the CPS. And if they look at what we've dug up so far and the pm report they'll walk away from it."

The DCI mulled over what Howley had said before answering "Are you sure about this Howley? I can't call the CPS with supposition and personal judgement." His anger was barely contained as he fought with the reality of what Howley had told him.

"I'm as sure as I can be at this point. There are still some leads to chase up but at the moment I'd say we need to be very cautious and consider that Knowles' may not have done this. DS James is meeting with Miss Sterling from the CPS later so he'll fill her in on the investigation."

"Ok Sergeant keep on looking into this. And don't forget that Knowles is still the number one suspect. Do not start to discount him from your investigations."

"Of course Sir."

"Good. I want to be kept in the loop on this Sergeant. As soon as you find anything or make any progress I expect you to call me." Before Howley could respond Sutherland ended the call.

Howley sighed with relief and he drew air deep into his lungs; he felt like he'd been holding his breath for the whole conversation. As he relaxed a little more his erstwhile, stood on, cat joined him on the chair. The mewling and purring distracted him for a few minutes and he indulged the moggy with a gentle ear rub. His adrenaline purged, he forced himself out of the chair and took his feline companion to be fed.

Cat food served, Howley left the cat and went back to his files. He needed to find something to place someone at the scene. He reviewed the evidence desperately searching for something previously missed. Collected at his crime scene were several footprint photos and some cigarette butts. There was a chance the cigarette butts had belonged to the killer, but equally they could be the eschewed dregs of any passerby. There had been no attempt to retrieve DNA from the butts because there had been nothing to match. Any DNA recovered could potentially be matched to the DNA database but all it really proved was that the smoker had dropped the cigarette ends there.

He rubbed his eyes and yawned loudly. His thoughts were pulled from the files on the table and he remembered the cash box he'd retrieved from Knowles' house. He dashed to his car and brought the cash box in. He then took a screw driver from a drawer and began to prise it open. After a few minutes of persuasion the box popped open.

Howley peered into the box and saw a collection of photos. Some were recent photos of Kyle with Andy Lewis at the Etihad stadium. The remainder were faded snaps from what appeared to be the early nineties. Kyle with his father, and his brother, and a tall, handsome, fair haired boy. The three teen boys were on many photos and Howley looked on the back of the photos for any scribblings that might give a clue to the third teen. On one photo he found: Kyle, Ryan and Aiden 1993 Talacre Beach. The three boys were gooning at the camera; their innocent looks belied their already blossoming criminal lives.

After a few more minutes Howley put the photos back into the box still no closer to knowing who Aiden was or why the pictures had been locked away.

CHAPTER THIRTY

Ryan Knowles fidgeted nervously as he paced the length of his garden, sucking desperately on a cigarette. He felt scared and alone; his phone had been ringing constantly as anxious gang members turned to Ryan for support. With every call his façade of strength slipped and by the end of the day he was ignoring the calls.

The garden was large and Ryan paid a gardener to keep it tidy. In the centre of the neatly manicured lawn was an ornamental pond, filled with koi-carp and oxygenated by a miniature Eros, who peed nonchalantly into the water. Ryan stepped onto the lawn and across to the pond. He stared aimlessly into the water, watching the fish. The tranquility of the fish calmed him and he resolved to be proactive. He sent a text to Aiden: **who's the prosecutor? Can you find their address?**

Aiden had responded almost immediately. **Grace Sterling. I'll find the address as soon as poss. What's the plan?**

Ryan replied: **A frightener. Your idea- Prodigy. Then a remand appeal when she's shitting it.**

He then dialed Danny, the prodigy, Barnsley. Ryan had given Danny the nickname, Prodigy, years ago when he'd first found out about Danny's proclivity for arson.

The phone rang several times before Danny answered. "Hello." Danny was sat at his kitchen table, soldering a new, illegal, satellite tv decryption device he was hoping to sell on the estate, when Ryan called.

"Hello Prodigy, how's it going?"

Danny's skin shivered when Ryan called him that. He knew he was going to be asked to start a fire somewhere. Part of him was excited at the prospect and part was reticent about letting that part of him take control of his consciousness.

"I'm alright. What are you after?"

"Got a little job for you. A simple frightener down in Macclesfield."

"Is it a house or business?"

"It's a home visit. A barrister from the CPS, you might know her, Grace Sterling?"

"I don't know the name and I don't care. You sure you have the right address?"

"Yeah it's a hundred percent right."

"Ok, send it me on a text. When do you want it doing?"

Ryan thought for a minute and then said: "Tonight. I want her shitted up. Get yourself down there as soon as it's dark and get it done."

"Tonight? That's a bit short notice. Can't it wait 'til tomorrow?"

"I'm fed up of doing nothing, get it done tonight Prodigy. Oh and Prodigy do this and you're straight with me and Kyle."

Danny couldn't quite believe what he'd heard. "Seriously? No more payments? All square?"

"Absolutely. So are we right? Can you get to Macclesfield tonight?"

"Consider it done."

Ryan ended the call and felt better. Kyle might not be thinking straight but he was.

CHAPTER THIRTY-ONE

After leaving Howley at the betting shop, Ollie made the short drive to Benchill and soon found Adam Grey's house. Grey's house was adjacent to a small, croft type, grass area that was populated with dog walkers and football playing kids. The twenties built house was the sort of simple design that a child would draw if asked to sketch a house. The brown-red bricks had worn the years the well and only the modern upvc windows gave any indication of the decade.

Ollie parked the car and made his way up the path to the front door. The white upvc door had a half-moon frosted window at the top and an electronic bell sat on the frame. Ollie pressed the bell and heard it play a serious of digital bell sounds that Ollie could hear clearly from where he stood outside the house. There was no response. Ollie knocked loudly on the door and again waited. There was still no response. He moved to the right of the door and looked in through the window into the lounge. The lounge was empty and there were no signs of habitation, not even an empty cup on the coffee table.

Ollie moved round to the side of the house and unlatched a gate. He stepped into the garden and peered through the window into the kitchen. In the sink were a few cups and plates but there was no other signs that anyone had been in the house. He took a few steps backwards and looked up at the first floor windows and again saw nothing to indicate anyone was home. He checked the door handle, and found it locked, before returning to the front of the house.

As he stood looking up at the upstairs windows at the front of the house he was joined on the street by a neighbour.

The man was about sixty and had a thinning head of grey-white hair. He walked with a stick and wore a v-neck jumper over a shirt and tie. "If you're looking for Adam you won't find him here. He's not been here for a few days."

Ollie nodded. "Yeah I am. When was the last time you saw him?"

The neighbour didn't answer immediately. "Erm, Tuesday morning I think. Why? Are you the police or something?"

Ollie reached into his pocket and showed the neighbour his id badge. "DS James, gangs and organised crime team."

"Oh, ok."

"So do you know Adam well?"

"Not really but everyone on the street knows he's one of the Knowles gang. There's usually people in and out of there all day. We all think its drugs but we can't report it 'cause he'll find out and…"

"And he'll probably hurt anyone who snitches." Ollie finished the sentence.

"Yes, so it's nice that he's not here for a few days."

"I can imagine. Do you know if he goes away anywhere? Holidays maybe?"

"I've heard him brag about a place in Spain he goes to quite often."

Ollie nodded. "And would he tell anyone here if he was going there?"

The man shook his head, "no. But he'd make a point of telling anyone who'd listen when he got back."

"Did you notice of he'd taken a bag with him Tuesday morning?"

"I didn't see anything. You could try asking the woman who lives opposite but she probably won't want to say anything about him. He's got everyone round here pretty scared of him."

Ollie had heard the same story several times and knew there was little point trying to ask the neighbours too much about Adam Grey and his movements. He turned to the helpful man. "Listen I know how hard it is for you living here but if you see Adam or hear where he might be please call me." He handed the man his card. "You can call me in confidence."

The man took the card and nodded. "He doesn't scare me. I'll ring you."

Ollie admired the man's resolve and wished there were more like him. "Thank you, I really appreciate it." He offered the man his hand and they shook hands.

Ollie thanked the man again and climbed back into his car. He sent Grace a text to say he'd meet her and then headed away from the estate.

CHAPTER THIRTY-TWO

Grace left the office and took with her a selection of files to work on at home. She decided to take a train from Victoria and treat herself to a coffee for the journey. She quickly made her way along Deansgate and headed to the old corn exchange. Grace ordered a coffee from her favourite Starbucks and then headed into the station.

As ever Grace's wait for the train home was brief, the wearied faces and loose ties of the evening crowds looked familiarly tired. Hooded urban-rap star wannabes traded bars over mis-matched ipod tunes on the main concourse, but posed no menace to anything but sensitive ears. The diesel-slick brickwork looked and smelled comfortably normal and as, the too short for commuter time, sprinter pulled in, Grace felt her muscles begin to relax.

Grace, too tired to care, let her commuter competitors take victory in the sprint for seats and she stepped on the carriage in last place, grabbing a worn leather handle and tensing her calves as the train shuddered out of Victoria.

The first of many stations brought the train to an ugly, uncomfortable halt. As ever more people seemed to board than leave, and her chances of a runners up seat seemed slight. Another stumbling departure almost caught her out and tepid coffee splashed onto her hand. With a skill only women have, she conjured a tissue and quickly dried the sticky mess. Her bag was beginning to feel heavy now and her attention turned to the blunt trauma of hard leather handles hacking at her shoulders. The dull blades butchering delicate skin made her wince and she was forced to deftly swap shoulders.

After another three trudging stops there were a few free seats that Grace could take. She looked down the car and picked a seat with a table and power point. She tottered precariously through the shuddering car and flopped into the seat. She exhaled a loud sigh a she did and felt a sharp tug at her leg that meant her tights were now ruined. Safely seated and with a good thirty minutes to endure she eased back into the seat and sent a text to Ollie: **I'll be home after seven if you want to come over and go through your latest case findings?**

After her train journey and a short walk Grace was soon at home unwinding. Her legs stretched out on the sofa and a mug of tea balanced on the arm. A Hartmann overture streamed into the lounge through tiny Bose speakers and she hummed along subconsciously. She was calm, controlled and focused. She sipped her tea and used a highlighter pen as she scanned through some work she'd taken home. A half hour of concentration and her peace was interrupted by the piercing trill of her phone. She looked at the number flashing across the screen but didn't recognise it. The first three numbers gave away that it was someone from the cps. She considered screening the call but the trill continued and she finally acquiesced to its request. She pressed answer. "Grace Sterling," her professional response.

"Hi Grace its Matt."

Grace frowned quizzically. "Hi Matt, can I help you with something?"

"Erm no, I just wanted to see if you were ok. You seemed a bit perturbed earlier. Just thought I'd apologise again and remind you of my offer of help with the Knowles' case."

"Oh, ok. No I'm fine. I was just a bit taken aback but I understand you have been frustrated by Knowles' brief a few times." She answered as calmly as she could.

"Great, thanks for understanding. And don't forget if I can help in anyway just let me know."

"Thanks Matt, I won't forget." She ended the call.

As she worked her way through the work she'd taken home she thought about Matt. She knew he'd have felt slighted by her getting the Knowles' case. In the past few years he'd failed three times to convict Knowles; she decided to ask him about those cases and about the defence his brief devised.

Her eyes stung with the efforts of the day and she put her work down and closed her eyes. She cleared her mind of work and thought about Ollie as she floated into a shallow sleep that would refresh and recharge her.

* * *

Near Wythenshawe Park, Danny (prodigy) Barnsley was browsing the internet and updating his facebook status. At just thirty Danny looked much older, he had already been bankrupt, imprisoned and sidelined by society. A string of failed businesses and relationships had led him to his lonely existence. His chances of a respectable, normal life had all but vanished and he now did anything he could to get by.

In 2009 he took a loan from Kyle Knowles. It came as no surprise to him when he couldn't make the weekly repayments. Unfortunately, he was soon, very, surprised by Kyle's approach to collecting from anyone who defaulted on their loans. A broken finger was soon followed by a hammer to the kneecap. After weeks of torment, pain and the loss of many of his possessions he made Kyle a proposition. He told Kyle about his hobby: fire starting.

Danny pulled on an old black, leather jacket, worn and infused with a smell of oil, before shuffling his rucksack onto his back. He grabbed his keys and helmet and descended to the rear of the bedsits. In the grey soup of twilight, the concrete garages looked harsh and the swamping, burgeoning, shadows were bubbling up ready for the night feeders, waiting to hide in their grip as they drip deadly substances into battered veins. Danny moved to a green painted garage door, unlocked three padlocks and slid a hardened steel chain from a maze of stops and brackets. With the over-sized chain over his shoulder he lifted the garage door up. The benzene odours of petrol, mixed with the worn and broken molecules of old engine oil, welcomed him. He reached for a light switch and he flinched as the fluorescent tube popped and gagged into life.

Under the tube lighting Danny could now see his motorcycle. A 1995 Suzuki GSXR1100, the number one choice of hooligans in the nineties. He pushed the key into the ignition, pulled the choke to full and dabbed at the starter. The motor span up instantly and as it warmed he pushed it out of the garage. As it waited for him it burbled, and revs rose and fell by minute amounts. He relocked the garage and squeezed into his helmet. Climbing onto the bike he twisted the throttle and then pushed the choke off. He selected first gear and rode off in search of the barrister's home.

After an hour's riding, of a very indirect route, Danny arrived at a small row of shops he had identified earlier. He rode the bike close to a Chinese takeaway and parked it. After locking it to a railing he took off his helmet and joined the queue in the takeaway. As he approached the counter he shouted over "Chicken cashew, noodles and spring rolls please.

Be back in twenty." The girl repeated the order back and he left his helmet on a small table before walking outside.

Walking across the car park, towards the entrance of Grace's apartment block, Danny was completely alone. No one looked out of their windows, no one was driving in or out and there were no barking dogs to warn of his presence. As expected, the door had a magnetic release that the occupants of the building operated remotely from their intercoms; great systems, but not too tough to overcome. Danny knew that with a large enough magnet he could de-stabilise the magnetic field of the holding lock, by applying the same polarity from his tennis ball sized magnet to the lock. This creates a repulsion force greater than that of the attraction force that creates the lock. Danny placed his magnet against the lock and pushed the door, it didn't move. He turned the magnet 180 degrees and tried again, this time the door opened and Danny slipped into the lobby area.

The lobby was sparsely decorated, functional, clean and housed several post boxes for the residents: very Americanised, no self-respecting professional wants a postie wandering the halls of their apartment building. Danny imagined the over-paid, self-obsessed, flat dwellers collecting platinum card bills, over small talk about Jamie Oliver inspired dinner parties. He was actually sneering at the thought and was more than happy to be bringing an air of destruction to the insipid living quarters. A quick glance at the boxes confirmed Grace's flat was on the first floor and he ran silently up the stairs.

On the first floor corridor Danny found Grace's door. The corridor was well lit but had no CCTV camera, the walls were decorated with ornate wallpaper and he walked on plush red carpet. As he readied himself for his work he walked back away from his target and took a penknife from his pocket. He deftly unfolded the main blade then used it to break the bulbs in the wall lights in this part of the corridor.

In darkness, he crouched in a corner just past Grace's door. Opening his old Berghaus the faint smell of flammable liquids stung his nose as he pulled out the flask and tin he had packed earlier. From the small tin he pulled out the impregnated polishing cloth and rolled it between his fingers to make a crude looking rope.

With several lengths of rope made, he took out a roll of gaffa-tape and made several sticky balls. Moving silently but quickly Danny stuck the gaffa tape balls to the door and then pushed the crude ropes onto the gaffa tape, eventually framing the centre of the door. With this done he added a further piece of inflammable rope to form a crude fuse.

Content with his ignition source Danny opened the metallic flask and began pouring the liquid into a pool at the centre of the doorway. He watched for a moment to ensure that the liquid crept beneath the door and into the apartment. Satisfied with his work he stood up and lit a cigarette.

Repacking his bag he took a few long draws on the cigarette and then crouched back to his rudimentary fuse. With a final piece of gaffa he fashioned a delayed ignition with the remainder of his cigarette. He blew gently at the ashen end and the ignition source moved a millimetre closer to the inflammable cloth-rope. Convinced the improvised ignition source would work as planned, he hurried away from the door and out of the building.

* * *

Grace felt refreshed after her nap and was sat comfortably on her sofa, legs drawn beneath her, cradling a large mug of tea. Her lounge was comfortably decorated with neutral paint and cream leather. A large plasma TV had replaced a fireplace and she was numbing her mind with the ramblings of Sarah Beeny. A small plate with three jaffa cakes was perched on the arm of the sofa and after a sip of tea she put down the mug and grabbed a jaffa. On the coffee table lay her notes from work.

As the TV told her how much fun it was to waste thousands of pounds on old barns and stables, she nibbled her biscuit and sipped quietly at her hot tea. She checked her phone and found a text from Ollie: **I'll come over and bring you up to speed on the investigation sometime after 7.** She smiled and found herself basking in the warm feelings she associated with the good times with Ollie.

It was already seven and Grace padded from the lounge to the bathroom; she wanted to shower before Ollie arrived. She turned the tap and waited for the water to warm up; satisfied with the heat of the water she stepped into the shower. She dug her nails into her scalp as she scrubbed her hair and was soon feeling invigorated. She stepped out of the shower and toweled herself dry. After brushing her hair through she dressed in a comfortable pair of pyjamas and flopped back on the sofa, waiting for Ollie.

As she checked her watch, the quiet was broken with the screech and wail of the building's fire alarm. She slipped on her shoes and swiftly made her way to her door. As she approached it a flame whooshed up from the base of the door. The heat and intensity took her breath and she scampered backwards away from the licking flames. The flames crept into her flat, threatening to devour anything they could reach. She ran to the kitchen and pulled a fire extinguisher from the wall and sprayed the invading flames. The flames shrunk back, but the centre of her door was burning through. She aimed the extinguisher higher and it feebly spat the last of its gas, before failing.

The heat was intense and a thick black smoke filled her flat. She coughed as the smoke plumed towards her and she covered her mouth with her hand. Her cheeks had reddened with the heat of the licking flames and her eyes streamed with tears. She was trapped.

She screamed. "Help! I'm in number ten! Help!"

***

Danny was two roads away from Grace's flat when he heard the fire alarm screech into life. He had noticed smoke detectors throughout the building, but Grace would be unable to evacuate her flat. He continued his walk back to his bike without looking back and was looking forward to his Chinese takeaway.

CHAPTER THIRTY-THREE

Ollie drove into Macclesfield and onto the road where Grace lived. The evening's dark blanket had slid onto the town and only the orange glow of street lights gave any illumination. The still air was fresh and Ollie had been driving with his window open to enjoy it. As he rounded the corner to Grace's flat he was faced with two fire-engines and an ambulance.

Blue lights flashed brightly as dozens of people were stood around the vehicles and being guided into the rear of the ambulance was Grace. Ollie gunned the motor and quickly pulled up next to the ambulance. "Grace! Grace, are you ok? What's happened?"

Grace turned when she heard Ollie's voice and pulled away from the paramedics as she made her way to Ollie. "Oh Ollie, thank god you're here. There was a fire, my door was on fire…I tried to put it out but it was too big." She blurted.

Ollie pulled her close to him and wrapped his arms around her. She was shaking and he held her tightly. "It's ok Grace…deep breaths…I'm here."

One of the paramedics approached the intertwined couple. "Excuse me but I really need to check you're ok Miss Sterling, you'll need to come to the hospital."

"I'll bring her over in a minute." Ollie said.

The paramedic nodded and left them alone.

"Are you ok Grace? How did you get out if your door was on fire?"

"I'm fine. I still have that escape rope you fitted for me last year. I can't believe it, you weren't even here and you saved my life."

"Well I'm glad you didn't throw it out. So are you hurt? How did the fire start?"

"I'm ok. I just hurt my ankle when I dropped from the rope."

"Could've been worse. What about the fire?"

"It came from under my door…and then my door burned through." She cried as she spoke. "I couldn't get out Ollie; I…"

"I know Grace. It's alright now though, you're safe."

Without thinking she nodded. "I always felt…feel safe with you."

"Come on let's get you checked out. And after that you can come and stay at mine until your place is sorted."

"That's nice of you to offer but … I was going to ring my parents."

"Madeline and Sam? Are they even in the country?"

"Well, no, but …"

"Where is it this time? New York? The Caribbean? South Africa?"

"Rome. But I can just stay at their place."

"On your own?"

"It's familiar."

"So is my place."

"Ollie ..." A cough took over her insistent statement.

"That's settled then. You'll stay with me."

She didn't have the energy or inclination to resist. It was too easy. Too natural. She gave into the pressure from his safe arms and let her head collapse onto his chest.

"Thank you." Grace murmured, her eyes momentarily closing as she struggled to stop the tears.

"Come on, hospital then home." Ollie ordered as he slowly walked her to the rear of the ambulance.

"You are coming with me?" A wave of panic flooded through her usually confident voice.

"Yes. Of course I am."

Ollie helped her into the ambulance and sat beside her. The paramedics triaged her and made sure she was secure. Ollie held her hand throughout and kissed her forehead several times for reassurance. Ollie looked out to the fire engines and recognised the white helmet of the fire-station manager. He kissed Grace. "I just need a word with the fire brigade. I'll be one minute."

Grace nodded. Ollie stepped off the ambulance and approached the station officer. The station officer was wiry and had deeply piercing blue-violet eyes. His wrinkled face wore the wisdom and worries that only long service in the brigade bring and his strong hand could crush a billiard ball. Ollie reached into his pocket and showed him his warrant card. "D.S. Oliver James, have you got a minute?"

The station officer inspected Ollie's warrant card before extending his hand. "Hello sergeant; S.O. Clive Bixby. What can I do for you?"

Ollie accepted the firm handshake. "The woman whose flat was burnt out is a CPS barrister working a high profile case. Have you had a chance to see what the ignition point was?"

"Interesting that you should ask. I've just come from the flat and the source appears to be the door. There are no electrical points there and no obvious points of ignition. We've collected some samples from around the door and we'll run them through the gas-chromatograph and mass-spectrometer. There was a distinct smell in the area that will probably turn out to be white-spirit."

"I had a suspicion you'd say that."

"Well if we find anything we'll liaise with the arson task force, based at Old-Trafford. The borough arson liaison officer will bring you in if there's a link. But I'll let you know either way. Do you have a card?"

Ollie handed him a card with his contact details on. "Thanks Clive. I'd really appreciate that…" He looked over at the ambulance and could see the paramedics were anxious to move. "Look I better go I need to go with her to the hospital."

"Ok sergeant. Look after her she was pretty shaken up."

Ollie jogged back to the ambulance and the paramedics closed the doors behind him. The driver maneuvered away from the flats and headed to Macclesfield district hospital.

CHAPTER THIRTY-FOUR

Amy Lawrence was trying to distract herself with television. The family liaison officer had left her and she was alone; her throat was sore and her nose red. She opened another tin of beer and sipped straight from the can. The sharp, bitter taste felt good after a day of sweet tea and sympathy. She was glad that the liaison officer had been with her all day, but she had to try and survive on her own.

As she stared at the anodyne images radiating from the screen her focus drifted and she had no idea what the show was about. In her hand she fidgeted with the card Ollie had left her as she thought about Andy. Tears began to well in the corners of her eyes and she reached for a tissue.

The television wasn't distracting enough and Amy's tears evolved into a full blown cry. Her body shook with grief and she felt an inconsolable emptiness as she thought about Andy. She prowled the flat looking for anything that would distract her, but nothing could ease the pain.

She moved into the kitchen and found a bottle of vodka. She swigged vodka from the bottle and then carried it back to the lounge. As she dropped into the chair her phone rang and Amy answered. "Hello."

"Hello Amy. Are you alright?"

Amy thought for a second, "erm yes. Who's this?"

After a pause the man answered. "It's Ryan."

Amy knew who Ryan Knowles was but had never spoken to him before. "Oh, 'iya Ryan."

"How are you doin'?"

"I'm not. It's fucked up."

"I know. 'ave you got anythin' to help you through? Do you want some weed or something stronger?"

Amy occasionally smoked cannabis and thought about the offer. "Yeah I might have some weed. I could do with something to help me sleep."

"Ok I'll sort you out; I wanted to talk to you anyway. Can you meet me in the park later?"

"Yeah. It might be good to go out."

"Yeah you should get some air. I'll be near the bandstand in a couple of hours."

"Ok, I'll see you in a bit."

Amy put down the phone and took another swig of vodka. The dusk of the early evening had given way to the full darkness of night and Amy pulled the blinds shut. She looked at her lounge and began to pick up mugs and biscuit packets. She tutted at the crumbs on the coffee table and grabbed a handheld vacuum from the kitchen. She vacuumed the crumbs and wiped the table before sitting down again and finishing her can of beer.

She sobbed quietly as she thought about Andy; the stresses of the day had been physically demanding and her eyes burned with exhaustion. She tried to sleep but her anguish was too great. She looked at Ollie's card again and wondered if she should call him. She'd made a promise to Andy and to Kyle but things had changed. She toyed with her phone and the card as she battled with her conscience.

* * *

Blackening skies diffused and muddied the light over Wythenshawe Park. Trees moved awkwardly with chuffling winds, as grey squirrels bounced between grasping branches. Amy watched the bolder greys leap to gardens in search of unguarded bird feeders. Across the park she recognised a gaggle of hooded youths, swigging cider and passing round a joint; only a few months ago she would have been doing the same. Their chatter, vulgar and coarse, carried and three times she heard the name Knowles. She cringed and shuddered when she did.

"Amy, over here." A voice beckoned from the park edges. She squinted through rhododendrons and saw a flash of red sports-wear. She didn't recognise the caller but felt she knew the voice. Glancing round there were no other visitors to the park and the coarse teens were distant rumblings now. "Is that you Ryan?" She stuttered.

"Yeah, if that suits." The red top answered quizzically. He fidgeted where he stood and cold droplets of leaf-caught rain flicked down his warm back. He shivered and frowned.

Amy stepped off the footpath and onto the wood chipped planting area. Soft and cold on her trainered foot, she aimed for the hiding man. Through the green, Indian, invading, plants she pushed; her shoulder soon soaked with collected rain-water; she could now see the world-shy man who had called her and asked her to meet here. His sporty clothes and shoes sodden he looked cold and angry.

The caller didn't move, he leant back on a tree branch and wanted Amy to come to him. She crept closer to him, his dark eyes never moved from her as she looked at him desperately trying to work out how she knew him. He was wearing a blue and red tracksuit, adorned with Nike labelling, and was foot-shod in matching trainers. At his feet were three cigarette butts and a chewing gum wrapper. He was built well and reminded Amy of a bouncer, but that's not how she knew him, and he could be any number of Knowles gang members she had come across. What struck her as different were his hair and his face. There was something different, he seemed cleaner somehow, his hair wasn't the usual clipper-cut style and his teeth somehow too healthy. She thought for a minute and realised that Ryan would probably live in a huge house somewhere away from his old neighbourhood, he would have expensive tastes now and private dentists. She was sure this was Ryan, brother to Kyle and running things in his brother's absence.

She took one last step and was standing next to him.

"I was startin' to think you weren't coming." He scowled.

"Sorry, I missed the bus and it took ages for another one." She quickly responded. "Why did I have to come here? Why couldn't you bring the weed to mine? What's this about?" She asked nervously.

"Andy." As he spoke his name Amy started to cry. Her throat was constricted and she could barely stand but she blurted-
"What? What about him? I... I know Kyle didn't kill him, he wouldn't, he liked Andy. Why do you want to see me about him now?"

"People tell me you've been acting strangely; there's talk of rumours coming from you about Kyle and your Andy." He told her in a calm voice that had a currently creepy air to it.

"What rumours? What fucking people? Course I'm acting strange, my…my Andy was fucking murdered!" Her tears now filled her eyes and bronze foundation was laid to waste by rivers of pain cutting through her cheeks, exposing her pinked skin. "Why the fuck have you called me here? What do you think I've done?" Her anguished cries were now barely recognisable a human; jolts of grief shook her frail body and choked her throat. Every word was spat out as she fought to make her point.

Watching Amy he felt little for her. He had his own problems and now it was time for him to be loyal to Kyle. As the girl wretched and cried, babbling and spitting as she did so, he turned himself away from her slightly and took a four inch lock-knife from his jacket pocked. He breathed deeply as he unfolded the polished, glinting blade. The poor wretch was still shuddering out her hysteric cries, her chin virtually on her chest and eyes too blearly with briny tears to have noticed his actions. As he turned back towards her he wondered if he was actually doing her a favour, her misery would soon be ended, her inconsolable grief would give way to blissful ignorance. It was him who would have to deal with life after this, not her. Life was torturous round here, hers even more than his. He would soon free her from that pain.

"Ok Amy, you can stop crying now. I just had to see if myself that the rumours weren't true." As he spoke he lifted her chin gently and her sorrowed eyes looked at him. She sniffed and blinked hard, confused and angry with this callous man in front of her. "Andy was loyal Amy, too loyal. Kyle trusted him, confided in him. In fact I think Andy was soon to receive recompense for his loyalty. But you see, I have been loyal far longer, my recompense is well past due. I'm sorry Amy, he had to be removed." As he watched her work out what he'd just said he brought the knife up and pushed it through her clothes and into the soft flesh beneath her ribs. She tried to speak but as he twisted the blade she collapsed to her knees.

He pushed her over as he pulled out the knife and she fell wounded into the chippings. She held her hand over the wound, but the butchered flesh ached and throbbed as if the blade was still there. She tried to catch her stolen breath but gasped in failure. He knelt and pushed a knee into her soft gut; touching the wound he rubbed the tepid blood between his fingers. Shock paralysed Amy and she could only watch, wait and hope. His hand was now on her chest and she fought so hard to move and tried to buck him as he neared her breast.

He sneered, "silly girl, I'm really not into chavs. What the fuck do you take me for?"

She lifted a hand and he simply wafted it away. He continued to caress her chest just below her bra, then he pushed a hard finger into the muscle between her ribs. She twitched in pain. "Ah, that will do."

He placed the tip of the knife into the same spot and held the knife vertically with his left hand. With a swift move he used his right like a hammer and forced the knife through the intercostal muscle, forcing the blade into her lung. Blood bubbled from the wound as the punctured lung hissed like a car tyre.

Amy was gone, the pain too much she passed out. He repeated his bloody task several times until satisfied she was dead. He stood over her body and looked at her face. It never ceased to amaze him how alive they looked after they're killed. He took a deep breath and spoke to her corpse; "Sorry Amy, I'm really sorry about that chav remark, you were quite pretty in your own way. But I just can have you running about raising doubt about Andy's killer."

He made no attempt to hide her body and walked out of the rhododendrons and onto the hard tarmac path. The fecund aroma of old orchard trees was heavy-laden in the air as he made his way to the old bandstand.

He felt sure no one was about but quickened his pace as he saw the Victorian bandstand. He arrived at a jog and found a large sports bag. From the bag he pulled jeans, a shirt and a pair of boots. He quickly changed and took his tracksuit and trainers to a corner of the bandstand, normally used by drug takers. He used the jacket to clean the knife then threw the clothes into the corner. From his pocket he took his lighter and set the clothes alight. He lit a cigarette and watched as the bloodied clothes were consumed and transformed into ash. He felt for the knife in his pocket and patted it as if it were a pet or friend and smiled happily to himself.

CHAPTER THIRTY-FIVE

On a freshly vacuumed floor laid a swiftly made pile of clothes. Soft silk intertwined with cotton and denim. Fine, wool jacket pressed against nylon, lycra mix. On the hotel-chain purple bedding, lay a human mix, just as bizarre, that moved animal-like oblivious to anything but their intimate act. Skinhead and hate tattoos mixed with salon perfect curls and soft moisturised skin. Unkempt grubby nails dug into soft, clean, pale skin as manicured, polished and painted nails felt fragile on coarse bedding. On her knees she looked trapped by this opportunist predator pushing into her, shouts of joy easily confused for those of terror. As the grim dog-like man thrust himself to a primal finish she arched back allowing his length to push on her G-spot. As he grunted and barked his tumultuous end to the passion she felt herself shudder as his throbbing finally gave her G-spot the stimulation she craved. They finished their wild mating and collapsed smiling, red-faced and spent.

Their primal ritual finished the couple lay exhausted on the hotel bed. Manicured nails on soft hands traced the outlines of inked artwork deep in his flesh, as hairy, grubby, digits maul, teen-like at sensitive breasts. Ruth was too tired and too happy to care. She let her hand wander lower and stroked his now flaccid penis and was saddened that it wouldn't respond. He turned onto his side. "Just gimme ten minutes sweetheart." He said hoping the little blue pill he was about to take would work quickly. "I'm just going to get a drink of water."

He stood from the bed and walked into the bathroom. He swallowed down a Viagra and headed back into the room. He looked and admired the soft, peach flesh of his recent triumph. He smiled as he thought about her. She'd been a revelation to him, a total animal in bed, so voracious he could barely keep up.

He slid back into the bed and she was instantly stroking him again. He kissed her and tried to distract her from her sexual appetite with a question. "So what time do you need to be in the office in the morning?"

"For about half eight? Why are you going to wake me with a naughty surprise?" She ran her hand back down to his groin hoping to find him more responsive. "Is there something wrong? Can I do anything to help you?"

He laughed nervously; she was more sexually overt than any women he'd ever been with. He was glad he'd got hold of some Viagra. "I'm fine, we have all night."

"And I don't want to waste a minute Jack."

"Don't worry we won't waste anytime. So where have you been today? Stuck in the office or have you been in court?"

"I was in court. But I was thinking about you. I wanted to be on top of you."

"You'll get yourself fired if you're not careful. So who were you prosecuting?"

Ruth wasn't really interested in talking about work but answered anyway. "It was just a remand hearing for Kyle Knowles. You know the gang leader?"

Jack feigned ignorance. "Oh yes I've heard of him. He's a big gangster type on my estate."

"Yes that'll be him." She kissed his neck and then let her kisses trail down his body. As she approached his penis he felt it respond to her touch and his erection grew. He rolled fully onto his back, pulling her on top as he moved. She eagerly grabbed at him and skillfully slid herself onto him, allowing him to penetrate deeply. He sighed with pleasure and satisfaction.

They finished their primal dance and Jack collapsed, exhausted and happy. Ruth lay her head on his chest and smiled broadly. Jack felt her relaxing. "So was Kyle Knowles remanded?"

A post-coitally happy Ruth answered. "Yeah, he didn't even challenge the application."

"Really? Is that normal?"

"Well, I haven't been to many remand hearings for murder so I don't know. But the barrister I was working for thought it was strange."

Jack stretched and yawned. "So do you think he'll be found guilty at the trial?"

"Probably. There's a ton of evidence against him."

Jack smiled to himself. "That's good. People like that should be locked up for good."

Ruth laughed. "Listen to you, Mr Morals."

"Well I have a few morals left." He joked.

Ruth kissed his chest and Jack reached for the television remote control, then turned it on. They watched tv and had sex until they were finally too tired to do anything but sleep.

CHAPTER THIRTY-SIX

While Grace rested for half an hour in the hospital, Ollie made his way back to her building to collect his car. The fire brigade were clearing their equipment away and Ollie was allowed into Grace's flat.

The building looked no worse for the fire and the residents had all gone back to their apartments. Ollie took the stairs and as he climbed higher he detected a slight smell of smoke, it was like someone had left the window open as they barbecued. He turned onto the short corridor in which Grace's apartment was and the smell increased.

Grace's door was nothing more than a few chunks of charred wood and the floor was scorched and burnt. The damage was tightly confined to an eight foot radius from the door. The edges of the comfortable old sofa had been licked by searing flames but they'd been unable to take hold and it sat resolutely proud of its battle scars. Ollie had seen a few arson attacks and this looked a lot like one. A sharp intense fire, started with an accelerant, lots of smoke and lots of heat but short lived. The accelerants burnt fast and soon ran out of fuel and as a result the flames consumed the door but failed to take hold further into the apartment.

Ollie went through to Grace's bedroom and filled a case with her clothes before moving into the bathroom. He grabbed her toothbrush and scooped a shelf full of bottles and tubes into the bag. Content that he'd collected enough girly necessities he returned to the living room. In the living room Ollie put Grace's laptop back into her work bag, along with a stack of papers and files Ollie found on the table.

Ollie gave the apartment another cursory glance before leaving and heading for the apartment's maintenance store. He took some plywood, screws and tools and secured Grace's apartment. He then left the building and headed back to the hospital.

The drive to the hospital was short and Ollie was soon parked. He rushed through the brightly painted corridors and found Grace waiting impatiently for him. "Sorry, I had to board up your doorway before I left."

Grace's impatience quickly turned to gratitude. "God I hadn't even thought about that. Thank you Ollie; I don't know what I'd have done without you."

"I'm sure you'd have managed fine without me."

"Maybe, but I'm glad you were here."

"I was only ever a phone call away…" He stopped himself. "Anyway, not to worry; are you all set to go?"

"Yes I've been given the all clear. No real smoke inhalation and my ankle is just a sprain and is all bandaged up now."

"That's good. Now can you walk or do I have to carry you?"

"Was that a chivalrous offer?"

Ollie laughed; "Of course M'Lady"

"Well that's very sweet of you but I can walk."

"Oh thank god, I wasn't sure I could carry you that far." He joked.

Grace gave him a playful punch to the arm. "You're a cheeky bastard."

"Ouch, yes I am. But you always knew that about me." He offered her his arm and she linked him as she stood. "Ok M'Lady let's go."

Ollie walked Grace from the hospital and out to the car park. The cool night air exposed their breath and Ollie held Grace closely to keep her warm. She was grateful for the extra warmth and they walked as one towards Ollie's car.

"Oh god Ollie I forgot you had that sick-green coloured car. I hope nobody recognises me in it." Grace jibed and laughed.

"Oh you're such a model of good taste in your pyjamas and slippers. Just get into my beautifully coloured car." Ollie retorted.

"You're very touchy Oliver. And what exactly is wrong with my pyjamas?"

Ollie grinned widely; "nothing, I'm sure they're very nice pyjamas, a lovely shade of pink." He looked her up and down. "Where are the unicorns?"

"Ha, ha very funny. Actually the unicorn ones are at home…" As she said the words her demeanour changed. Her eyes filled with tears. "Do I have a home Ollie?" She said as she cried.

Ollie quickly reassured her. "Yes, I was just there Grace. It's not too bad I promise. A new door and some paint. The insurance will cover it."

Grace felt slightly reassured. "Are you sure? The flames were huge."

"I'm sure. It looks like an accelerant fire all flames and smoke. It didn't set anything alight in your apartment. It's a bit smoky smelling but it can all be sorted."

"Oh thank god. Will you take me there tomorrow? I want to get my laptop and work things."

"It's ok, I've already got them in the car. And some clothes, and most of your bathroom."

"You're so good Ollie; thank you. Did you pick up the papers on the coffee table? I thought they'd all be burnt."

"I got them all. No damage done. Although the inside of my car now smells like a barbecue."

"Thank you. I'll clean your car out I promise." She thought for a minute. "Unless you want to change it for a more sensible colour?"

"Funny, glad you still have your sense of humour. Now come on, get in, it's freezing."

Grace shivered and nodded before climbing into the car. Ollie quickly started the engine and turned on the heated seats for Grace.

* * *

Ollie pulled onto his driveway and killed the engine. Grace was asleep in the passenger seat and he gave her a little nudge. "Hey sleepy, we're here." He whispered.

Grace roused from her sleep and looked up at Ollie's house. The semi-detached house was typical of the eighties new builds; Ollie's being slightly different only in his extension of the garage. The front of the house had a small garden and whilst it was neatly looked after it had no flowers or any interesting features. Grace remembered trying to persuade him to plant a rose bush, but he insisted any spare time was for fixing old cars, not pruning flowers.

Ollie could see she was thinking about something. "You ok?"

"Yeah, just looking at your boring garden. I see you never put any flowers in."

"No I've never got round to that. Maybe next summer."

Grace knew he didn't mean it. "Yeah, maybe next summer." She mocked.

Ollie chose to ignore her mocking tone and pushed open his car door. "Come on Sterling, let's get you in and make you a bed up."

"Yes sir." She retorted. "When did you get so bossy?"

Ollie laughed. "I've been listening to self-help tapes: how to deal with annoying barristers."

"Annoying? I'm hurt."

"Yes, I'm sure that's the worst thing anyone has said about you."

Grace shrugged her shoulders and stepped out of the car.

Ollie opened the door to his house and the two of them stepped inside. Ollie led Grace to the lounge and asked to wait while he put some bedding on the spare bed. Grace sat on the sofa and looked around the room. It was exactly as she remembered it, simple and comfortable. Shelves were home to books and a few photos and his film collection on DVD or Blu-ray were neatly stacked in Swedish, floor-standing units. The beech-wood laminate floor was a little more worn and he'd bought a new cream and brown rug, but otherwise the room was exactly as it had been when she was last there.

CHAPTER THIRTY-SEVEN

Howley was woken by a piercing ring tone. His senses jarred and reset as he moved rapidly from sleep to awake. An early morning call wasn't a new thing but they were getting harder to deal with. He flailed his arm in the direction of the noise and picked up the phone. He pressed answer. "Hello."

"Good morning Steve, its John. We just got a call. There's a dead body at Wythenshawe Park; it looks like a murder and it's your turn to pick it up."

Howley paused for a second as he further gathered himself. "Ok, where about in the park?"

"On the perimeter path near the bandstand."

"Ok, I'll be there as soon as I can." Howley ended the call. His back ached and his head throbbed. He felt old and tired. He'd noticed that he could no longer jump from bed and into usefulness with the instant vigour of his youth. He needed longer to come round and for his brain to engage fully.

It was still dark out and Howley pushed himself from the bed. He looked at the clock, ten past six, and shook his head as he wondered why these calls never came at a reasonable hour. He slumped from the bed to the bathroom and quickly washed, before dressing himself quickly.

Despite being a long standing member of the gangs and organised crime unit he, like Ollie, was still required to work other cases and despite his involvement on the Knowles case he would have to attend crime scene. The forensic medical examiner would have also had an early morning wake up call and would probably be at the scene already though it would be unlikely they'd be able to tell him anything at the scene.

Dressed and ready to go Howley made his way to the kitchen. He then clicked the kettle on and grabbed a mug from the cupboard. He sprinkled some instant coffee granules into the cup and a dash of milk while he waited for the water to boil. His cat mewled at his feet and he gave it a gentle stroke on the head, before opening a tin of cat food and spooning it into the bowl.

The kitchen was spotless; it had been that way since the death of his wife. The beech wood worktops gleamed the way they had when they'd been fitted. His wife had died a month later and Howley had barely used it since. A new dinner service, six of everything and a new set of cutlery all sat untouched in cupboards and draws.

Howley thought about his wife. Her fight with cancer had been brief and painful. Her death had brought her relief from the pain but Howley's had never gone. He remembered their happier times and smiled at the fond memories. At his feet a sated cat nuzzled him and brought him back to reality. He petted the cat and then poured the hot water onto the coffee and milk.

He tipped the coffee into a travel mug and made his way from the kitchen and out of the front door.

* * *

The early morning winter sun hit the roadside trees almost horizontally and strobed, painfully, into Howley's eyes as he drove to the crime scene at Wythenshawe park.

Relief from the stabbing sun only came as he turned off the Parkway, too late to stop the now entrenched migraine.

Detective Sergeant Howley parked next to the SOCO van at the newly found crime scene. He dragged himself out of the car by the door pillar and grimaced as a rush of pain flooded across his back. Still dressed in the same suit, and creased shirt, he wore the day before he hobbled, tramp like, to see the first officer on scene. He found the entrance to the mobile police station that had been hastily erected by SOCO and was greeted by a face he knew. The officer, PC White, was a twenty year veteran of uniform and was integrity itself. He offered him his hand to shake and he took it warmly. Howley was happy he would deal with White and not one of the younger breed he was starting to despise. White offered him a seat in the office-van and he took it gratefully.

"Been a while John, when did you get here?" Howley probed.

"Yeah, too long. I got here at six but we received the call at five thirty. The girl was found by a dog walker, she's in the other mobile unit, and I secured the scene." PC White responded. Howley gritted his teeth as more back pain surged and teased his nerves. He nodded at White indicating to him that he should continue.

"Ok, so we've got one dead female. White, about nineteen, fully clothed, in expensive track suit, and no immediately obvious signs of a struggle, but she's face down so you will have to wait for the SOCO to have a look at her front to ascertain if there is any stab or gun wounds. Paramedics declared life extinct earlier but had the sense to leave the body alone. Her mobile phone is missing and there's no identification on her."

Howley nodded again and asked White: "So where's the body?"

"Come on, I'll take you over." White answered.

Howley felt pain with every jarring step out of the van but refused to show it as he followed PC White to the body.

The wisened men pushed their way through a growing crowd of forensic techs and eager hopeful reporters towards a blue and white taped area. In front of the blue and white tape stood two young uniforms, puff-chested for the cameras. They saw White and Howley and raised the tape to allow them access. Three metres in was a sun bleached blue inflatable tent; pegs held the edges down to prevent the stare of morbid onlookers. The forensic medical examiner, FME, was about to take the body back to the morgue and one of his assistants began constructing the plastic screening that would continue to give the poor victim her privacy. Howley gave a nod to the FME who nodded back in recognition. Howley asked the tired looking doctor, "Anything on her front?"

"Yes DS Howley, several stab wounds on her torso. Would you like the time of death?"

"That would be great please doc."

"Thought you would. Well, rigour has set in so I'd estimate approximately six hours but you will have to wait for the pathologist for a more accurate time dear boy."

"That's a dark hour for a young girl to be out." Howley said. He sighed and a new pain spread over him. "Is it possible to tell if the stabbing killed her yet?"

"I can't say for certain but it looks like her lung may have been punctured. That can sometimes be enough depending on internal bleeding and a few other factors. The pathologist will confirm more in the post-mortem report. However, when we rolled her over there was evidence of post-mortem bruising on her abdomen which is fairly normal where there is internal bleeding."

"Ok thanks." Said Howley quietly.

While Howley and the doctor had been talking, the assistants had rested Amy in a body bag and hauled her onto the stretcher. Howley trudged to the stretcher and unzipped a few inches over the face. He looked at the greying pale face of the girl. She looked like any number of young kids he had seen in the area. He felt a charge of sadness in his chest and with a deep breath closed the bag.

* * *

Howley sighed with exasperation as he waited for the results of the finger printing.

He left the SOCOs searching and went to find a coffee. In the canteen he saw Craig Lindley. Craig, tall and blonde, was a long standing CID member and like Howley had been involved with gang crime cases for a long time. "Hey Craig, how you keeping?" Howley asked his colleague.

"I'm good, Sutherland has me busy trying to push on from Kyle Knowles, he now wants Ryan." He replied. "Oh and I'm bloody knackered after picking up a floater in the ship canal the other day."

Howley nodded knowingly and then frowned "Sutherland has no idea. There's no chance of Ryan sticking his head above the trenches now."

"Well you know how he is. He's got Kyle, but he's insisting that Ryan has now taken over." He looked at Howley who was shaking his head, "I know, I know, I've tried to tell him" he continued "but he's convinced that Ryan is capable of taking over."

Howley laughed sarcastically and responded: "He won't get anywhere with Ryan, Andy was the most likely to have taken some sort of control but clearly we have issues there..." He suddenly stopped talking as his mind made links. His eyes narrowed and he quickly returned to the conversation "Craig, what was the name of that girl Andy was involved with? Damn I should know this Ollie went to see her."

Craig looked quizzically at his colleague but answered "Amy, I think. Can't remember the surname, but definitely Amy. Why?"

"You're sure it was Amy?" Howley asked excitedly.

"Yeah, certain. Blonde kid. Why are you asking Howley?"

"I think that Amy is in with the pathologist. Found in Wythenshaw park." He answered solemnly. "Gotta go, thanks for that Craig." He grabbed his coffee and headed back to his desk.

Back at his desk Howley reached for the phone and called Ollie.

CHAPTER THIRTY-EIGHT

Ollie's phone buzzed across his bedside table and woke him from a comfortable sleep. He leant up on his elbows and smiled as he realised Grace was still in bed with him. Her hair was strewn across the pillow and her pale face was serenely beautiful as she slept. The phone buzzed again and Ollie picked it up. "Hi Steve."

"Hey Ol. I just picked up a dead body at the park."

"Unlucky mate, was it an early call?"

"They always are. But that's not the reason for the call. I'm pretty sure it's Amy Lawrence and she's been stabbed in a similar way to Andy."

It took a moment for what Howley had said to register. "Oh shit, how sure are you?"

"Well it's just a vague memory of her and a hunch at the moment, I'm waiting for a confirmed identification. SOCO are running the prints as we speak."

"Well I was with her yesterday. Have you got the SOCO pictures of the body?"

"Yeah, from a dim and distant memory I have of her I'm pretty sure it's her, but get yourself in here and confirm it."

Next to Ollie, Grace was stirring from her sleep and turned to face him. She smiled broadly at him. "Morning."

Howley heard the female voice. "Who's that? Am I interrupting something?"

Ollie rolled his eyes "Its Grace. She had to spend the night here. I'll explain later."

"I'm sure you will." Howley said with a mock tone of disapproval.

Ollie ignored the tone. "Right, I'll be there as soon as poss."

Grace frowned at him and asked: "Who's that? Is it Steve?"

Ollie shushed her through a smile and whispered; "yes it's Steve."

Howley heard the whisper. "You're a terrible whisperer Ollie. I'm going back to SOCO to see if they got a hit from the fingerprints. I'll see you soon." Howley ended the call.

Ollie put his phone down and turned to Grace. "Did you sleep alright?"

Grace nodded. "I did. Thank you for staying with me."

"It was my pleasure."

Grace grinned mischievously; "yes I thought I felt something poking me in the back this morning." She laughed as she spoke.

"Very funny. I was, and remain still, a perfect gentleman. Now if you'll excuse me I need to get dressed and go to work. I'll call in at your office later and collect your work for you."

"Thank you. Will it be ok if I ask Matt to come here tonight while we go over the Knowles case and a few others?"

"Yeah, no problem."

As Ollie headed to the bathroom Grace whispered in his direction. "You didn't have to be a gentleman."

Ollie showered quickly and moved into the bedroom to dress. Grace wasn't in bed and Ollie could hear her in the kitchen. He picked a grey suit and a crisp white shirt and dressed quickly. He stepped quickly downstairs and entered the kitchen.

Grace had made coffee and Ollie took a few scalding sips from his cup. "Thanks for this, but I really need to get going."

Grace nodded. "It's ok I just thought you might want a quick coffee. Why don't you put a little cold water in it and drink it quickly?" She suggested.

Ollie nodded and took his mug to the sink. He quickly gulped the drink, grabbed his car keys from the shelf and moved towards the door. As he passed Grace he gave her a gentle kiss on the cheek before leaving the kitchen and heading for the front door.

* * *

Ollie drove angrily through the, dawdling, morning traffic from Sale to Wythenshawe and arrived at the station. He signed in and made his way to the gangs and organised crime unit.

The room was buzzing with activity, following a raid in Salford that turned up some cocaine and a cache of sawn-off shotguns. Ollie dodged the effervescent officers and support workers and side-stepped his way through to his and Howley's office.

In the office Howley was waiting for Ollie and had the pictures from the crime scene laid out on his desk in readiness. Without speaking Ollie strode straight to the pictures. One look and he recognised Amy Lawrence. "That's Amy."

Howley nodded. "I thought so." He chewed his cheek and thought for a moment; "do you think this is related to Knowles?"

Ollie instinctively knew it was. "Yeah, I'd put my house on it."

"So what now?" Howley asked.

"I think the first thing we need to know is whether Amy's stab wounds and Andy's were made with the same knife. That'll give us a starting point."

"Ok. Well technically it's your turn to go to the morgue but I'll go over there and see if Christine can push the death doc to get a move on."

"Good idea. I need to try and track Adam Grey down and nip into town for Grace."

Howley smiled and raised his eyebrows; "ah yes, the lovely Grace. Now, why was it she was at your place this morning?"

Ollie shook his head told Howley about the fire. Howley listened intently and began to make links in his head. "Prodigy." Howley blurted.

Ollie frowned. "What?"

"It sounds like the work of Danny Barnsley. He's been quiet for a while, which is why you haven't heard of him. But he's a pyro that Knowles uses. He was nicknamed prodigy because of that song, fire starter."

Ollie was furious; "Knowles will pay for this. What an evil shit-bag; I'm going to the remand centre…"

"Slow down; Kyle wouldn't have done this. This has Ryan written all over it."

Ollie didn't answer he simply nodded and frowned.

"Ollie you need to stay calm. I know you want to go and hurt somebody but you'll get nowhere like that."

Ollie thought for a moment; "I know that Steve. It's just…its Grace she was so scared. She could've died."

"And that's exactly what they wanted her to feel. You can't give in to that; you've got to see past it and do your job. If you kick off and slap Ryan about you'll be pulled off the case." Howley said calmly.

Ollie knew Howley was right and he sighed. "You're right. So what do you suggest?"

"If I were you I'd go and lean on Prodigy. He's weak and it won't take much to get him talking."

"Ok, where will I find him?"

"He lives in a flat above some shops on the estate. We've got the address on the system."

Ollie turned to his computer. "Thanks Steve, I'll get the address and then I'm going to go and have a word with Danny Barnsley."

Howley looked at his partner curiously. "You sure I can leave you to do this alone? You're not going to go all revenge crazy and do something stupid?"

Ollie laughed; "no Steve I won't be doing anything stupid. Go on, go and see what you can find out from Christine."

"Ok, if you're sure."

"I am." He said as he typed his login details into the computer. "Let me know what you find out at the morgue. Maybe make your way into town later and we'll grab a sandwich at that place on Deansgate, you know the one that has the underground type logo?"

"Yeah I know the place. I'll give you a call later."

Howley left the office and Ollie searched through the gangs and organised crime database for Danny Barnsley. The computer soon came up with the intel held about Barnsley and Ollie read through it. He wrote Barnsley's address down and shut down the computer.

CHAPTER THIRTY-NINE

Howley pulled his battered Mondeo onto a grass verge. The home office pathologist's admin offices were a collection of shaky partition walls inside a porta-cabin. The damp, fungal atmosphere was partly masked by the strong aroma of coffee filtering through cheap coffee machines. Most post-mortems were carried out by the hospital pathologist, more concerned with anaesthesia malpractice than murder. They dealt with the majority of unexplained deaths within the region. In the case of suspected murder a specialist forensic pathologist was called in from the home office. The modern hospital had no room for the team that the home office pathologist needed and Howley had seen too many temporary offices erected here over the past few years.

As he waited for one of the home office assistants to acknowledge him he saw a face he recognised. "Michael" he shouted across to the man. With that a tall, thin man in his thirties looked over at Howley.

"Detective Sergeant Howley, our paths cross once more." Said the man.

Michael was the mortuary assistant who was tasked with liaising and assisting the home office pathologist, when he was needed. His rangy body and slight stoop was as clichéd a look for a mortuary assistant as Howley had ever come across, yet there he was, six foot five of Adams-Familyesque mortuary assistant. Despite his somewhat unfortunate appearance Michael was not a strange death obsessed loner and Howley had always found him a useful ally.

"I'm afraid so Michael. Is Christine about?"

"No she's in court this morning. But I'm covering for her. I take it you're here about the young lady who joined us this morning?"

"Yeah so, who have the home office sent us? Anyone we know?"

Michael walked over to Howley; "he's been here before but I'm not sure you had the pleasure; Dr Paisley?"

"I've heard the name but never met him personally. What's he like?" Howley asked.

"Usual home office attitude: no manners, no grace and in a rush." Said Michael.

Howley chuckled, "typical. Ok, so where is he? I really need the pm report."

"He's in the mortuary, I think he is checking his findings before releasing the report. Come on I'll take you down there."

Howley followed the lank man through the porta-cabin and into the main hospital building. Very few people visited this corner of the hospital, the breeze block walls were not clad but merely painted in a pale blue wash. The colour coded walkways didn't stretch as far as the mortuary and doors only had numbers here. Fluorescent tubes cast a cool light onto the mortuary corridor and the meticulously clean floor squeaked under Michael's Birkenstocks. Howley's pace slowed as he followed the rangy assistant. Over twenty years of service and Howley still found it uncomfortable in the morgue. The distance between him and Michael inched wider as he readied himself for the next part of the walk.

The double doors ahead were chipped and scratched from countless collisions with clumsily driven gurneys. The patients travelling this way weren't afforded the delicacy of transport expected elsewhere in the hospital. The odd bump and bounce were silently ignored. Porters numbered only one to a patient and friendly chat was absent during this journey.

Michael waited for Howley with the door pushed ajar. Howley looked beyond Michael and saw reflected tubes on a silvered wall. He flared his nostrils to disguise his sharp intake of breath and stepped towards Michael. Michael pushed the door open further. Sixteen, over-sized, stainless steel draw fronts filled the wall. Their rippled surfaces twisted reflections in a macabre fun house way and a red card beneath the handle told, any who passed, the draw was occupied. Howley counted seven red cards as he dawdled closer to Michael.

"Care to join me DS Howley?" Michael said as a nudge to Howley. Howley just nodded and picked up his pace.

As they crossed the threshold into the main mortuary Howley quickly chose to walk closer to the wall, away from the draws. His shoulder brushed the breeze block as he kept the stainless steel body cabinets as far from him as he could. The chill of the negative temperature casks only exacerbated Howley's discomfort and he picked up his dawdle and almost jogged ahead of Michael.

More battered and otherwise non-descript doors led Howley and Michael into the post-mortem room. Michael spoke first:

"Hello Doctor, sorry to interrupt, this is DS Howley. He is the lead officer in this case." The pathologist looked up from his desk. "Doctor Paisley, Howley. Howley, Dr Paisley." Michael said as way of introduction.

"Hello Sergeant, I suppose you're in a frightful rush for my post-mortem report?" He continued without waiting for a response. "Well you have impeccable timing because I've just completed it. You can take a copy from the printer in just a few moments." His glib tone irritated Howley but he'd learnt from experience it was usually better to bite his lip in this situation. Pathologists tended to develop a glib and often eccentric outlook; their patients needed no friendly bedside manner so pathologists tended to become anatomists with set routines for investigation.

Lip well and truly chewed Howley replied "yes that would be great, thanks. But can I ask a few questions?"

"I thought you might. Yes, if you must, go ahead." He said.

Howley looked at Amy's body wrapped in surgical green on the post mortem table. The stainless steel table was designed to allow fluids to collect and drain at one end and beneath Howley could see a grotesque filter tray. Congealed, clotted, blood and fatty deposits lay, trapped, ready for disposal. He shivered involuntarily then looked to the pathologist.

"At the scene there were several stab wounds evident, were they enough to cause her death?" Howley asked.

"Oh yes, her lungs were punctured. It resulted in a pneumothorax, air accumulated in her pleural space and she probably died within minutes of being stabbed." Paisley answered.

"Ok, what about time of death?" Howley probed.

"Ah, glad you asked that. That's very interesting I can give you a pretty accurate time of death. When I arrived and pulled her from the cold storage her body was covered with over fifty insect bites. I doubt these would have been visible at the scene so your FME wouldn't have been able to make any assessment for you. Anyway, these bites have a very specific time of visual exposure so I can be fairly confident in confirming your FME assessment of two A.M." Paisley responded smugly.

"What about the bruising the FME saw? What caused that? A blow to the body?"

"More likely a vicious kick to the body after her death." Paisley said. "It's all in the post-mortem report Sergeant."

"Ok thank you. What about the weapon used? What can you tell me about it?"

"Ah yes I was wondering when that would come up." He peered at Howley through the top half of his bifocals as he spoke. "The stabs were made by a narrow blade about one hundred millimetres in length and fifteen wide at its widest. There were not heavy hilt marks from the knife so it's probably a lock knife or similar."

Howley nodded. "And in your opinion would you say it could be the same weapon that was used to kill Mr Lewis; I assume the liaison officer drew your attention to the similarity in the cases?"

"Indeed she did Sergeant. And yes in my opinion it could well be the same weapon. But as I said, it's all in the report."

"Thank you doctor." Howley said and then followed Michael back to the temporary offices and collected a copy of the post-mortem report. He thanked Michael for his assistance and headed back to his car.

Sitting in his car he browsed the report, there wasn't much more to it than the pathologist had told him. He looked at the photos of the stab wounds; every bloodied slit was in the intercostal muscle, each one carefully placed. Every picture he looked at reminded him of Andy's wounds. This cast huge doubt over Knowles's guilt. The more he sat and looked, and thought, he felt certain this was the same killer. He was positive that Amy's killer had also been Andy's. That meant Sutherland was wrong, Knowles hadn't killed Andy.

He knew he had to tell Sutherland and that meant Sutherland looking over his shoulder. The ambitious DCI wouldn't take his word for it, nor would he be happy about this latest development. No amount of righteous knowledge would disguise the career damage this will do to Sutherland. Everything he had done would have to be airtight. He sighed and swore, "Fuck!" Howley knew this case would soon be the property of Sutherland.

Amy's body had revealed no trace evidence from her assailant, just the results of a clinical attack. As he thought about the crime scene in the factory he realised that it had been a more personal attack. Andy had been tortured before the clinical kill. But those precise stab wounds tied them inextricably together, torture or not this was the same killer.

CHAPTER FORTY

Ollie took his anger out on his car and drove it hard to Danny Barnsley's flat. As he approached the row of shops and flats he saw somebody cleaning a motorcycle outside a short row of garages and remembered the intel he'd read about Barnsley owning a bike. He glanced at the man again and he fit the description he'd read; it was Barnsley.

He drove past the garages and flats and pulled up a little further along the road. Despite the warm autumn sun there were few people around and there was a quiet calm about the area. He left the car and strolled towards the garages, where he'd seen Danny cleaning the motorcycle. He slipped along the back of the flats where the garages were and saw Danny Barnsley crouched at the front wheel of his bike, cleaning it with a small brush. Ollie moved closer and Barnsley didn't look up from his task.

Ollie quickened his pace and walked deliberately at the crouching man. Danny looked up as he heard the footsteps of the oncoming Ollie but it was too late. Ollie raised his knee swiftly into Danny's ribs and knocked him to the floor. Danny looked up bewildered to see Ollie stood towering above him. Ollie raised his foot and planted it gently on Danny's neck.

"Hello Danny. We don't know each other yet. I'm D.S. James."

"Get off me!" Danny protested. "You can't do this; it's police brutality. You're assaulting me. Get off you twat."

Ollie increased the pressure on Danny's neck and gave him a maniacal smile. "Well that's not very nice. Here I am trying to make friends and you're calling me a twat and accusing me of brutality. I thought we'd get off to a better start than this."

Danny tried to push Ollie's foot from his neck but failed. "Fuck off. Let me go."

"Tut tut Danny. Your manners leave a lot to be desired." He resisted the urge to crush Danny's windpipe and eased the pressure a little. "Ok, so you're not the friendly type. Well that's ok; it's lucky for you that I am. Surely you can see that? I mean if I wasn't I would've crushed your neck by now for setting fire to my friends flat."

Danny's eyes widened with fear; "I didn't set fire to anything. Now get off me."

Ollie shook his head and took a sharp intake of breath. "You're telling me lies Danny. That's not very nice." He pushed his foot deeper into Danny's throat as he spoke.

Danny squirmed and tried again to push Ollie's foot from his throat. He twisted his body and bucked violently, kicking out trying to hit Ollie. "Just get off me. You're killing me."

"Oh no Danny if I wanted to kill you I'd wait till you were at home alone and then set fire to the place. A fitting end for a fire-starter don't you think?"

"I wasn't trying to kill her. It was just a flash fire on the door. Please get off me."

"Ah, so now the truth comes out. Very good; now we're getting somewhere." Ollie took his foot from Danny's throat and knelt beside him. "So I'm guessing you'd never heard of

Grace Sterling until when? Yesterday? So who sent you there?"

Danny rubbed his throat but said nothing. He breathed rapidly as if fighting off a panic attack.

"Oh Danny you're not going to make me regret letting you go are you? Come on was it Kyle or Ryan?"

"I...I can't tell you. I did the fire, but it was just a frightener."

"It's not that simple Danny. You really do need to tell me who sent you."

"I can't...I did that fire...but it's the last one. I don't need to do it anymore."

Ollie worked out what he meant. "So you're off the hook with the Knowles now?"

A look of panic surged across Danny's face. "I didn't say that."

Ollie grinned: "well you sort of implied it Danny."

Danny frantically shook his head. "I didn't. I told you I did the fire; just arrest me for it."

"Oh we'll get to the arresting part soon. But first you have to tell me who sent you."

"Nobody sent me. I just wanted to start a fire." Danny said nervously.

"And you rode all the way to Macclesfield, and randomly chose where you started the fire? I don't know Danny; I'm getting the feeling you're lying to me again."

Danny pulled himself up onto his elbows. He was thinking about his predicament and Ollie could see the machinations of thought in his eyes. Before Ollie could prompt him again he spoke. "What's in it for me?" He asked.

"Oh I see; you've watched TV and think if you give me something I give you something. Well it's not really like that. However, I might be able to do something for you."

Danny saw an opportunity opening up; "really?"

"We got off to a bad start but I'm warming to you. So yes why not."

Danny was as weak as Howley had suggested and all he wanted at this point was relief from Ollie's relentless questioning. "Ok, so what can you do for me?"

Ollie frowned as he thought. "Ok Danny if you tell me who sent you I'll make sure your sentence is as small as it can be. I'll vouch for you and say you were forced to do it. How's that?"

Danny shook his head: "that won't stop me getting killed. What protection can you offer me?"

"We can keep you safe Danny. Just tell me who sent you."

Danny couldn't cope with the constant pressure of Ollie's interrogation and he finally acceded. "Ok. It was Ryan."

Ollie felt his anger forging its destructive path through his nervous system and he took a deep breath to suppress and control it. He turned to Danny. "Was Ryan being told what to do by Kyle?"

"I don't know. He just called me and said if I fired the lawyers place my debts would be wiped. I only spoke to him on the phone."

Ollie looked at the stressed Danny and nodded. "Ok Danny; I believe you."

Ollie reached behind him and unclipped a pair of rigid handcuffs from his belt. "Put your hands in front of you. I'm going to arrest you for arson."

Danny complied with the request and offered his hands in surrender. Ollie cuffed him and radioed for a van to pick him up. "The van will be here in five minutes. You'll be processed and you can make a formal statement. If you want any chance of bail, admit the charge and I'll speak to the magistrate for you." Ollie looked at Danny who was nodding nervously. "Do you understand me?"

"Yeah I'll admit to it." He spoke quietly. "But what about Ryan? If I'm bailed he'll find me and kill me."

"Don't worry about Ryan." Ollie paused as a plan formulated in his mind. "I won't be talking to Ryan just yet. No one will even know you were pulled."

A cool wind was funneled into the garages and soap suds blew from the bucket Danny had been using to clean his motorcycle. Ollie looked at the dejected Danny and then at his motorcycle. "Do you want to put it away before you're taken to the station?"

"Can I? Please?"

Ollie nodded and then released Danny from one half of the handcuffs. He stood over Danny as he wheeled the bike into his garage and recuffed him as soon as the garage door was locked.

The police van arrived in silence and two uniformed officers stepped out. Ollie greeted them and handed Danny over to them. "Take him in the back and don't let any of our other guests see him please."

"Ok, understood."

As Ollie watched Danny being driven away he thumbed his phone to call home. After several rings Grace answered. "Hello."

"Hi Gracie it's me."

"Hey you. Are you checking up on me?" She asked playfully.

"As if I'd dare." He said through a laugh. "But seriously, I just thought you might like to know I've just arrested the arsonist who attacked your apartment."

Grace was shocked into silence and couldn't quite believe what Ollie had just said. "How? …I mean, that was quick; how did you know who to arrest?"

"Steve threw out a name and it turned out to be right."

"Who was it? Was it because of the Knowles case?" She asked anxiously.

Ollie knew her curiosity was working overtime, but he couldn't tell her about Danny and his link to Knowles. "I can't tell you yet. If there's a link and you know about it; and know this guy's name; you'll have to give up the case."

Grace toyed with the phone cable and sighed with reluctant acceptance. "I get it Ollie, ok, fine. But you can't keep it from me forever." She said with obvious annoyance. "But I can use this Ollie. I can bring it into the case if I speak to the judge and let the defence know about it."

Ollie was shaking his head and smiling at her tenacious approach. "Look, we'll talk about it later but right now I need to head over to Sunlight House and pick up your files."

Grace knew he was trying to change the subject and decided to allow him to on this occasion. "Ok. Oh and Ollie, thank you."

* * *

Ollie left the garages and headed into Manchester. The traffic was light and Ollie parked his car near St John's Gardens, a short way from Sunlight House. As he locked his car his eye was drawn to a BMW 330ci, that he recognised as Matthew Doherty's. The deep-gloss, black paint was spattered with mud and Ollie tutted disapprovingly as he walked past it.

Leaning against the wall of Sunlight House, smoking a cigarette was Matthew Doherty. His navy suit was pristine and his shirt electric white. He saw Ollie walking towards him and nodded. "Good morning D.S James. Grace rang earlier; she said you'd be in to collect her work. I've put it together ready, I'll take you up for it."

Ollie smiled and nodded. "Thanks, and call me Ollie."

"Sorry, Ollie, court room habit. So how's Grace doing? She sounded ok on the phone but you know what she's like she'll never admit to anything that might be seen as weak."

Ollie raised a knowing eyebrow and smiled. "She really wouldn't. But yes she's fine. She wasn't hurt and she'll be back in her apartment in a couple of weeks."

"Oh, that's great news." He stubbed out his cigarette and disposed of it in a bin. "Come on up I'll get you that work."

"Cheers." Ollie walked with him into the building and into the lift. "Is that your beemer three-thirty across near St John's?"

"Yeah that's me."

"I thought so; nice motor. You need to wash that mud off it though." Ollie joked.

Matthew laughed. "Trust a detective to notice."

The two men walked out onto the fifth floor and Matthew swiped them both into the CPS office. Ollie had been to the CPS office several times and nobody looked twice at him as he followed Matthew to his desk.

On the desk Matthew had left a thick pile of files, wrapped together with industrial looking elastic bands. He handed the files to Ollie along with a small USB device that looked like a memory stick. "These are the files she wanted and she'll need this security dongle to log onto the system from an outside network." Matthew explained.

Ollie nodded. "Ok, great, thanks Matthew."

"You're welcome."

Ollie had a thought. "Are you coming to see Grace later? She said something about you helping her with some cases."

Matthew shook his head; "no we managed to sort it out over the phone. But tell her she can call me anytime if she needs anything."

"I will."

Ollie left the CPS office and took the lift down to the ground floor. He left Sunlight House and strolled towards Deansgate, and the café he'd told Howley to meet him at. He made his way onto Deansgate; The Great Northern Warehouse filled Ollie's view and he admired its red brick façade. Along Deansgate each windowed arch was filled with a shop or a café and less than fifty yards from the junction of Quay Street was The Bake Station, nestled comfortably into one of the arches.

The dark, maroon, red paintwork framed the large window front stylishly and the Bake Station logo, borrowing heavily from the London underground, proudly adorned the middle of the window. The café had entrances on Deansgate and also within the leisure complex that inhabited the bulk of the old warehouse. Ollie pushed open the door and saw Howley sitting with his back against the bare-bricked wall nursing a tall latte cup and scouring the menu.

Ollie ordered a black coffee and joined Howley at the table. "How'd it go at the morgue?" He asked.

Howley frowned; "hello to you too Ollie. Yes I'm fine." He said sarcastically.

"God you're a touchy old git."

"Insults too, how quickly you've forgotten that I was your mentor and sage."

Ollie sniggered, "ok, I'm sorry Yoda. How are you Stephen? Was your morning fruitful?"

"You'd think I'd be offended by the Yoda jibe, but to paraphrase: when this old you are, this good looking you will not be."

"I won't argue with that. So did you find out anything at the morgue?"

"I did indeed. It would seem that Amy's wounds are consistent in type, and in weapon type, with Andy's." He continued to explain what he'd found out at the morgue.

"So what do we think? Did Amy's killer kill Andy? If so does that mean Knowles is innocent?" Ollie asked after listening to the report.

"Yes and yes. I know it's not beyond the realm of possibility but the two killings are so similar I'd find it hard to believe they were carried out by two different people." Howley proffered.

"I agree. I think we need to pay a visit to Risley and see Mr. Knowles."

"Yes I think we do. We'll go there after lunch. So how did you get on with the estate's favourite pyromaniac?"

Ollie told Howley about his encounter with Danny Barnsley as he ate a brie and bacon baguette and sipped at his coffee. Howley nodded knowingly, unsurprised by Ollie's encounter. "So what are you going to do about Ryan?" Howley asked.

Ollie grinned: "don't worry about Ryan Knowles. I'll be dealing with him soon enough."

Howley frowned: "Why haven't you brought him in yet?"

"I'll bring him in soon; but if I go barreling in there now Danny will end up hurt or worse and I'll have nothing on Ryan. As soon as Danny is processed and bailed I'll see to Ryan."

"Understood." Howley said, between bites of his roast beef sandwich. "If you grab us both another coffee to go we can make our way to the remand centre."

"I bought the last coffees." Ollie retorted.

"Yes, but that was because I was stuck in an abandoned factory while you were cozying up to Gracie."

"Fine, I'll get the coffees to go." Ollie conceded.

Coffees in hand the two men walked purposefully to Ollie's car and headed out onto the motorway towards Warrington and Risley remand centre.

CHAPTER FORTY-ONE

Risley Remand Centre violently interrupted the gentle greenery of North Cheshire; the tightly meshed fencing separated the two worlds and Ollie slowed his drive in search of a place to park near the entrance. With the car parked Ollie and Howley made their way to the pale brick reception.

A fair haired man in his mid-forties was behind the desk. He wore an older style uniform, a shirt and tie, eschewing the more modern polo shirts of his colleagues. His keys rattled as he stood to take his perfunctory glance at their identification badges. "Thank you gentlemen. So what can I do for you today?"

"We'd like to interview Kyle Knowles please." Howley said.

The officer looked through his day book and saw no visitor requests for Knowles. He chewed the inside of his cheek and sighed loudly. "There's no request for Mr. Knowles to be brought up to the visitor suite today. Have you made a request?"

Howley knew the officer was being pedantically obstructive but remained calm. "No, we're really sorry but we're just following up a lead. Usually we'd ring ahead and let you know but this is urgent. If you'd be good enough to bring him up we'd really appreciate it." Howley said in his most sincere voice.

The man had appreciated Howley's sincere, contrite tone and nodded his head; "well it's not normally how we like to do things but ok, I'll have Mr. Knowles brought up. There's no visiting for another hour, so you can interview him in the visitor suite."

"Thank you, we really appreciate this."

"You're welcome D.S. Howley. Just give me a few minutes and I'll take you through to the visitor suite." He sat down behind the desk and picked up the phone.

After a few minutes the officer took Howley and Ollie through to the visitor suite. Orange, plastic chairs were lined up, in twos, on opposing sides of steel framed, laminate wood topped tables. The linoleum floor had recently been mopped and the smell of the cleaning fluids reminded Howley of his visit to the morgue. Sitting at a table in the middle of the room was Kyle Knowles, watched by a fearsome looking prison officer.

Knowles was dressed in a prison issue, grey jog suit but instead of the simple blue plimpsolls, issued with the jog suit, he was wearing an expensive pair of Nike trainers. This was a sign of status amongst the inmates and a privilege that could be earned from the prison officials. Kyle hadn't been inside long enough to have earned the privilege and it was clear his reputation afforded him privilege and status. The almost foetal-like posture he displayed in the station was now gone and he sat arrogantly confident in the shadow of the supervising prison officer.

Knowles looked up at the two men and smirked. As they sat down to face him he addressed Howley. "Hello Sergeant, what brings you here?" He said sardonically.

"Hello Kyle. Now before we start I have a duty to tell you that you're still under arrest and that you can request your brief be present." Howley said.

Kyle shook his head. "It's ok Sergeant I think I'll manage."

"Well that's good to hear." Howley paused for a moment wondering where start. "So Kyle..."

"...You've worked out it wasn't me haven't you?" Kyle interrupted.

Howley was taken aback but nodded cautiously. "Well I wouldn't go quite that far Kyle but we certainly need to ask you some more questions."

Knowles grinned and winked; "you're so coy Mr. Howley. My old-man was right about you. So what do you want to know?"

Howley ignored the bravado from across the table and jumped straight in. "Who killed Andy?"

At the mention of Andy's name Kyle's arrogance peeled away visibly and whilst he didn't adopt the slumped hopelessness of the station, his face greyed and his petulant sneer faded. "I don't know. All I know is that it wasn't me. I don't know why anyone would kill Andy." His voice trailed off and there was grief in his voice. Howley thought he heard a stifled cry.

Ollie could see that Kyle was wobbling. "Was it Aiden?"

Kyle stared bewilderingly at Ollie. "My cousin Aiden? Are you kidding?"

"No joke."

"It's gotta be a joke. You're barking up the wrong tree."

Ollie shrugged his shoulders; "ok you're convinced, but I need to follow up every lead. Where can I find Aiden?"

"I'm not letting you hassle my family. Just forget Aiden."

Howley glanced at Ollie and gave a gentle head shake. "Ok Kyle, tell me what happened between you and Adam Grey."

Kyle's eyes betrayed him and both Ollie and Howley saw that Adam's name had jolted something in his mind. "Nothing...I haven't seen Adam in ages."

Ollie frowned; "so you didn't hit him with a meat tenderiser?"

Knowles quickly retorted. "No."

"So we've been given duff information?" Ollie pressed.

"Looks like it. Me and Adam are good mates."

"I don't know; the source is pretty reliable."

"Well I don't know who your source is, but it never happened." Kyle said.

Howley was getting bored of Kyle's uncooperative responses. As he'd watched him block Ollie's questions with his usual disdain he could see that behind the superciliousness something was eating at him. His tone had been flat and his thick mancunian accent softer and less aggressive. He was doing his best to put on a front but Howley could see through it.

Howley sighed as he thought and then touched Ollie on the shoulder; "I don't think our friend here is going to be of any help." He then turned to Knowles.

"Kyle I know it's normal for you to deny everything and to protect the people in your organisation but all we're doing here is trying to find out the truth about Andy's murder. We don't care if you hit Adam…Unless of course that gave him a reason to kill Andy. When we interviewed you the other day in the station, you asked me if I was still an honest cop who did things right. Well I am, and that's what I'm doing. And yes you were right, it looks like we've turned up evidence that puts you in the clear, but we don't have any leads on who might have done it." He stopped and looked at Kyle. "Oh and if you're interested it looks like whoever killed Andy also killed his girlfriend Amy."

Kyle's face drained. "Amy? She's dead?"

Howley nodded; "yes Kyle. Stabbed just like Andy. But as long as you're not implicated I don't suppose it matters does it?" Howley stood to leave and Ollie did the same.

Kyle was stunned by the news and looked up at Howley. "Sit back down; I'll tell you what you want to know." He covered his face with his hands and rubbed hard, making his face red.

Howley and Ollie returned to their seats. "Ok Kyle let's start with your cousin, Aiden." Howley asked.

Kyle tutted loudly. "Aiden didn't do this. He wouldn't"

"Then let us confirm that and cross him off the list of suspects. What can you tell us about him?"

"He's my cousin; on my ma's side of the family…" He stopped and thought about what he was saying. "Look Aiden didn't do this. He used to be a bit nuts, when we were kids, but that was before he went off to university…"

"What did he study?" Ollie interrupted.

Without thinking Kyle answered. "Law." He realised he'd given too much away and shut up quickly.

Ollie nodded and Howley took the hint. "Ok Kyle so you don't want to tell us about your cousin; then tell us about Adam Grey." Howley said.

Kyle was relieved that the conversation had moved away from his cousin. "Yeah you were right, me and Adam had a bit of a fight a few weeks back…But it was over straight away."

Howley was listening closely; "so what about Jack Haworth? Any problems with him?"

Kyle's eyes flickered. "Jack Haworth is a little snake. He's a little shit who hasn't the balls to kill Andy." He said with a dismissive tone.

"What if Jack was angry about the way you'd treated Adam? Rumour has it Jack and Adam were looking to expand business against your wishes." Howley asked.

"They were pushing their luck. Adam got the message; Jack was going to get it…"

"…What do you mean? He got the message?"

"Let's just say Adam won't be stepping out of line again." Kyle said with certainty.

"So the fight? That was more of a beating?"

"I suppose you could put it that way." Kyle smirked.

Ollie could see that Howley had opened Kyle up. "Ok Kyle so I have an idea I'd like to run past you; is that ok?"

"Be my guest."

"So I think you gave Adam such a beating that he was humiliated enough to seek revenge. I think he killed Andy because he was your right hand man and he tried to frame you so you'd be out of the picture." Ollie checked Kyle was paying attention. "You see we found rope, that looks to be the same as the rope found around Andy's neck, in the boot of Adam's car; the trouble is nobody has seen or heard from Adam for a couple of weeks. Of course that could mean he is in hiding. Alternatively, he could've done this with Jack Haworth, in fact Jack could have done it alone because you beat up his friend so badly that he went into hiding."

Kyle was concentrating: "the same rope?"

"It looks that way."

Kyle tapped his fingers nervously on the table; his breathing had quickened and his pupils had dilated. "Jack…It must be Jack." He blurted.

"Why Jack and not Adam?" Howley asked.

Kyle clenched his jaw and then spoke. "Adam's not in any fit state. It must be Jack. That weasely little shit bag. You'd better get to him before I have him seen to…"

"Alright, that's enough." Howley said forcibly.

Kyle seethed but said nothing.

Howley turned to Ollie; "is there anything else?"

Ollie wanted to question Knowles about the arson attack on Grace but knew he'd have to wait for that. "No, I think that's everything for now."

The detectives stood and Howley looked down at Knowles; "I can tell you're cut up by Andy's death but don't think we're looking for his killer for you. You've hurt so many people you don't deserve any sympathy. I'm just doing my job."

Knowles didn't respond and the two detectives left the visitor suite.

* * *

Sitting in the car the Howley spoke first. "So what do we make of that?"

Ollie sighed; "he's still hiding something about Adam Grey but seems genuine about Jack."

"Yeah I think so too. We need to double check Jack's alibi…"

"And I think he gave us enough to do a search for the mystery cousin too. Even if he has nothing to do with this case, someone, somewhere, will want to know about his involvement with Knowles."

Howley nodded; "god I hope he's not a prosecutor." He added.

"Don't even think it. That would be a huge shit-storm."

"It really would." He paused for a second in thought; "assuming cousin Aiden is about the same age as Knowles…and Knowles is about the same age as our Gracie…"

"I see where you're going; I'll ask her later."

Howley winked at Ollie; "thanks."

"No problem. So shall we go to the Flying Horse and double check Jack's alibi?"

"Yeah, I'll ring the office and get the intel officers looking for the cousin while you're driving."

Ollie said nothing and started the engine. He pulled the car away from the prison and back out onto the roads of North Cheshire.

CHAPTER FORTY-TWO

The aged, leather, wingback complained quietly as Matt flopped on to it. He pulled his tie from round his neck and yawned loudly. He thought back to his encounter with Grace earlier and smiled. She'd been more amiable than he had remembered her being. He wondered if he should ask her out for coffee or dinner. He knew she was involved with Ollie James, but he was just a cop.

He rubbed his eyes and pushed himself out of the chair. The burden of a suit and tie prevented him from relaxing properly. He padded to the bedroom and shed the professional skin of the day; dressing in worn denim and a favourite New Order t-shirt he started to feel human again.

Unburdened, Matthew took out a can of lager from the fridge and micro-waved a frozen chicken curry. At the beep of the nuclear cooker he took his gourmet meal, retook his place on the leather chair and punched at the keys of the TV remote. As he shoveled the processed meal into his hungry body he flicked through a myriad of nonsensical celebrity based shows until he finally settled for a show about the traffic police. The sickly food satisfied and the sharp beer stung sensitive teeth. A few minutes into the TV cop show his phone rang. He looked for handset, eventually finding it on an old oak book case.

"Hello," he said as he put the phone to his ear.

"Hello mate," the caller replied. He recognised the voice and responded.

"Hey bud, how's it going?"

"Not great, why don't you come to the old boozer? I'll buy you a pint. I could do with a friendly ear."

Matt bit his cheek, he knew there would be trouble or a favour involved, there always was. "Yeah, ok. Tonight?" He asked tentatively. He waited for a reply hoping the voice on the other end of the phone would say 'tomorrow.'

"Tonight is good, half eight or so?"

Matt noted the time on his dvd recorder, six thirty, "Ok, I'll see you there." He went to say bye, but before he had taken a breath the phone clicked dead and there was no one there to hear his farewell.

Matt put the handset into the base unit and returned to his meal. The sickly curry had suddenly lost its appeal and he put the plate down onto the coffee table.

With time to kill before his trip to the pub Matt decided to ring Grace Sterling. There was no harm in saying hello and seeing if she needed some help. He looked through the contact list in his phone and scrolled to her number. He hesitated nervously before pressing the call button.

* * *

Grace was bored; she hated being kept from work. Her boredom had been eased at points during by the day by dipping into Ollie's DVD collection; but even the eclectic mix of John Cusack to Bruce Willis had its limitations. She padded into the Kitchen and worked out how to use Ollie's nespresso machine and took a coffee back into the lounge.

Grace thumbed the TV remote until she found something suitably trashy to distract her and then pulled her feet up onto the sofa and tried to relax. She smiled as she sipped the rich tasting coffee; Ollie was such a coffee snob and she remembered how long it had taken him to choose his coffee machine.

On the TV, attics were being raided as families hoped an expert would tell them they had some sort of rare antique, that they could auction for thousands of pounds. Of course they'd claim some sort of sentimental value before surrendering to greed and sending their cherished possession off to auction.

The fawning presenter's excited appraisal was interrupted by the aggressive ring tone of her mobile phone. She grabbed her phone from the coffee table and answered the call. "Hello."

"Hi Grace, its Matt."

Grace was suddenly worried that there was something wrong at work; "hi Matt. Is there a problem at work?"

"No, no problems; relax."

Grace was immediately relieved. "Good, I just wondered with you calling me."

"I'm just calling to see how you're getting on. I didn't get a chance to talk to you earlier."

"That's very sweet of you, but I'm fine. Just bored and missing work."

Matthew laughed. "You're the only person I know who'd miss work after just one day. Relax and get better."

"I'm not really ill Matt. Just a little smoke inhalation."

"It must've been awful though. You must've been scared out of your wits." Matthew said with concern.

"It was terrifying but it happened so quickly…And then Ollie was there and I was ok." As she spoke she realised that she wasn't merely putting on a front; it was the truth. With Ollie she was ok; better than ok.

Matthew felt a jolt of envy, when she mentioned Ollie, which he turned to a feeling of disdain for Ollie. "Well as long as you're alright. I gave D.S James the files you wanted and a dongle so you can log onto the system."

"Thanks for that, I knew if Ruth asked you, you'd be able to sort them out."

"You're welcome." He chose to ignore the obvious about Grace and Ollie and said: "I'm glad you're ok. When you're back in work we'll have to get a coffee and you can tell me about the whole incident properly."

"That'd be nice Matt, thank you." Grace automatically replied.

"Ok then…Anyway, I'd better leave you to recover. If you need anything just give me a shout. Take care and see you back in work soon."

"Thanks and thanks for the call. You'll probably see me back at work tomorrow. I'm feeling ok and I'd rather be in the office being productive than stuck here worrying about work." Grace said.

"Are you sure you should? Nobody at work is expecting you to rush back."

"I know, but I'm just not comfortable being off work when there's nothing wrong with me." Grace explained.

Matthew laughed again. "Well you know best…So, I'll see you in the office at some point tomorrow."

"Yes you probably will. See you tomorrow Matt."

"Yeah, see you."

Grace ended the call and returned to the antiques on TV. A family had found a rare watch and had been told it was worth ten thousand pounds. Grace glared at the screen and shouted: "oh fuck off!"

CHAPTER FORTY-THREE

Ollie and Howley pulled up outside The Flying Horse and marched into the bar. The early evening crowd was much the same as the daytime crowd and nobody looked up to see the two detectives walking in. Ollie spotted Jack Haworth playing pool and headed over to him, while Howley moved to the bar.

The pool table had a blue baize surface set in a dark wood framing. On the wooden framing sat stacks of fifty pence pieces; the monetary representation of the queue for the table; and two half-finished pints of lager. As Ollie approached the table a few of Jack's companions eyed him. One of them caught Jack's eye and tilted his head in Ollie's direction.

Jack turned towards Ollie and smiled sarcastically; "I hope you're not here to assault me again." He said with the confidence only a crowd of supporters can give.

Ollie smiled and shook his head. "Not today I still have a warm glow from the last time."

Jack's grin disappeared and he handed his pool cue to a football-shirt wearing companion. "So what do you want Sergeant?" As he spoke more of his associates moved around the pool table.

"A quiet word or two." Ollie looked round at the increasing audience. "Come outside with me for a few minutes."

Jack sensed his audience were waiting for his response; "and if I say no?"

Ollie had picked up on the same atmosphere that Jack had. If he made Jack look weak in front of his entourage he'd be impossible to interrogate. Ollie quickly decided he didn't have time to interrogate an uncooperative Jack. "Just give me a few minutes Jack or there'll be a van full of uniformed coppers here all looking for a collar." He glanced at the faces in the crowd and saw a few worried expressions at the thought of the place being overrun with police. "I don't think we need all that aggravation for the sake of a few questions; do we?"

Jack nodded slowly and purposefully in an attempt to make himself look smarter and in control. His expectant observers bought it and waited for the sagacious response from Jack. "Fine, I'll give you a few minutes." The faces in the crowd relaxed and knowing nods were exchanged amongst the gathered audience. The crowd thinned and Jack turned to football-shirt. "You can finish the game for me."

Ollie waited for Jack to move and then led him out to the front of the pub. Dusk had thickened into evening and the aurulent glow of ancient street lights barely illuminated the paths and roads. Jack reached into his pocket for a cigarette and lit one. He drew a long drag and looked at Ollie. "So here I am. What do you want?"

"I've had an interesting conversation with Kyle Knowles today." Ollie said.

"Good for you. Why would I care?"

"Well maybe because Kyle was very chatty today and he thinks you killed Andy Lewis."

A look of dread crept quickly over Jack's face; "shit. Why? Does Ryan know?..."

"Calm down Jack." Ollie said calmly; "I'm here to find out the truth."

"I told you the last time you were here. I didn't have anything to do with it."

"You did, but there have been developments since then."

"What developments?" Jack asked quizzically.

"Well let's start with the mysterious disappearance of your friend Adam."

"How does that make me guilty?"

"On its own it doesn't, but then we have reliable intel that points to you as a person of interest." Ollie looked at Jack and tried to get a read on his reaction. It was hard to tell if his confusion and shock were genuine or a well-practiced act. "Oh and of course you have form for using a knife."

Jack looked blankly at the ground. "It wasn't me. I didn't kill Andy…"

Jack was interrupted by Howley's arrival outside. "Well it's nice to see you two are getting along. But we do have a problem."

Ollie raised his eyebrows; "a problem D.S. Howley?"

"I'm afraid so; Mr. Haworth here has being lying to you. He wasn't in the pub on the night of Andy's murder." Howley explained.

"Interesting." Ollie said.

"It is and I also asked around and made a few calls. It seems Jack hadn't been seen from around lunch time that day."

Jack remained silent and stared doggedly at the floor. "Nothing to say? That's not like you Jack; you have an answer for everything." Ollie said.

"I didn't do it." Jack muttered.

"I don't think I can just take your word for that." Ollie looked at Howley and they exchanged a knowing look. Ollie reached to his belt and took off his handcuffs. In one swift move he cuffed Jack behind his back. "Jack Haworth I am arresting you on suspicion of having murdered Andrew Lewis; you are not obliged to say anything but anything you do say will be recorded and may be given in evidence."

Jack tugged and pulled his arms in the cuffs; "fuck you. I didn't do anything. Let me out of these fucking things."

Ollie ignored Jack's protestations and spoke to Howley. "Let's get him to the station and question him straight away."

Howley nodded. "Good idea."

Jack had heard them and his face was red with anger. "You can't fucking do that. I've not done anything."

The detectives ignored him again and guided him into the back of Ollie's car.

* * *

At the station Ollie and Howley quickly had Jack processed and into an interview room. The room was cold and the fluorescent lighting popped and cracked for a minute before settling into its harsh, steady light.

Jack was slumped in his chair and sulking like a child. "I don't know what the fuck you're doing bringing me here but I already told you: I haven't done anything"

Ollie looked at Howley quizzically; "did you here that Steve? Mr. Haworth hasn't done anything. Shall we let him go?"

Howley laughed softly; "I don't think it's quite that simple."

Ollie nodded. "No, neither do I." He sat opposite Jack and reminded him that he was under arrest. "So do you want your solicitor? I'm quite happy for you to contact your own brief or we can get one in for you. But it will probably be morning before we can get them in."

Jack's face betrayed his discomfort and he quickly responded. "I don't need a brief; I've not done anything."

"Ok that's your choice." Ollie reached to the recording device, and followed the legal procedures needed, before facing Jack again and beginning the interrogation. "Why did you kill Andy Lewis?" Ollie asked bluntly.

"I didn't. I was…"

"Why did you kill Amy Lawrence?" Howley interrupted.

A look of shock and disbelief swarmed Jack's face; "Amy?... What the fuck? Is Amy dead?"

Ollie and Howley exchanged a surprised look. "Yes she was killed last night. Where were you last night?" Ollie said.

Jack's brow crinkled as he tangled with a thought. "I was with someone."

Howley noticed his hesitation and leaned into Jack. "If you want us to believe you didn't kill Amy or Andy you'd better start talking now." Howley said calmly. "Now Jack, where were you?"

Jack sighed through his nostrils; "I was with Ruth Johnson and I was with her when Andy was murdered."

Ollie frowned with confusion as he struggled to place the name, then it came to him. "Ruth Johnson who works for the CPS?" he asked.

Jack nodded slightly; "yeah."

"So you and her are what? In a relationship?" Ollie asked.

"Sort of. We met online and we meet up every now and again."

Howley looked confused; "so you're not in a relationship?"

Despite the seriousness of the situation Ollie wanted to laugh at his colleague; instead he rescued him. "It's ok Steve I think I understand." He looked at Jack again. "Ok so you met through an adult dating site and you meet for sex occasionally?" He asked almost rhetorically.

"Yeah, that's pretty much how it works."

"So you were trying to protect her by lying about your alibi for Andy's murder?"

"Yeah, she's been good to me and if anyone found out about her and me it'd be bad for her career." Jack's concern for Ruth seemed genuine.

"But you lied about an alibi for a murder Jack." Ollie said.

"I knew I didn't do it and if Kyle didn't do it I thought you'd find someone else...Probably Adam."

Howley's ears pricked at Adam's name. "Why Adam? What makes you think Adam would've killed Andy?" He asked.

Jack was suddenly looking uncomfortable; his face had lost its colour and he was fidgeting with his fingers. He shrugged his shoulders; "don't know. Just think it could be him."

"You're a terrible liar Jack." Ollie interjected. "You have more of a reason to think Adam killed Andy than you're saying. Now me, and my colleague here are going to go outside and make a few calls to check your alibi; when we come back in we want to hear the real reason you think Adam would have killed Andy."

The two detectives didn't wait for him to respond and simply left the room. Ollie made sure the door was secure and turned to Howley. "What do you think? Do you believe him?"

"Yeah I don't think he was involved in the murders; but he does know more about Adam Grey."

Ollie nodded; "agreed. Let's get him in a cell for a bit and we'll check his alibi out. Maybe he'll be more accommodating later."

"Ok, I'll grab the custody sergeant if you want to go and call Ruth Johnson?" Howley suggested.

"Alright, sounds like a plan. I'll go up to the office and see if I can get through to Ruth Johnson."

Howley made his way to the custody sergeant and Ollie left the custody area and trotted to his office.

* * *

The gangs and organised crime unit was sparsely populated and Ollie instinctively looked at his watch; seven o'clock. He realised he'd not told Grace when he'd be home and swore to himself under his breath; "fuck."

Ollie pushed open the door to his office and collapsed into his chair; he wondered if Grace had a number for Ruth. He picked up the phone and dialed Grace's number. As the phone rang he leant back in his chair and looked around the office. On his computer monitor was a bright orange post-it; Ollie peeled it off and read it: please call or see Greg Milner ASAP. As Ollie began to think about what Milner might want Grace answered the phone.

"Hello stranger;" Grace said as she answered the phone.

"Hey, sorry I know it's late. I should've let you know where I was." Ollie said apologetically.

Grace smiled to herself; "it's ok Ollie. You don't have to do anything like that for me. I'm a big girl and I'm a guest in your house."

"I know but I worry about you."

"That's very lovely of you…So have you called for a reason or just to chat?"

"Well, I wanted to let you know I was going to be here a bit longer and I also need a number you might have." Ollie explained.

"Ok thank you; I'll prepare some dinner for us. If that's ok?"

"You don't have to…"

"I know I don't but I want to…You said something about a number?" She asked curiously.

"I did indeed. I need Ruth Johnson's number."

Grace was confused and curious; "why do you need Ruth's number?"

"I have someone in custody who claims she is their alibi…"

"Alibi? What's going on Ollie? Is Ruth in trouble?" Grace was concerned.

"It's ok she's not in trouble. But I guess your boss will be less than impressed with the sort of company her lifestyle seems to have attracted."

"I'm confused; what are you talking about Ollie?"

Ollie tried to think of a delicate way of explaining. "Some people use internet dating sites to find love; Ruth uses a slightly different type of website for a more physical type of relationship."

Grace worked out what Ollie was saying; "oh…I see…So you're saying the man you have in custody is Ruth's fuck-buddy?" Asked an incredulous Grace.

"That's about the long and short of it, yes."

"Oh god. Michael will go nuts when he finds out. Is this person in custody anything to do with the Knowles case?"

"Well that depends on whether his alibi checks out…But either way, he's a known associate of the Knowles family."

"Shit. She'll be bollocked for this."

"I'm sure she will…So have you got her number?"

"Yes I'll text it to you just hang on a min…"

Ollie heard some beeping down the phone.

"There, you should have it on your phone now." Grace said.

Ollie moved the phone away from his ear and saw that a text had come through. "Thanks Grace."

"You're welcome… So what sort of time shall I expect you back?" Grace asked.

"If I get through to Ruth and she confirms our suspect's alibi then I'll just have a few questions to go through with him. So say a couple of hours." Ollie said.

"Ok I'll see what food you have in the kitchen and make us something to eat. Then you can tell me where you're up to with the Knowles case."

"Ok but if you change your mind about cooking I'll bring a take out."

"See you later Ollie."

"Yeah see you soon." Ollie said as he ended the call.

Ollie's eyes burned with fatigue and he yawned loudly in an attempt to reinvigorate his weary body. He grabbed a pen from his desk and turned to a fresh page in his notepad before calling Ruth Johnson.

* * *

Ruth twiddled with her hair as she updated her Facebook status. Her bright emerald eyes were bright and filled with the vitality only youth and ambition could create. Her chubby cheeks hid her age, and intelligence, and people often judged her too quickly. Dressed in comfortable shorts and a vest top, a celtic tattoo decorated the base of her back and a small, bright-red devil grinned mischievously on her shoulder.

She shared a house on Chester Road, five minutes from the city centre, and she spent most of her time in her room studying towards her full law degree. She went out with her housemates into the city, but not as often as she used to and her more recent leisure activities had been of a more intimate nature with Jack.

All her life she'd been the good girl, the hard working student, attentive child, regular church goer but after leaving her parent's home she'd found a new side to herself. She ended her relationship with her long-standing boyfriend and began to explore new ideas about her sexuality, attractions and relationships. After a few failed attempts she found what she wanted in Jack Haworth. He was older and from a very different background to her but she felt an animal attraction she'd never experienced before and she acted on it.

Still fidgeting with her hair she logged out of Facebook and checked her messages on the adult dating forum, nothing from Jack, she frowned. Her dismay at Jack's lack of comunication was broken by the sound of her phone ringing. She didn't recognise the number and answered tentatively. "Hello."

"Hello is this Ruth Johnson?" Ollie asked.

"Yes, who's calling?"

"Hi Ruth its D.S. Ollie James…"

"Oh, Grace's friend?" She asked with some confusion. "Why are you calling me?"

Ollie rubbed his forehead before speaking; "it's a little delicate Ruth."

"What is?"

"Well…I have someone in custody who is claiming to have been with you during the time of two crimes…"

Ruth knew instinctively who he was talking about; "Jack, its Jack isn't it?"

"Yes. Can you confirm or deny he was with you on the 8th for the night and on the 10th, also over night?"

Ruth blushed from her chest up; "yes." She said, almost whispering.

Ollie scribbled her answer onto his pad; "ok are you sure? Did anyone else see you?"

Ruth was overwhelmed with the cold, unnerving feeling of having been caught doing wrong. "Am I going to be in trouble?" She asked.

Ollie thought for a minute; "that all depends on what you knew about Jack. I'm sure Grace will talk to you about it...Now back to my question please; did anyone see you with Jack? Where were you? I need something concrete Ruth."

Ruth realised she didn't really know much about Jack and she suddenly felt stupid. "Ok...Erm, yes we were in the Premier Inn near the Trafford Centre. The desk staff would've seen us and I guess the CCTV would have caught us too."

"And you were there both nights?"

"Yes it where we always go..." Her voice trailed off as she realised she'd revealed more than she'd wanted too.

Ollie was satisfied that Jack was with Ruth during the murders but felt he was keeping something from him. "Ok Ruth, thank you. I might need a formal statement but I'm happy for now."

"Ok...D.S. James, do you think Grace will be ok if I call her now?" She asked hopefully.

"I would think so. I got your number from her so she's probably thinking about ringing you...Give her a call...Oh and Ruth do yourself a favour..."

"What?"

"Delete your adult dating account and distance yourself from Jack."

Ruth felt a pang of regret but knew Ollie was right. "I will."

"Good; you go and call Grace. Thanks for the information and good luck." Ollie ended the call.

* * *

Howley left the custody sergeant to lock Jack in a cell. He could feel all of his fifty six years as he walked and not for the first time he wondered if a more leisurely life would be preferable. He looked great for his age and his steel-blue eyes still sparkled but his love of the job and his stamina for the long days was waning.

He stepped through the doors of the canteen and found it all but abandoned. He shook his head; in his early career the canteens had been open all day and all night; and looked at the array of vending machines that stood as poor substitutes for the human beings who would make bacon sandwiches and strong tea for the hard working cops. He rifled through the change in his pocket and bought coffees and a selection of chocolate bars for him and Ollie to snack on.

He carefully carried the unhealthy food back to the custody suite and waited for Ollie to return from the office. He sipped some coffee and demolished a mars bar before Ollie returned. "Did you get through to her?" He asked.

Ollie nodded; "I did and she confirmed laughing boy's alibi."

Howley sucked air sharply through his teeth. "I bet she won't have much fun when she goes to work tomorrow."

"She certainly won't"

Howley lifted a coffee to Ollie and offered him a chocolate bar. Ollie chose a twix and sat down with Howley. "So what now?" Howley asked.

Ollie sighed and turned to his friend; "we find out what happened with Adam and see where he is."

"I think our friend through there knows more than he was letting on. We'll drag him back into the interview room and push him on it."

With a mouth full of chocolate bar Ollie nodded in agreement.

* * *

Sugary snacks and caffeine bolstered the energy levels of Ollie and Howley; feeling recharged they had Jack Haworth brought back into the interview room.

The interview room was lit only with the harsh fluorescents in the ceiling, as the night had fallen onto the day. Jack's skin was a pallid grey under the lights and his lined face shadowy. He looked expectantly at the detectives as he gnawed at his finger nails. His eyes darted between Howley and Ollie, anxiously hoping one of them would say that Ruth had confirmed his alibi.

Ollie and Howley sat opposite Jack and restarted the recording device. Ollie scratched the stubble on his chin and clicked his pen. Howley opened his notebook and tested his pen on the corner of a page. Jack's patience was failing him and his leg bounced involuntarily beneath the table; "so? What did she say?" He garbled.

Ollie raised his eyebrows; "what's wrong Jack? You seem worried."

Jack shook his head defiantly; "no, not worried. Just want to get out and go to the pub. I've got a pool game to get back to."

Ollie nodded with pursed lips in mock belief. "Ok Jack, I understand. The problem is we have two murders and you know more than you're letting on."

"I told you I didn't do anything. Did Ruth tell you I was with her?" An agitated Jack said.

"We have to fully confirm your whereabouts during the murders." Ollie paused for a moment; "how long that takes…well I suppose that depends on how long it takes you to tell us what you know…What do you think D.S. Howley?"

"I think you summed up the situation pretty accurately." Howley said.

Ollie smiled sarcastically; "yes I thought so."

Jack tutted loudly; he'd worked out what the two men were implying. "Oh you two are so fucking funny." He said as he glared at the two detectives. "I told you before; I don't know anything."

"I know what you said; but I don't believe you." Ollie interjected.

"Oh come off it; just let me go."

Ollie ignored his plea; "talk to me Jack. Where's Adam Grey?"

Jack sighed with frustration and anger; "I don't know."

"Really? But the way I understand it you two are good mates." Ollie said with disbelief.

Jack frowned; "we're mates yeah. But I'm not his mum. He doesn't tell me where he is all the time."

Howley leant forward and spoke softly. "Listen Jack you're no stranger to the interview room. You know we can keep you here tonight and start nice and fresh in the morning…Or you could cooperate and be in your own bed tonight."

Jack seemed to react better to Howley and he nodded slightly as if agreeing with him. "What do you want from me?"

Ollie recognised the breakthrough from Howley and eased himself back from the table a little, allowing Howley to take the lead.

"Ok Jack let's go back a few weeks. What can you tell me about Adam being attacked by Kyle Knowles?"

Jack clenched his jaw tightly and breathed hard down his nose. "We were at Kyle's pad taking some money in and Adam was in one of his funny moods…"

"Funny moods?" Howley interrupted.

"Yeah, really trying to wind everyone up. Picking hole in anything anyone said. That sort of thing…"

"Ok, I get it. So he's a wind-up merchant?" Howley suggested.

"Definitely. Lot of the time it's funny but sometimes he goes too far…"

"And he went too far that day?"

"Yeah, he went way too far." Jack said.

"How?"

Jack hesitated to answer; "nothing I say here will get out will it?"

Howley shook his head; "don't worry your name won't be mentioned out of this room."

Jack thought for a minute; "ok; Adam was being his usual self and coming up with smart arse answers to everything when Kyle got pissed off and told him to shut up. Adam told him to fuck off and Kyle threatened to twat him…Well you see there were a few of us there and Adam didn't like looking like a pussy so he said something…Something that got Kyle really mad."

"What did he say? And when you say really mad, is that when he attacked Adam?" Howley enquired.

"Why does it matter what he said?" Jack asked.

"Everything matters; it's the details Jack. That's what helps us catch the bad guys. So come on what did he say?"

Jack shifted nervously in his seat; his eyes flitted from featureless wall to featureless wall as he avoided the stares of Howley and Ollie. His hand fidgeted with the drawstrings on his hoodie and his knee was shaking again. "I can't tell you...It's more than my life's worth...You don't understand..."

"What am I not understanding Jack?"

"Kyle'll kill me if I say..."

"Kyle is still on remand. He won't know you've told us anything." Howley said in his still, soft, calm voice.

Jack wasn't sure and he sighed heavily; "I don't know. Kyle wasn't happy; he said if I said anything he'd fuck me over..."

Howley didn't care about Kyle's threats; "What went on Jack? What was said that caused Kyle to say that?"

"Look you didn't hear anything from me...So Adam had been saying to me for weeks that he had something on Kyle but he wouldn't tell me what it was. Then after Kyle threatened him he said to me something about Kyle being careful or he'd tell everyone his secret..."

"Hang on," Howley said; "what secret? I thought he insulted him?" He continued in confusion.

"I'm getting there just gimme a minute…So, Adam wouldn't shut up and Kyle finally blew up and said if he didn't shut up he'd twat him…Adam turned to Kyle and called him a faggot…he said 'you're a fucking faggot, arse-bandit, you're too busy sucking off pretty-boy Andy to bother about the business anymore…'"

"Hang-on;" Ollie interjected. "Did Adam really know that Kyle is gay or was he just trying to wind him up?"

Jack looked towards Ollie; "I saw him the day after…He said he'd caught Kyle and Andy together."

Ollie thought about what they'd just learned and suddenly things clicked into place. The lack of photos at Kyle's place, Kyle's grief and out of character behaviour and why killing Andy was a way to hurt him. Ollie understood why Kyle had been so stunned and silent when they first interviewed him and why he'd asked Howley to find the killer.

Ollie exchanged an understanding glance with Howley before returning his focus to Jack. "And did you believe him?"

Jack screwed his face up in thought; "not sure…When I thought about it I couldn't remember seeing Kyle with a woman…But then I remembered Andy had a girlfriend…So…So I didn't know…I mean what the fuck?.. Right?.. It's totally fucked up."

"It is indeed. So let's say this is true and the last thing Kyle wants is for this to get out?"

Jack simply nodded.

"Then Adam was a threat…yes?"

Jack frowned "erm…yes…"

"So why didn't Kyle simply have Adam dealt with?" Ollie asked almost rhetorically.

Howley had been chewing his cheek as he processed the information and spoke before Jack could respond; "Because Adam disappeared before he could get a chance…"

"Yes…But he didn't disappear so far away that he couldn't hurt Kyle by killing Andy." Ollie suggested.

"No but why then kill Amy?.. And how does she fit into this? Did she know about Andy?" Howley thought out loud.

Ollie rubbed his chin as his brain dealt with the information. He turned to Jack again; "where's Adam?"

"I don't know…I haven't seen him in days." Jack answered immediately.

Ollie sensed that he was telling the truth; "when did you last see him or hear from him?"

Jack's eyebrows tightened as he thought; "about a week ago. Maybe ten days."

"Did he say anything?" Howley asked.

"No…I mean he obviously said stuff but nothing about killing Andy if that's what you mean…"

"Did he say where he was or where he was going?" Ollie said.

"No, I thought he was at the bookies."

"And what did he say about Kyle?"

"Nothing really…"

"What do mean, nothing really?"

"Well…He didn't really say anything about what had happened and he wasn't scared of Kyle…But he just kept banging on…Saying Kyle was a fag and that no faggot would tell him what to do…No arse bandit would scare him off…Stuff like that." Jack explained.

"Did he talk about getting back at Kyle?"

"I can't remember…He said a lot of stuff…"

"I'm sure…Was he angry with Kyle?"

Jack nodded furiously; "he was fucking mental with him."

"Mental enough to want to hurt Kyle?" Ollie asked.

"I don't know…Maybe…" Jack said.

"Have you got Adam's mobile number?"

"Yeah…well it's on my phone."

"Ok, what about his addresses? How many places does he have? Where does he like to stay?" Ollie asked.

"He's only got one pad here and a villa over in Spain." Jack answered.

"What about girlfriends or family?" Howley said.

"He hasn't got any family…He used to see a girl in Benchill…Laura Giddins I think. She lived somewhere near Hollyhedge Park."

"So he could've run off to Spain or be hiding in Benchill?" Howley asked.

Jack's face tightened in thought; "I can't think of anywhere else. I've got the number to his place in Spain…But I don't think he'd go there…"

"Why not?"

"Last I heard, he was renting the place out…He was bitching about not being able to go over when he wants."

Howley nodded; "ok we'll have to check it out…What about this Laura Giddins? Do you think he'd be with her?"

"Not sure…I haven't heard him talk about her for a while…But they were together for ages, so he might be."

Howley turned to Ollie and raised his eyebrows. They both knew Jack's leads on Adam were tenuous and vague, but nonetheless needed following up. "What do you think?"

"Probably the same as you." Ollie said. He eyed Jack and nodded at him; "ok Jack. We'll release you…We'll take you to the desk and you can give me those numbers from your phone."

Jack's relief was visible and he nodded. "Ok."

CHAPTER FORTY-FOUR

Ollie and Howley left the station and stepped out onto the car park. The dark sky had fallen fully across South Manchester and wrapped its sinister claws around the urban sprawl. Howley breathed deeply and the sharp icy air stung his nostrils. The men walked in silence to Ollie's bright green car and quickly got in to it.

Ollie keyed the ignition as Howley spoke; "do you really think we're looking at Adam for this?" He asked.

Ollie screwed up his face in doubtful thought. "I'm not sure; something doesn't quite add up…"

"I've come to a similar conclusion. I can see that it all fits…But…" He paused; "but I don't see Adam as being that calculating."

"No…It's a big shift from mindless thug to being that calculating." Ollie agreed.

"Indeed…but we do have his sudden disappearance…And he does have a history of violence. So if we add the parts together we have motive and means. Then we have his disappearance which at the very least gives an impression of guilt. So if we look at the facts as we have, and know them we have to consider Adam as a viable suspect." Howley conjectured.

Ollie simply nodded and focused on directing his car towards Benchill and the address for Laura Giddins that Jack Haworth had given them. The moisture filled air fogged around the orange glowing street lights and ice crystals began to form within the fissured surfaces of the poorly maintained roads and in the distance Ollie could see the first gritting lorry of the autumn spewing its salty contents across the road.

Laura Giddins lived in one of five identical terraced homes, all with identical white upvc doors and windows. Ollie looked for number seventeen and pulled the car to a halt outside. Howley was looking at the house as Ollie slowed and saw the blinds move as its inhabitants spied on them.

Ollie led the way as they approached the door and he knocked firmly on the tarnished, brass knocker. The blinds moved again as curious eyes tried to ascertain who was knocking at their door. A few seconds later a mish mash of colour appeared behind the frosted glass and Ollie could hear the lock turning, before the door opened.

Standing in place of the door was Laura Giddins. Harshly scraped hair pulled at her face giving her a stern and angry demeanour. Her multi-coloured, track suit was frayed at the wrists and down the front were the tell-tale signs of cannabis burns, from late night smoking sessions. "What do you want?" She asked in a broad Mancunian accent.

Ollie smiled and introduced himself before asking: "when was the last time you saw or heard from Adam Grey?"

Laura's face was pulled tightly with disdain and she looked as if she had a bad taste in her mouth. "What's the stupid twat done now?" She spat.

"We're just trying to find him. Is he here?"

"Are you having a laugh? That fucking shit bag isn't welcome here…So no, he isn't here." She said with contempt.

Ollie and Howley were both convinced by her protestations. "Ok, ok I get it…So have you heard from him or maybe heard where he is?"

Laura frowned and pursed her lips; "no I haven't heard from him for months. Last I heard he was getting fat and smoking dope every day at the bookies."

"What about his place in Spain? Could he be there?" Howley asked.

Laura shook her head: "He wishes. He's so broke he had to rent it out. Some timeshare company uses it most of the time and he can only use it for a couple of weeks a year. No way is he there…Plus he's always too skint to get there anyway. Only place he'll be is at his pad or in the bookies."

Howley smiled gently with his lips pursed; "ok Laura, thank you." He handed her his card. "If you hear from him or hear anything about him please call me."

Laura took the card; "if it means you're going to nick him you can count on it."

"Thank you."

Ollie and Howley left the embittered Lauren seething, and muttering expletives, and climbed back into the car. The leather was cold and the windows damp from the cooling night air that had enveloped the car. Howley shivered and pulled his jacket tighter around himself. "So where does that leave us?"

Ollie sighed; "like so many leads in this case it leaves us with another dead end and more questions…We'll put a note out and a picture to all the stations in the area and get eyes out looking for Adam…But I think it's time to call it a day."

Howley was yawning; "it's been a long day. So yes, let's call it a day and start fresh in the morning."

* * *

As Ollie pulled onto the drive he saw the curtains twitching and Grace waved enthusiastically at him through the gap. He smiled to himself and his dour mood was forgotten. Before he'd made it to the door Grace had opened it and was waiting for him. "Hello stranger." She said cheekily.

Ollie grinned, "hello yourself. Sorry it's so late but you know…"

"No need to explain. I understand." She interrupted. "Come on I've made dinner for us. Have you got any wine?"

"Yeah, it's in the garage. I'll go grab a bottle. Red or white?"

"No you get comfortable. If I remember rightly you like to get out of the suit when you get home. So you go do that I'll find the wine."

"Yes boss." He said through a soft chuckle. He watched her turn on her heel and head to the garage and he climbed the stairs.

In his bedroom he quickly changed into some soft and comfortable jeans and a tee-shirt. He looked at himself in the mirror. His eyes were bloodshot and his pallor almost greyed with fatigue. He walked into the bathroom, scrubbed his hands and splashed his face with warm water. Feeling a little better he stepped quickly down the stairs and headed into the kitchen.

In the kitchen Grace was lifting a lasagne from the oven. On the table was a bowl of salad, two glasses and a bottle of Chianti she'd found in the garage. The lasagne smelled delicious and Ollie's stomach growled loudly in anticipation. Grace heard the gastric growl; "you haven't been eating properly have you? Let me guess, chocolate bars and coffee?" She said.

"I had a proper lunch."

"Well it doesn't matter there's plenty of lasagne. Sit down and pour us some wine; I'll dish up."

Ollie did as he'd been told and took a sip of the Italian wine. Grace filled his plate and he added some salad. Grace did the same; "you look tired Ollie. I'd forgotten how hard you work. Would you rather take this through to the lounge and watch some TV while we eat?"

"No it's ok." He took a mouthful of lasagne and raised his eyebrows. "This is good." He said with a full mouth; "you sure you cooked it?" He joked.

"Cheeky. I'll choose to take the compliment only."

"That's your choice." Ollie retorted.

Grace smiled serenely; "so do you want to tell me about work?"

Ollie grimaced at the thought; "it was a long and arduous day."

"Feel like sharing?" She pushed.

Ollie sighed in resignation. "The usual: arresting your arsonist; chasing down leads and visiting a remand centre."

Grace relaxed, happy that Ollie was letting her in. "Anything to do with the Knowles case? Is that who you visited?"

"Yes it was all tied to the Knowles case. There's lots gone on in the last couple of days and a lot of new leads that put someone else in the frame; and not just for Andy Lewis's murder..."

"Someone else? Ollie!" Grace said in a shocked tone; "why are you holding out on me?"

"I'm not holding out on you. It's an ongoing, fluid investigation...and with the fire...I'm just trying to get to the bottom of it all...Anyway the long and the short is that Kyle didn't do it...Or at least it's looking a lot less likely. There's still some bits of evidence to tie up to say with certainty but my gut says he didn't kill Andy."

"Ok, sorry I jumped on you. So if not Kyle then who? His brother? He's a sandwich short of a picnic that's for sure." Grace babbled.

"Slow down; no not the brother. Although, he is dangerous and is the reason you should stay here and not go to work for a few days..."

"I'm going back tomorrow Ollie. I'm going nuts doing nothing."

"Have your work sent to you. Or simply have a rest. I really don't think you should go into the city. Ryan has got shit bags everywhere." Ollie pleaded.

"Thanks for the concern but I'll be fine. And if what you're saying is true I need to be ready to do a lot more work; not least of which will be sharing your findings with the defence because I guarantee he'll push for Kyle to be released on bail."

"If we've found what we think we've found the case is completely on its arse and Knowles becomes your star witness." Ollie explained.

"Seriously?"

"Yes, it's looking like this was an attack against Kyle..."

"Hang on a minute;" Grace frowned in confusion. "What do you mean an attack on Kyle?"

Ollie took another fork full of lasagne and a sip of wine; he breathed deeply and rubbed his face hard. "One of Kyle's lackeys claimed that Kyle was gay and in a relationship with Andy Lewis. Now on the face of it, it's not unusual for these neanderthals to use the term gay in a negative way; and to say that someone is gay is a very negative insult for them. But Kyle's reaction and a few other things make me think in this case it wasn't just another abusive name calling but a genuinely derogatory attack on Kyle."

"Ok I think I'm starting to get the picture." Grace said.

"Good. So if Kyle is gay and Andy was his lover then killing Andy is an attack on Kyle. It's also one hell of a warning to Kyle which might be why he didn't contest you at the remand hearing."

"That makes sense; I suppose; sort of." Grace agreed.

"Ok so the lackey making the allegation and winding Kyle up is Adam Grey. Kyle assaulted him after the incident; and by assault I mean severely beat him with a tenderizing mallet; and as you can imagine Adam was less than happy about it."

Grace was mesmerized by the story that was unfolding; "so you think Adam killed Andy to get at Kyle?"

"Well if you add to the mix, that in the back of Adam's car, we found some rope and card that, superficially at least, match the rope and card we found on Andy's body, then yes it makes sense."

Grace nodded; "so have you arrested Adam Grey?"

Ollie shook his head; "yet another problem. Adam has gone missing."

"Ah, I see. So where does Ruth's…friend fit into all this?"

"Kyle pointed us in his direction when we were at the remand centre. Jack's alibi is good but he put us onto Adam."

Grace was astounded by how much Ollie had discovered in such a short time. She looked across at him and found herself impressed and proud. It was good cops like Ollie that made her job easier. He left nothing to chance and always provided good, strong evidence. "Sounds like Sutherland is not going to get his easy, high-profile conviction."

Ollie finished his lasagne and shook his head. "No, he's not going to be happy when Kyle is released."

"Shit…glad you're the one who gets to tell him that." Grace said through a laugh.

Ollie frowned at her; "oh you're so not funny. But I'll let Steve tell him anyway."

"I'm sure he'll thank you for that." Grace said.

"He's more of a diplomat than me." Ollie suddenly remembered something from the morning. "By the way Kyle claims his cousin is a lawyer. He'd be about your age, probably at law school about the same time; maybe even took the bar. Don't suppose you can recall anyone with the name of Knowles do you?"

Grace rolled her eyes; "seriously Ollie? Do you have any idea how many places offer law?"

"Sorry, just a thought."

"It's ok…I can't think of anyone off hand but I'll have a think."

Ollie nodded gratefully; "thanks. It's a bit of a stretch but we could really do with finding this elusive cousin."

Grace's eyes narrowed in contemplation; "are you sure the cousin is a lawyer? What about his brief could it be him?"

"No, his brief has no ties to the family…And Kyle was doing his best to keep the cousin's identity a secret."

"Ok, I'll ask around."

Ollie chewed the inside of his lip as an idea came to him. "Kyle seemed proud of this mysterious cousin…Do you think he could work for the CPS?"

Grace hadn't even considered the possibility; "anything's possible I suppose. If they don't have a criminal record and aren't directly related to a known criminal I guess they'd pass the background checks…But I can't think of anybody…"

"But isn't that the point?" Ollie interrupted; "that could be why Knowles is so secretive. If his cousin worked for a private firm it wouldn't matter; he wouldn't need to protect his identity. But if he works for the CPS then he has to make sure nobody finds out."

Grace wasn't sure if Ollie's theory was right but it certainly made sense. "Ok I see what you mean." She paused; "so let's assume Knowles cousin works for the CPS…with me…How are you going to find out who it is?"

Ollie tutted and sighed; "I have no idea."

"Can I do anything? At the office I mean…I know all the lawyers at the office…"

"It's ok Grace…I really think you should stay here and have a few days off. If the cousin is one of your colleagues then you could be in even more danger than I'd thought…"

"Oh shush about danger. You caught the arsonist; I'll be fine. I'm going to work tomorrow." Grace said with resolute indignation.

Ollie sensed her determined mood and chose not to challenge her any further. "Ok, but please be careful and don't try and go all Nancy Drew in the office. Steve and I will find the evidence."

"Ok, agreed."

"Thank you...So same sleeping arrangements as last night?" Ollie asked.

Grace desperately wanted to say no; wanted to tell him to share the bed with her but she simply nodded; "yeah. Thanks Ollie."

CHAPTER FORTY-FIVE

Grace left Ollie and trotted to the tram station in Sale. Following Ollie's warnings she viewed every one she passed as a threat. She eyed every awkward shape in a jacket, every sudden move and every upturned hood with suspicion. "Fuck you Ollie!" She cursed under her breath; her composure corroded by his warning. She inhaled sharply and chastised herself for being scared. Not entirely convinced she felt any better, she forced herself to slow her walk and resolved to maintain calm.

The recently developed Metrolink tram system had revitalised the old Victorian station and it was awash with tired looking commuters feeding the yellow ticket machines with coins and cards. The steel-framed structure had been repainted with thick, glossy paint and ugly, modern signage hid the architectural beauty as if there was no place for Victorian ideals in a modern world. Grace wished she could see more of the old and that the new would blend with, rather than clash with, the original station.

Her tram took her to Piccadilly without drama and she'd forgotten Ollie's warnings by the time she was stepping onto the platform. The brightly lit and modern station filled her view and the smell of Starbucks coffee jarred her synapses, the aroma reinforced a state of calm and a perfunctory glance at her watch told her she had time to collect a coffee to go. She ordered a latte and smiled as she watched a teen couple kiss.

Leaving the young romantics behind, she deliberately strolled towards the station exit. Her straight back and languid stride served as a message of defiance. She hadn't believed Ollie's perceived threat was real and she refused to be frightened away from enjoying her city as she always did.

From Piccadilly she strolled through the main shopping areas of the city and was at Sunlight house within ten minutes. The main reception area to the building was busy with visitors signing in to visit the various companies who shared the building with the CPS. Grace smiled at the building's receptionist, as she passed, and took the lift up to the fifth floor.

* * *

Ollie felt a pang of regret and anxiety deep in his gut as he'd watched Grace head off to work. He wished he'd tried harder to make her stay away from work and away from the city, where Ryan Knowles' thugs could be waiting for her on any corner. But even as he had the thoughts he realised he could never have stopped her from going in. She was as stubborn as she was smart and with her mind made up, she was never going to listen to him.

With Grace gone he reclaimed the bathroom and quickly had the shower up to temperature. He shaved after he'd showered and then wandered around from room to room as he brushed his teeth. He looked in his bedroom were Grace had been sleeping; she'd made the bed and left the room looking immaculate; and then moved into the spare room, where he'd slept. On the floor was a post-it note. He instantly recognised it as the one Greg Milner had left on his monitor. He picked it up and took it with him as he finished in the bathroom.

Ollie picked out a fresh, mid-grey, suit, a white shirt, a grey tie and quickly dressed. He picked up his phone and sent Steve Howley a text message: **meet me in SOCO. Milner**

wants to see us. With the message sent he walked outside into the overcast, damp day.

It didn't take Ollie long to drive to the station. The morning traffic was quieter than usual and he'd barely had time to listen to Chris Evans' top-tenuous before he'd arrived. He parked his car and climbed out in time to see Howley pulling onto the car park. Ollie gave his partner a nod of greeting and waited for him to park up.

"Morning." Ollie greeted Howley.

"Morning. How's Gracie?" Howley asked.

"She's a stubborn pain in the arse…But she's fine."

"So you two are getting along then? Did you get much sleep?" Howley winked as he asked.

"Get your mind out of the gutter. We were in different rooms…"

"Oh now that's disappointing…" Howley mocked.

"Funny. So sorry to disappoint your lascivious gossip need but we have work to do. I don't suppose Greg told you what he wanted?"

"No I've not heard from him since we found the rope and card in Adam Grey's car."

"Ok let's go and see him shall we?" Ollie asked rhetorically.

The two men made their way into the building and signed in. Once in the building they quickly ascended the stairs to the first floor and into SOCO.

The pungent, chemical aromas of the myriad tests and procedures they undertook in the mini-labs stung their eyes. Through the window onto the work area they could see Greg Milner and Howley raised a hand to wave at him. Milner saw the two detectives and made his way to the door.

Milner let the men into the SOCO work-room and grabbed the ever expanding Knowles evidence file from his desk. He had a look of excitement about him as he prepared himself to tell the detectives what he'd found. "Thanks for coming up chaps. There've been some developments here that you need to know about."

"Ok, so what have you found Greg?" Howley asked.

"Yesterday I managed to pull some prints off the cardboard sign we found around the unfortunate young man's neck. They don't belong to Kyle Knowles…"

"We thought that might be the case but it's good to have it confirmed." Ollie said.

"Indeed. So after your discovery of the card in the car of Adam Grey I ran the prints against the ones we have for him on file and there was no match…Now the card and the rope are of the same type but other than that I can't match them specifically. So I can't definitively place Adam Grey at the murder scene."

Ollie and Howley were shaking their heads in collective disappointment as they realised that yet again a good lead had led to a dead end. "Ok thanks Greg. Was there anything else?" Howley asked.

"There is one other thing; it's a bit of a good news, bad news thing though." Milner said. "At the factory we recovered several cigarette ends; I collated them into type and then further collated them into samples that might give up usable DNA."

Ollie and Howley nodded; "so is that the good news or the bad?" Ollie asked.

"I'm getting there. So at the second murder scene in the park we also collected some cigarette end samples. This time there was only one type, Marlboro. At the factory we also collected Marlboro samples and they did seem to be the most recent. Although that's an unscientific assumption. Both samples from both scenes have usable DNA on them. If we have a matching DNA profile on file we'll be able to put someone in the frame."

"Ok all good so far; what's the bad?"

"The bad is the usual bad…It could take up to three weeks to get the DNA processed." Milner said apologetically.

Ollie and Howley both rolled their eyes in exasperation. "Nothing new about that." Howley said.

Ollie accepted the delay and was used to DNA taking so long but he was thinking about something else. "Greg, where did you look for a match on the prints?"

Milner was puzzled by Ollie's enquiry; "the fingerprint database; why?"

"What about the law enforcement database?"

Milner's forehead crinkled with more confusion. "No, nobody touched it so I didn't need to…Is there a problem?"

Ollie shook his head; "no, no problem. Can you run it against the exclusion database please?"

"Of course…But, why? What are you thinking?" Milner queried.

Ollie rubbed his face and sighed; "we had a tip off about a cousin of Knowles. I think he might work for the CPS."

"You've got to be joking…What makes you think that?"

"Knowles was almost bursting with pride about his cousin but he wouldn't reveal where he worked. There was something about his smug demeanour that just has me thinking he's got someone in the CPS." Ollie stopped and looked at the bewildered expression on Milner's face; "I could be wrong. But if I'm not…"

"If you're not, then the Knowles family has a dirty little secret in the CPS." Milner said knowingly; "but what makes you think anyone working for the CPS, even if they're part of the Knowles pack, would commit murder? They'd be taking a massive risk."

"I know it's a bit of a push to believe it, but so far everything in this case has been back to front and as Adam Grey's prints aren't on the card then the only other person of interest to follow up is this illusive cousin." Ollie looked at Howley and Milner; neither of them were ready to object or challenge his reasoning. "So maybe we don't find a match for the prints, but we have to check; I have a strange feeling about this. Please run it against the law enforcement exclusion database."

Milner screwed his face up in an apologetic gesture; "I would, but we won't find anything on there…"

"What do you mean?" Ollie asked anxiously.

"The CPS fingerprints aren't on our system. There was a big fuss about it and being lawyers they managed to keep their prints out of the database. So now if they're likely to have left prints anywhere we have to apply to access a different database. Basically they argued that there was very little chance of their prints being near a crime scene and so they're not automatically in the exclusion database." Milner explained.

Ollie slammed his fist down hard on the desk; "for god's sake why is nothing straight forward in this case? Who do I have to see to get access to the CPS finger print database?"

Milner's eyes darted frantically around the room avoiding direct contact with Ollie's. He shifted nervously and he paced to the door of his office. He turned the lock and returned to Ollie and Howley. "Technically you have to see a judge…" He lowered his voice to a whisper; "but I can log in…It's a bit of a grey area but I suppose I could run a check and if we get a hit you can then make an official application…"

A small smile spread across Ollie's face and he placed a reassuring hand on Milner's shoulder. "Greg I know how hard it is for you to do this and I promise if we get a hit I'll make a proper application and nobody will ever know you bent the rules."

Milner took solace from Ollie's reassurance and he nodded a thank you. "Ok detectives let's see what we find."

Milner turned to his computer and logged into the database. Within seconds the computer was matching and comparing the fingerprints. "It shouldn't take too long, but remember it is looking at all the CPS prints, not just the ones in Manchester."

Ollie and Howley simply nodded and waited.

* * *

Grace stepped off the lift and saw Matt standing near the window pacing frantically as he held his phone to his ear. He looked agitated as he listened to intently to the voice on the phone. Grace waved in his direction but he didn't notice her.

Grace fumbled for her swipe card and stopped at the door to search her bag properly. Her bag was a mess of pens, tissues, keys and make-up. She rifled through the mess distracted by Matthew's behaviour, and intrigued by his call. She strained to listen as she continued to rummage.

She could hear enough to know the voice on the phone was shouting, but she couldn't make out anything else. Her hand had stopped moving inside the bag; all her concentration was on Matthew. The newly focused concentration worked and she heard Matthew responding to the caller in a muted voice. She heard him say: "it's ok Ryan, I'll sort it."

Her stomach suddenly felt cold and a wave of nausea flooded through her body. The sudden realisation that Matthew was involved with Knowles jolted her senses and the panic that engulfed her forced her to drop her bag.

Matthew heard the clatter of Grace's bag and turned on his heel to look at her. His face was taught with anger and he marched to Grace. "Hey Matt…you ok?"

Matthew glared at her; "what did you hear?"

Grace shook her head. "Nothing, you just looked concerned."

Matthew raised his eyebrows. "Oh really? Because you were stood listening long enough."

"I wasn't listening; I was trying to find my swipe card." Grace said anxiously.

Matthew's rage had grown and he grabbed Grace's wrist. His grip was tight and Grace was instantly in pain. His grimaced face snarled at her; "I know what you heard." From his jacket he pulled a gun. Grace's eyes widened with fear as he pushed the muzzle into her ribs. "Move, towards the stairway."

Grace nodded and moved as he pushed her with the gun and a tight grip on her wrist. Her steps were slow and deliberate but Matthew wanted to move away from the office doorway as quickly as possible. He twisted her arm behind her and pushed her through a door and onto the stairway landing.

The door snapped shut behind them as the automatic door closer pulled it. The landing was sparse and the green carpet, barely touched, looked and smelled new. Matthew pushed Grace against the wall as he held her wrist increasingly tighter. His rational thoughts had gone and his only thoughts now were destructive.

Grace could see he was trying to think. "Why are you hurting me Matt?" She asked.

Matthew sneered at her; "shut the fuck up."

Grace kept quiet and let her focus drop to the floor. She had seen plenty of rage driven incidents in court and could see Matthew was in the same state of mind. His eyes had the malevolent look of a psychotic and he was fidgety as he tried to come up with some sort of plan. Matthew's hand was shaking and his grip on Grace loosened. Grace felt it, but remained still; she knew trying to run would only anger him.

All the floors above the CPS offices were empty and there was an echoing silence on the sixth floor as Matthew wrestled with the problem he'd just created. He looked at Grace; "you couldn't have just gone into the office could you? You had to be a nosey bitch; a fucking annoying, nosey bitch." He stopped and raised his hand. "I should beat the shit out of you right now...You've never been anything but a fucking pain...and so fucking prissy. I saw the way you looked at me when I called Knowles' lawyer a faggot. You're such a fucking goody-goody."

Grace remained silent, not wanting to enrage him further. She'd been frightened from the moment he grabbed her; as she watched him grow more unstable and more unpredictable she began to fear for her life. She kept her eyes facing the floor and listened to him ranting.

Matthew grabbed her chin and pulled her head up so he was looking directly at her. "So how much do you know?"

Grace shook her head slightly. "Not much. Ollie found out that the Knowles have a cousin in the CPS." She stopped.

"I guess that's you?" Her inquisitive nature pushed through the need for self-preservation.

Matthew half-smiled; "so if you hadn't heard me on the phone you wouldn't have known it was me. Fucking typical…What else do you know?"

Grace could sense that he wanted to talk. It made sense that he would; he was a lawyer he would feel in control if he was talking and arguing. "Ollie and Howley thought that Knowles' cousin killed Andy Lewis and Amy Lawrence." She hesitated; "did you?"

"Oh yes I killed them both." He said with a smile on his face; it felt good to tell somebody what he'd done.

Grace could see that Matthew was getting some sort of catharsis from admitting to the killings and decided to risk pushing him further. "I don't understand. Why?"

"God, even now you're a nosey bitch. But I'll humour you." He grinned almost manically. "Kyle is ill. I take it your super Sherlock worked that much out?"

Grace was confused and frowned. "Ill?" She asked.

"Yes. He's gay. It's an illness and he needed help."

Grace didn't know what to say. "Oh, I see." She said meekly.

Matthew sneered dismissively as he shook his head at her. "Oh I know you don't see it as an illness. You're too politically correct and liberal to see the truth."

"The truth?"

"Yes. Normally I don't mind the poofs or the dykes but I could see what it was doing to Kyle. Until Andy Lewis turned up he was in control; he kept a tight grip on his feelings and on the business. Then that fucking ponce Lewis turned up and straight away Kyle struggled to keep a lid on his sickness. I tried to help him back then; I took him to our old church and asked him to speak to the priest, but even priests have gone soft on ponces these days."

He looked at Grace to make sure she was still listening. "Do you have any idea what would have happened to him if everyone had found out he was ponce?" He looked for a response and Grace quickly shook her head. "No I don't suppose you would;" he continued. "If any of his collectors or enforcers suspected he was gay all his power and control would have vanished. Every one of them would've challenged him; he maybe could've beaten a few challenges but even those idiots would soon have pulled together and over-turned him."

Grace sensed Matthew was happy to keep to talking; "so you killed Andy to put Kyle back on track?"

Matthew nodded. "That's right. Kyle was going soft; he needed to sort himself out. With Andy out of the way he can run things right and he can reward me for all my hard work."

Grace frowned in confusion. "Your hard work?"

Matthew smirked; "oh yes. Do you really think Kyle has avoided conviction all these years without help? Come on Grace, wake up. Put the pieces together."

"Of course and whenever you were the prosecutor you purposely made an error to make sure he got off."

He gave her a slow, mocking hand clap. "Yes Grace, well done."

"But why did you try to implicate Kyle? And why kill Amy?"

Matthew's malice filled smirk softened and he turned to face Grace directly. "I wanted to punish him. I warned him about Andy and he ignored me, flaunted him in my face. He brought him up through the ranks and made him powerful." His anger returned as he spoke. "Without me he'd have been somebody's bitch in Strangeways now. I kept him out and I made sure he took the business in the right direction. With Kyle locked away and suffering I can control Ryan. It's time for a Doherty to take over." He stopped talking and stared out of the window towards Deansgate.

"All those pubs and clubs across there have our doormen. Our doormen make sure our dealers are supplying the drugs. I help the owners make sure their licenses are granted. It's a symbiotic relationship from which all parties benefit. Kyle would still be warring with the other gangs for three or four clubs without me. Of course Kyle's skill set can still be useful when the competition try to move in, but it's hardly a unique skill."

Grace listened as Matthew angrily, but calmly, confessed. But it wasn't a contrite confession it was the conceited, self-satisfied, bragging of a proud man. "What about Amy?" She tentatively asked not wanting his anger to be turned towards her.

"Amy was a weak link. When Kyle refused to cut Andy out of his life and the organization I helped him come up with a cover. Amy was a sort of cousin of Andy's and we paid her to act as his girlfriend. Ryan and Kyle arranged it but I heard she was close to cracking. I didn't want more doubt over Kyle's guilt. If your boyfriend had found out about Kyle's relationship with Andy then the evidence I'd left would have been worthless. Of course, when I killed Amy I didn't know that DS James had already started to doubt the evidence."

Grace nodded and realised that Matthew's psychopathic behaviour was all perfectly rationalised in his own mind. Like Andy, and Amy, she was an obstacle getting in the way of his plan and he knew that Ollie and Howley had no idea that he was Knowles' cousin. She had to keep him talking; Ollie was picking her up for lunch. He would find her. He would rescue her. "So you killed Andy and implicated Kyle at the factory; that throws the police off but what about Kyle? Won't he want payback? Won't he find out?"

Matthew laughed at her and shook his head. "Typical fucking Grace; you have never recognised my intelligence. Do you really think I haven't thought this through?"

"Sorry…I just thought…"

"You just thought I was stupid. You're a condescending bitch." He raised his hand as if to hit her then let it drop to his side. "Well for your information Kyle thinks Jack Haworth killed Andy."

Grace recognised the name. "Ollie questioned Jack Haworth, but he had an alibi for the time of the murder."

Matthew laughed again. "Oh yes, he was fucking that little hottie who was working as your assistant. Apparently she likes a bit of rough. But Kyle doesn't know that. All he knows is that Jack was unhappy about a kicking he gave to Adam Grey and he wanted Kyle to pay for it."

"I imagine getting a kicking is part of the risk of working for Kyle."

"It is, but Adam knew, or at least thought he knew, about Kyle and Andy. He said something to Kyle and got a real beating for it. Not just a slap, Ryan told me he was close to death."

"So Kyle thinks Jack killed Andy in retaliation for beating Adam? Why didn't he say something to the police?"

"Oh come on Grace, you know that's…" Matthew was interrupted by a noise from the stairwell and he yanked Grace to her feet. He pulled her to the other side of the building and they slipped out onto the rear stairs.

* * *

Milner's computer beeped loudly as the fingerprint search made a positive match. Milner turned to face the screen and pressed a few keys before turning back to face Ollie and Howley. "We've got a match. Three fingers, no doubt about it…"

Ollie leant forward, his eyes wide in anticipation; "who is it?"

Milner scrolled down the page; "Matthew Doherty."

Ollie's anticipation turned to anxious anger as he realised Grace had gone into the office. The office where Matthew Doherty was; where he'd been all along, pressing Grace for information in the guise of friendly office support. Ollie then remembered the mud on Matthew's car; mud like that at the factory. "Shit…Why didn't I make him? Come on Steve we have to get across to Sunlight House."

Howley stood and Ollie did the same. The detectives moved quickly from the office and then Ollie sprinted past Howley towards the car. "I'll meet you at the front door…" He shouted.

Howley's adrenal gland was working frantically and a flood of strength buoyed his tired body and he too was running towards the exit. He ran past the front desk and shouted to the uniformed civilian manning it to sign him and Ollie out. He stumbled a little as he pushed through the front door and out on to the street.

As he climbed into the car his mind turned to the cash box and the pictures of Kyle with Ryan and the handsome young blonde boy. As he pictured the boy he started to remember the features and it was clear to him that it was Matthew.

"Shall I get some uniform there to back us up?" Howley asked as Ollie accelerated hard away from the station.

"Have them on standby. He doesn't know we've made him; if he sees uniforms and blue lights he'll bolt…or worse." Ollie explained.

"Ok. Is Grace at Sunlight House today?"

Ollie nodded as he pulled the car on to the Parkway and pushed his floor hard to the floor. "I tried to get her to stay at my place but she was having none of it. She was on the seven thirty tram…"

"She's always been a workaholic. You couldn't have kept her off another day unless you'd locked her in. You couldn't have stopped her Ollie…"

"I know, I know…God why wouldn't she just listen. Just this once."

"Because that's not who she is." Howley winced as Ollie's frenetic driving brought them too close to other cars for Howley's liking. "Just focus on getting us there…Please."

Ollie remained silent and continued to carve his way through the traffic. The ever-present congestion around the city centre created a monstrous slow moving mass of steel and Ollie thumped at his steering wheel in frustrated anger.

"It's ok Ollie; we'll get there."

* * *

Grace's eyes scanned the open landing; she frantically searched for some sort of escape but could see none. The sparse décor and bare steps echoed every resonant breath she took and Matthew's nervous foot tapping sounded like a tympanic underscore of terror. Grace took a deep breath and held it as she listened for any signs of life on the rear staircase; after a few seconds it was apparent she was alone with Matthew.

"What now Matt?" Grace asked.

Matthew's foot tapping halted and he glared at Grace with dark, unfeeling eyes. "Well Grace, you've become a real problem for me haven't you? So now I have to decide what to do with you."

Grace shuddered as her courage briefly gave sway to an urgent surge of fear; her lip quivered and her eyes glossed, ready to cry. But she clenched her jaw tightly, squeezed her fists till her nails broke the skin on the palm of her hands. She refused to acknowledge the fear. She returned Matthew's harsh glare; "what do you mean? Do with me?"

Matthew's brow creased in confusion; "do you really need me to spell it out Grace?" He stepped closer to her and he could smell the delicate tones of Jo Malone's Bluebell perfume, the same scent she wore every day for work. In one swift move he grabbed her chin brusquely and pushed his gun to her temple with the other hand. He could feel her shaking as her courage finally surrendered to the pervading fear. "Ah there it is. You know exactly what I mean." He said coldly.

Grace nodded and sniffed as tears filled her eyes. "Yes…I do."

Matthew pushed her head back with her chin and then spun her round: "Move, we're going upstairs." He pushed the gun into her back and she complied.

* * *

The oppressive grey sky touched the roof tops of Manchester's city centre, enveloping the Beetham tower in a haze of difficult light and granite opacity. Ollie was racing along Deansgate, heading to Quay Street and hoping the pedestrians would stay off the road for just a few minutes more. He approached the lights on red but chose to take the left turn regardless. Howley braced himself with his legs and held tightly to the seat sides as Ollie focused on getting them to Sunlight House.

Ollie pulled the car up behind the Opera House theatre and he and Howley climbed out of the car. "So what's the plan here?" Howley asked.

Ollie chewed his cheek: "Let's go in the front door. We're working the same case as Grace so if you go in the front, keep it official looking and I'll go in the back corner. Get the receptionist to unlock the back door and then if he bolts when he sees you I'll have the back covered. If it's all quiet I'll meet you on the fifth." Ollie went over it again in his head; "we'll arrest him together. Hopefully we can contain him to his office."

Howley agreed: "Ok. Sounds good...Ollie, why didn't you ring Grace and tell her?"

"I need her to carry on as normal. He's been hiding in plain sight for years; even the slightest change in how she behaves and he'll pick up on it..."

"And if he's already worked it out?" Howley suggested.

"Let's just hope he hasn't..."

"Yes, let's." Howley said with little optimism.

Ollie gave Howley a good luck slap on the back and headed round the back of Sunlight House. The rear entrance was quiet and only a swipe card lock prevented entry from the portico. Only the smoked glass of the doors gave any real definition to the entrance. Ollie pushed open one of the heavy glass doors, walked into the barren portico and waited for the lock to release and allow him into the building.

From Quay Street Howley entered Sunlight House through the more usual entrance. There were a few people gathered near the lifts and Howley overheard them, they were going to an insurance company on the fourth floor. He walked calmly past them and approached the receptionist, a twenty something blonde with a spray tan and a fondness for Pandora bracelets. He showed her his police badge; "hello Susan. If you look at the monitor for the back door you'll see my colleague waiting to get in. Would you be a dear and release the lock please?" She did as he'd asked. "Thank you, we're going up to the fifth, to the CPS, there's no need for you to ring up. We're expected."

"Ok." Said the confused receptionist.

"Thank you." Howley said as he stepped to the lift.

Howley pressed the five button and breathed deeply as he tried to control the adrenaline that was energising him. The lift rumbled and shook gently as it ascended towards the fifth floor and Howley wished it would move faster.

As Howley had stepped into the lift Ollie had entered the building and started climbing the stairs to the CPS offices. The stairs were empty and Ollie could hear only muffled sounds from the offices he passed. The dark wood staircase was barely used and the eighty year patina was barely noticeable and Ollie's shoes squeaked against the varnished treads.

The lift stopped at the fifth floor and Howley moved out onto the landing area. He looked across and into the CPS offices, everything seemed normal and calm. He approached the secure entrance and pressed the buzzer.

"Hello."

"Hello its D.S Howley, I'm here to see Grace Sterling."

"Ok Sergeant, come in I'll try and find her."

Howley heard the door click and pushed it to enter the offices. As he walked in he was met by Ruth Johnson. Her usual happy face was glum and serious, Howley had a good idea why, and she barely managed a smile when she saw him; "Hello Sergeant Howley I haven't seen Grace yet; I'd assumed she was taking another day off."

Howley's face paled in an instant and his stomach knotted tightly. "You're sure you haven't seen her?"

Ruth frowned; "I'm sure. I was in her office earlier." Ruth saw the worry in Howley's face; "what's wrong?"

Howley composed himself; "nothing's wrong. Is Matthew Doherty in?"

"Matt was in early but I haven't seen him since about half eight. I thought he'd gone out for a smoke because his briefcase and coat are still here, but he hasn't been back in."

Howley was increasingly concerned and he frowned as he processed the information; he looked around and noticed black and white monitors showing the open landing area outside the CPS offices. "Do they record as well?" He asked the worried Ruth.

She nodded; "yes…What's going on?"

"I'll explain after I see the video for this morning. Do you think you can set it up for me to look through while I make a call?" He said reassuringly.

"Ok." Ruth then moved to the controls next to the monitors and began to find the morning's recording.

Howley stepped away from her and called Ollie: "Ollie, there's a problem. Grace hasn't been seen in the office and Matthew Doherty is missing too."

"Shit. Has she called in does anyone know anything?" Ollie asked.

"I'm with Ruth she hasn't seen or heard from Grace; but we're about to look at CCTV recording from this morning. It might show us where Matthew went or if Grace got to the office..."

Ollie stepped from the rear staircase and on to the fifth floor; he ran to the CPS entrance and hammered on the door. Howley opened the door and Ollie followed him to the monitors and Ruth. "Have you got the footage for this morning?" Ollie asked.

"Yes I'm just about to play it."

"Ok Grace should've been here around twenty past eight so start about quarter past. Can you play at double or four times?"

"Yes, I'll play at four times and stop if I see Grace." Ruth said.

Ruth began the play back and after a few moments Grace appeared in shot. They watched in horrified astonishment as Grace's kidnapping unfolded before them. "Shit, he's got a gun...He must have taken her somewhere in the building there's no way he'd have hit the street without creating a panic." Ollie said as he tried to see which way Matthew had pushed Grace. "I think they've gone upstairs...Come on Steve..."

On the twelfth floor blood had trickled from Grace's nose; the deep crimson so bright it screamed the obvious. Like a surrendered animal she was waiting for the inevitable final blow. She wondered how much longer he would toy with her before he finally ended her life the way he'd ended Andy's and Amy's. Her trousers were torn at the knee from stumbling on the stairs and she struggled to breathe after a hard punch to her side had cracked a rib. Despite this, she'd remained resolutely silent; not once had she cried or screamed.

Matthew prowled; scouring the view from the windows and jumping at every noise he heard or thought he heard. The cool composure he'd held when he murdered Amy and Andy was long gone and he'd become even more dangerous and unpredictable. He stared at Grace and scowled; "you really are an annoying bitch."

Grace simply stoically sat, suffering quietly. She looked up at the dangerously pacing Matthew. He noticed her movement and pounced on her. He pushed the muzzle of his gun hard against her forehead and his thumb played with the safety catch. Grace shuddered and sobbed. "Oh shut the fuck up." He snarled.

Grace clenched her jaw and spoke softly; "I'm sorry."

"I'm sure you're really sorry. Who wouldn't be in your position? But it's too late for sorry; now's the time for little bitches to suffer." He kicked her hard in the side as he spoke; "god it feels good to hurt you. You've always been a prissy little know it all. Little miss morally correct; little miss brown nose. Do you know how many big cases you were given over me?"

Grace said nothing.

"No I don't imagine you do. You've probably gotten used to having it all handed to you on plate. Well I know. It's over twenty. More than twenty good opportunities taken from me, because of your brown nosing. You fucking goody-goody bitch."

Grace remained silent.

"Nothing to say? No lecture about hard work and doing the right thing?" He smirked at her. "No? Oh well I am glad because I'd rather not listen to such sanctimonious shit anyway. Because you know why you really got all good cases don't you?"

Grace didn't speak.

"No? Well I'll tell you. Michael just loves your ass. He gives you all the breaks and all the good cases because he likes your ass and he wants to fuck you. Now don't get me wrong I quite like your ass too and I'd most certainly enjoy fucking you." He looked over at Grace who suddenly felt a new threat; "oh don't wet yourself bitch I'm not going to fuck you now…Sadly there's no time for that." He laughed to himself.

Grace's resolve held and still she said nothing.

"I've known you for years and never known you be so quiet. I much prefer you this way, it's so much nicer than hearing your self-righteous bullshit."

* * *

Ollie and Howley sprinted the stairs as they searched for the kidnapped Grace. The floors above the CPS offices were echoing caverns of grey marbled floors and Victorian, cast-iron heating pipes. Despite the inherent urgency the two men stepped lightly, minimising the noise they made as they checked every corner hoping to find Grace unhurt.

As they moved from the eleventh floor on to the stairs to the twelfth Ollie could hear hushed mumblings resonating through the empty space. He placed a finger to his lip and Howley nodded and listened. "They're just above us." Ollie whispered.

"So what's the plan?"

Ollie's gaze vanished from Howley and he suddenly stood and he hurtled up the stairs. "Ollie! Get back here!" Howley whispered as loud as he dared, but it was too late Ollie was gone. Howley grimaced as he filled his burning lungs with a large gulp of air and followed Ollie.

Ollie burst through the doors and in to the twelfth floor office space. Matthew was jolted from his ranting and he turned towards Ollie, firing the gun at him as he did so. A small caliber bullet seared past Ollie as he was diving for the floor. "Get the fuck away from here before I put the next bullet through your girlfriend's head." Matthew screamed.

Ollie desperately looked for some cover as he shouted back; "let me see she's ok…"

"Fuck you Sherlock!"

Behind Ollie Howley was lying flat on the parquet flooring watching through the double doors that led on to the main office area. Ollie put his hand behind him and motioned to Howley to stay back. "How do you see this turning out Matthew?" Ollie asked.

"Well Sergeant I'm going to take your bitch of a girlfriend here and walk down the stairs and away from here. And if you or your ancient partner try and stop me I'll kill her and then I'll kill you."

As he spoke Howley had crept back down to the eleventh floor and was running across to the rear staircase.

"So you maybe get out of the building. What then?"

Matthew was dragging Grace up off the floor and pushing her towards the rear stairs. "You don't need to worry about that. Where's your partner? D.S Howley isn't it?"

"He's at the station. He wasn't with me when we got the hit on your fingerprint…"

"Fingerprint? What fingerprint?"

"Yours. It was on the sign you put around Andy's neck." Ollie explained as he wondered if Howley had made it to the other staircase.

"You don't have legal access to my fingerprints." Matthew said angrily.

"Really Matthew? You're playing the lawyer now?" Ollie mocked as he tried to gain Howley more time.

Matthew pushed Grace hard and she stumbled. "I've never played at being a lawyer…Now, move back towards the door. If you make one step this way Grace goes bye-bye."

Ollie stepped back but kept his eyes on Matthew and Grace. "Grace; are you ok?"

Grace nodded dolefully. Matthew pushed her again. "I didn't say you could talk to her…Shut the fuck up and keep moving back."

Ollie nodded and stepped off the marble, elevated floor and onto the warm parquet of the vestibule. "Ok Matthew I'm at the door; take it easy, don't hurt Grace…"

"Don't hurt Grace? Are you fucking joking? It's too late for that now just stay back and she might live."

Ollie stood at the door; forced to watch as Matthew pushed Grace towards the rear staircase. Grace was limping and Ollie thought he could see blood on her face. "What have you done to her? Is that what you are Matthew? A woman beater? Just like the rest of your family, bullies and woman beaters?"

Matthew's eyes widened with anger and he pushed Grace so hard she fell to the floor; "I am so much better than any of my family. You really have no idea do you? Do you think Kyle and Ryan had any idea?" As he spoke Grace was shuffling towards the door; Ollie saw her peripherally and kept his eyes firmly on Matthews.

"What do you mean?" Ollie asked hoping Matthew would keep talking.

"Oh come on; do you really think an illiterate queen could have taken over all the door business in the city? Without me Kyle and Ryan would still be mugging old ladies on pension day and selling weed to stoners in the park." Matthew bristled with pride as he continued; "those two morons did as I told them and the business grew into a multi-million pound enterprise." Behind him Grace was almost at the door.

"So you were the brains and they did the dirty work? And of course you dropped the ball on any prosecution they faced." Ollie said.

"Well done Sergeant; and the public think the police are all stupid."

Grace made a lunge for the door just as Matthew finished speaking. He turned quickly and ran after her, crashing through the doors.

Ollie raced across the office, his feet slipping on the marble floor, as he frantically tried to help Grace. As he approached the doors they'd gone through he heard a gun shot and a scream of pain; "Grace! Grace…Are you ok? Steve!"

Ollie flung the doors aside and ran onto the landing. Howley was applying pressure to a bloody wound on Matthew's abdomen and Grace was holding the gun in her hand, shaking and sobbing. She looked up at Ollie and the gun fell from her hand; "Ollie, oh my god Ollie, thank god…"

"It's ok Grace, I'm here." Ollie reassured her. "What happened?"

"It was Steve…He…" Grace broke down and tears streamed down her face before she could explain. Ollie embraced her and held her tightly to his chest while she cried.

Howley looked up, his hand was covered in blood; "call an ambulance Oll, I don't know if he'll make it but let's do our best to get the real murderer to court."

Ollie looked at the abhorrent lawyer and every part of him wanted to let him die. He'd hurt Grace, threatened to kill her. But he knew Howley was right. He nodded at his partner and gently sat Grace down before taking his phone from his pocket.

After calling for an ambulance Ollie called DCI Sutherland and explained what had happened. Sutherland had listened to Ollie and immediately jumped in a car and headed to Sunlight House.

While they waited for the ambulance and Sutherland, Ollie held Grace and soon her sobbing stopped. She picked her head up from Ollie's shoulder and turned to Howley: "Thank you Steve. You're so brave."

Ollie reached over to his longtime friend and partner and rested his hand on his shoulder. No words were exchanged, there was no need.

EPILOGUE

THREE WEEKS LATER

Ollie made coffee, in a newly bought machine, and carried it into his lounge. On the sofa, Grace sprawled across three seats; wrapped up in a white dressing gown and sporting fluffy slippers; she was relaxed and her bruises almost healed. Ollie smiled at her: "move over slacker." He joked.

"Hey I'm not a slacker I'm recuperating." She pouted.

Ollie laughed; "my apologies. Please move over, recuperating slacker."

"That's more like it." She pulled herself up into a seated position and Ollie joined her on the sofa. "So what's the news from the station?" She asked.

Ollie made himself comfortable and sipped from his cup. "Well, it never gets boring watching Sutherland trying to resurrect his political career …" He tailed off, wondering whether to share the next piece of information.

"And?" Grace pressed him with a playful poke to the ribs.

"As of this morning Matthew Doherty's recovery has been deemed satisfactory enough to move him from the hospital to a more secure location where he'll await trial."

Grace pursed her lips as she considered whilst pouring the coffee.

"We've got the whole division breaking down his involvement in the Knowles' activities…"

"What about all his work with the CPS?" Grace interrupted.

"There's a huge investigation going on and Steve and I have been asked to give evidence."

"He was involved in a lot of cases it's going to be a mess."

Ollie raised an eyebrow in agreement. "Probably."

"And the other Knowles is safely locked up after trying to help his brother."

"Ryan's on remand for conspiracy and Danny is on bail for arson."

Grace nodded. "I suppose that's as much as we can hope for at this stage. What about Kyle?"

"He was released and charges dropped…" The chirrup of his phone interrupted him; he looked at the phone and saw it was Howley. "I better take this it's Steve."

"Say hi from me." Grace nodded.

"Steve, can't you manage one day without me?"

"Hello Oliver; I think you better get yourself over here. You're not going to want to miss this."

Ollie frowned. "Miss what? What's going on?"

"Lindley pulled a floater from the ship canal about three and half weeks ago. The DNA came back and it's Adam Grey. The injuries are consistent with a meat tenderiser, Kyle Knowles' meat tenderiser. We're going over to arrest him." Howley explained.

"I'll be there in half an hour."

Ollie ended the call and gulped his coffee; "I've got to go."

"I understand." Grace said.

Ollie leant across and gently place his hand on her face before kissing her gently. "I'm sorry Gracie…But it's Kyle Knowles, we're bringing him in for murder…Again."

THE END

4626468R00170

Printed in Great Britain
by Amazon.co.uk, Ltd.,
Marston Gate.